DISCOVER WHY EVERYONE LOVES
PARNELL HALL'S SIXTH
STANLEY HASTINGS MYSTERY—

JUROR

"Deft . . . a tale of murder and duplicity neatly
woven with the workings of the New York justice
system.—*San Antonio Express-News*

"Laughs, witty dialogue, and a style that captures
the grit and fear of life in Manhattan."
—*Richmond Times-Dispatch*

"Stanley Hastings is one of the most appealing
detectives . . . and a magnet for murder."
—*Booklist*

"A cleverly crafted tale . . . and very, very funny . . .
Read!"—*Cedar Rapids Gazette*

"A crafty plot and readable dialogue—an unbeatable
combination . . . this is a good story . . . Hall hits
the mark again."—*South Bend Tribune*

(For more critical acclaim, please turn the page . . .)

JUROR

PARNELL HALL

AN ONYX BOOK

ONYX
Published by the Penguin Group
Penguin Books USA Inc., 375 Hudson Street,
New York, New York 10014, U.S.A.
Penguin Books Ltd, 27 Wrights Lane,
London W8 5TZ, England
Penguin Books Australia Ltd, Ringwood,
Victoria, Australia
Penguin Books Canada Ltd, 10 Alcorn Avenue,
Toronto, Ontario, Canada M4V 3B2
Penguin Books (N.Z.) Ltd, 182-190 Wairau Road,
Auckland 10, New Zealand

Penguin Books Ltd, Registered Offices:
Harmondsworth, Middlesex, England

Published by Onyx, an imprint of New American Library, a division of
Penguin Books USA Inc. This is an authorized reprint of a hardcover edition
published by Donald I. Fine, Inc.

First Onyx Printing, May, 1992
10 9 8 7 6 5 4 3 2 1

PUBLISHER'S NOTE
This novel is a work of fiction. Names, characters, places and incidents are
either the product of the author's imagination or are used fictitiously. Any
resemblance to actual events, locales, organizations or persons, living or
dead, is entirely coincidental and beyond the intent of either the author or
publisher.

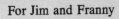

For Jim and Franny

1.

I GOT JURY DUTY.

I know that shouldn't sound like an earth-shattering event—everybody gets jury duty—but the thing is, I'm not *supposed* to get jury duty. Because in point of fact, everybody *doesn't* get jury duty. Some people are exempt.

Now, I hate to say that, because it immediately conjures up a picture of an elite upper class, with sufficient political connections to pull a few strings and wriggle out of the duties and responsibilities dumped on the poor, unwashed masses. But such is not the case. Jury duty exemptions are actually based on hardship.

One reason jury duty is a hardship to some is that it pays squat. By last count, the stipend for doing jury duty was up to a whopping twelve bucks a day. You don't have to be a math major to figure out that falls somewhat short of the minimum wage. But since jury duty is an obligation, not a job, the judicial system's able to get away with paying it.

For most people, the twelve bucks a day isn't a hardship. That's because they work regular jobs and have an employer who pays them a salary, and during the two weeks of jury duty it's the employer who takes the loss, continuing wages to people who are not there. So for those jurors, the twelve bucks a day is actually a bonus.

The people who take it on the chin, of course, are the people who are self-employed. If you work for yourself in a one-man operation and you aren't there, you don't earn. For that reason, anyone can be exempt from jury duty if he happens to be the sole proprietor of his business.

I'm the sole proprietor of mine. Stanley Hastings Detective Agency. Don't get me wrong, it's not really an agency. It's a one-man show, and I'm him. Or I'm he, if you want to be grammatical. At any rate, I'm the sole proprietor, the sole employee, the sole source of income. I work my butt off day after day trying to feed my wife and kid. In New York City, that ain't easy. I'm always behind. For me, to close up shop and earn twelve bucks a day for two weeks would be a disaster of such epic proportions that I might never recover. In short, I am exactly the sort of person the laws about juror exemptions were designed to protect.

So when I got my notice of jury duty, I immediately called the number on the form that you were supposed to call if you had any problems or questions. This being a government agency, I only had to tell my story four times before I finally got transferred to the right person who should have been hearing it. She was a nice woman, sympathetic and understanding. She said there was no problem, on the basis of what I told her I should be exempt, and all I had to do was come in and bring in my most recent tax record to show that I was, indeed, the sole proprietor of my business and that would be that.

So I did.

But since I started this whole thing by saying I got jury duty, you have to know something went wrong. And, of course, something did. Which it shouldn't have. Because I *am* the sole proprietor of my business, and have been for several years. As I said, I'm a private detective. Not a grand and glamorous one like you see on TV, but a private detective nonetheless. I work for the law firm of Rosenberg and Stone. Don't get me wrong—I'm not *employed* by the law firm of Rosenberg and Stone—my agency is. Stanley Hastings detective agency is subcontracted by Rosenberg and Stone to investigate some of their accident cases. For this, I am paid a flat fee as an independent contractor. At the end of the year I get a 1099 form from Rosenberg and Stone listing my gross earnings. From this amount I deduct my expenses and then pay my taxes. And four times a year I pay estimated taxes because I have no withholding. I also pay Unincorporated Business Tax. In short, I do everything a sole proprietor of his business should do.

So what went wrong?

Well, I wasn't always a private detective. I've been doing it for the last few years, but before that I've been many other things. Before I was a private detective I was a failed writer, and before I was a failed writer I was a failed actor.

It's the acting part I want to talk about. You see, twenty years ago I was in Arnold Schwarzenegger's first movie.

That probably surprises you, because most people think Arnold Schwarzenegger's first movie was *Pumping Iron,* but it wasn't. He did another movie way before that, and the only reason you don't know that is because nobody's ever heard of it. The movie was called

Hercules in New York. It starred Arnold Schwarzenegger as Hercules. Only Arnold Schwarzenegger wasn't a household word back then. Aside from being Mr. Universe, which only those in the bodybuilding biz would know, his biggest claim to fame was appearing on the inside cover of Marvel comic books, standing there flexing his muscles and supporting a curvaceous, smiling girl in a bathing suit who was sitting on his bicep, as an advertisement for Joe Weider's weight building course.

Someone, somewhere, got the bright idea that this young man should be in a movie, and damned if he wasn't. The plot of *Hercules in New York* involved Zeus, king of the gods, zapping Hercules with a thunderbolt and knocking him off Mount Olympus (shot in Central Park), and Hercules falling into the harbor and winding up in New York, and having various capers with a bunch of Damon Runyonesque crooks.

Schwarzenegger wasn't bad, by the way, if you can imagine an Austrian actor with a thick accent, playing a Greek god in a production of *Guys and Dolls*. Had it been left that way, the movie at least would have been high camp. But the producers weren't happy with Arnold's accent, so they dubbed his voice. They also knew the name Schwarzenegger would never do, so they changed his name to Arnold Strong. This was largely because the co-star in the movie was Arnold Stang, the little guy with glasses who used to do the Chunky commercials, which made for cute billing—''Arnold Strong and Arnold Stang in *Hercules in New York*.''

And where do I come into all this? Well, as I said, I had a part in the movie. It wasn't much, but as a struggling actor, I was damn glad to get it. I played ''Skinny Hercules.'' I had a horse and chariot and I wore a leopard skin and I stood outside a movie theater, and the horse and chariot and I were all supposedly an advertisement for yet another fictitious Hercules movie. During the chase scene, Schwarzenegger runs from the theater, steals my chariot and takes off after the Damon Runyon-type crooks. I chase the chariot down Broadway, waving a hotdog I just bought from a Sabrett vendor and screaming, "Come back with my chariot!"

"Come back with my chariot!" Pay attention to those five words, because they are important. They were my only line in the movie. By saying them, my status in the movie was upgraded from "Silent Bit," which at the time was seventy-five bucks a day, to "Day Player," which was a hundred and twenty. Not only that, being a Day Player made me SAG eligible, and I immediately joined the Screen Actors Guild, in the hope that this movie might launch a few careers.

My career never took off.

Arnold Schwarzenegger's eventually did.

But not because of this movie. No one I know has ever seen this movie. *I* have never seen this movie. But it does exist, and still does play now and then somewhere on late-night TV. I know this because every time it does I get a forty-dollar residual check as a bonus for having said those five immortal words, "Come back with my chariot!" and having been upgraded to Day Player status. So each time the forty bucks arrives in the mail—thirty-two something, actually, after taxes—I'm pleased of course, but I'm also somewhat wistful, when I think about what might have been.

But I digress. The point is, as soon as I found out I could get out of jury duty I grabbed my tax records and rushed straight down to do it.

Apparently, getting out of jury duty isn't exactly a novel idea, because there were about thirty people ahead of me. After waiting for two hours, I finally found myself in a glass partitioned cubicle sitting across the desk from a crisp, efficient-looking woman, who took my juror duty notification slip, inspected it, and said, "You're applying for an exemption, Mr. Hastings?"

"That's right."

"On what grounds?"

"That I'm self-employed and the sole proprietor of my business."

"Did you bring your tax return?"

"Yes, I did."

I opened my briefcase and handed her my last year's tax return. I did so with absolute confidence. I pay an accountant a hundred bucks a year to fill out my tax return. I'm sure he saves me more than that, and even if he didn't, it would be worth it, just for the peace of mind of knowing the thing had been done right, that I wouldn't be audited and suddenly find I owed a bunch of back taxes plus penalties and interest and the whole shmear.

The woman took my tax return and riffled through the pages. She nodded her head—I didn't know what that meant, but it looked promising. Then she riffled through the 1099 forms stapled to the top of the front page.

She stopped, frowned, pointed to one. "What's this?" she demanded.

I shrugged. "A 1099 form."

"No, it isn't."

"Oh?"

"No. It's a W2."

I leaned across the desk and looked. It was indeed

a W2 for my forty-dollar residual for *Hercules in New York*.

"Right," I said. "That's a residual check I got for a movie I was in."

The woman shook her head. "I'm sorry, Mr. Hastings. You don't qualify for exemption."

"Why not?"

"Because you're not self-employed."

"Yes I am. Look at my return. I run my own business. I pay Unincorporated Business Tax."

"Yes, but you have a W2 form."

"So what?"

"You're not self-employed. You have an employer. This movie production company. They paid you as an employee and withheld taxes."

"Forty dollars."

"The amount doesn't matter. The fact is, they paid you."

I smiled and held up my hands. "You don't understand. See, I didn't work for this company last year. I worked for no one but me. I worked for that company twenty years ago. I did one day's work as an actor in a movie. The movie played on television one night last year, so they sent me a residual check. But I didn't do any work for it. See?"

She saw all right. She shook her head. "If you have a W2, you're not self-employed."

I frowned. How quickly one's opinions could change. I realized what I had taken for intelligence and efficiency in this woman was actually the precision of an automaton, a government employee incapable of independent thought.

"Whoa," I said. "Didn't you hear me? I did no work last year, except for myself. I did *not* work for this company last year. I am self-employed and have been for several years. Being on a jury would be a tremendous financial hardship for me. I am exactly the sort of person this exemption system was set up to protect.''

Now she got angry. How dare I question her authority? Her lips set in a firm line, and her eyes were hard. ''Mr. Hastings,'' she said. ''Perhaps *you* didn't hear *me*. You have a W2. You are *not* self-employed.''

I took a breath. So much for trying to make *her* understand. ''All right,'' I said. ''Let me talk to your superior.''

I expected her to be furious, but at that point I didn't care. I just wanted to get away from her and find a genuine human being I could talk to. A person who could think and reason.

It was not to be. The woman may have been furious, but she didn't show it. She actually seemed somewhat pleased. She drew herself up, stuck out her chin, fixed me with her eyes, and said with just a trace of a smug smile, ''I *am* my superior.''

I'm sure there are lots of people in the world who could have gotten past that. I'm not one of them. I was absolutely floored. Those four words stopped me dead. ''I *am* my superior.'' What the hell was it? It's not a non sequitur. It's not a paradox. It's an absurdity, yes, buy even more than that, you know what I mean? At any rate, I couldn't deal with it. And I couldn't deal with her. And I couldn't deal with her superior, since her superior was her.

So I was stumped. And that was it. The end result was, my five words, ''Come back with my chariot!'' and her four words, ''I *am* my superior,'' somehow through algebra, calculus and the new math, added up to the two words, ''Dorked again.''

I got jury duty.

2.

I WAS ORDERED to report to Room 362 at 111 Centre Street, which I figured to be The Criminal Court Building. My call was for ten o'clock, so I hit the subway at nine. I knew I was overprotecting, but I didn't want to be late my first day. I rode down to Chambers Street, walked over to Centre Street, and up Centre to 111.

I could see the courthouse as I walked up Centre Street. You can't miss it. It looks like a courthouse—a big stone building with marble pillars and long, wide marble steps. It's the one you see in all the courtroom movies, the one Al Pacino sits on the steps in front of at the end of *And Justice For All*. It felt good seeing it, it being so familiar and all. Kind of like meeting an old friend.

Only it wasn't the Criminal Court Building. It was *a* court building, but it wasn't the Criminal Court Building. At least it wasn't 111 Centre Street. It was 60 Centre Street, and it was the Supreme Court. The Criminal Court Building turned out to be a building two blocks up the street. I didn't know that, because it had never been in any movies, and the reason it had never been in any movies was because it was just your ordinary, tall, rectangular building, just like any other office building, and what movie director in his right mind would want to film there when he could wheel his camera around and shoot the sucker with the marble steps on down the street?

Not only that, The Criminal Court Building wasn't 111 Centre Street either. It was 100 Centre Street. 111 Centre Street was a building of no distinction whatsoever across the street.

Which really bummed me out. Which was silly, of course. Because once you get inside, one building is just like another, and what difference could it possibly make anyhow? I guess it was just that I was still so miffed about having to serve at all that I was programmed to be bummed out. That and the fact I somehow sensed that this was just the first of a series of disappointments.

As I said, my jury duty summons told me to report to Room 362 on the third floor. I did, and found a large assembly room with a bunch of seats all facing forward and a counter up front. About twenty people were already there, milling around, sitting in the seats, reading newspapers and drinking coffee from the concession stand downstairs or from the coffee machine in the front of the room.

There was a woman behind the counter, and I wondered if I should go up to her and hand her my summons. A sign on the counter said PLEASE DO NOT APPROACH THIS DESK DURING ROLL CALL. Which immediately made me feel stupid if what I thought was a counter was really a desk. It certainly looked like a counter. Whatever it was, I wondered if I should approach it. It certainly didn't look like roll call, which I assumed wouldn't be until ten o'clock.

While I was standing there thinking all this, a man

went up to the counter or desk or whatever, and handed his summons to the woman behind it. When she appeared to accept it, I figured maybe that was the thing to do. I walked up to the counter and waited until she'd finished with the man. When she had, I handed her my slip.

I always feel self-conscious and out of place in new situations, and I fully expected the woman to give me a withering look and say something like, "Your summons says ten o'clock. We're doing the nine forty-five people now."

But she didn't. Giving her the summons was the right and proper thing to do. She took it, tore off the perforated three-by-three-inch square corner, and handed the larger part of the slip back to me. Then she checked my name off a list, and put the three-by-three-inch square stub on top of a pile of others. I didn't know it then, but that three-by-three-inch stub would control my destiny from here on in.

It was going so swimmingly, I dared venture a question. "What do I do now?" I asked.

She smiled. "Have some coffee, have a seat, do whatever you like, just be back for ten o'clock roll call."

I nodded. Have some coffee. That sounded easy enough. I wondered if I should go downstairs for coffee or risk the machine. I opted for the machine. I fed two quarters into it, selected coffee light, no sugar, and was rewarded with a paper cup of coffee and a dime change. I took a sip of the coffee, found that I could drink it.

Fine. Now what did I do next?

I took a look around. The room was beginning to fill up. Of the people there, many were reading newspapers and many had brought books. Obviously, old hands at the game who had come prepared. I, of course, had brought nothing.

Those who hadn't brought newspapers or books were chatting in small groups. I'm shy at meeting people, particularly in new situations. And the people talking together were obviously not on their first day of jury duty, but had formed acquaintances during their days of service. I was an outsider, an intruder, the new kid on the block, and a schmuck who didn't know the system. So rather than deal with the people, I dealt with the room.

There were two open doorways on the right wall. One proved to be a small reading room with desk cubbyholes and chairs. The second proved to be a TV room. The TV was on and a half dozen people were watching it. The program was an early morning talk show of the variety I would not watch if you paid me. A young woman was being interviewed. I couldn't hear what she was saying, but a graphic appeared on the bottom of the screen reading, HAD AFFAIR WITH HER BOSS. Why that qualified her to appear on television was beyond me, but somehow it did. And there she sat, the graphic proudly proclaiming her title, just as if it had read NYU SOCIOLOGY PROFESSOR or MANHATTAN BOROUGH PRESIDENT.

So much for the rooms on the right. On the front wall, to the right of the counter/desk, was a corridor with several doors leading off from it. No jurors were wandering down it so I figured I shouldn't. I figured right. It later turned out that was where the offices and juror examination rooms were. You only went there if asked.

To the left of the desk was an alcove with a bank of six phones, and a corridor leading to the Men's and Women's rooms. I filed the information away for future reference and continued my inspection of the room.

Though I had brought nothing to read, there was certainly no dearth of reading material. There were signs all over the place. I've already mentioned the one on the counter/desk. There was another one there saying, WE ARE NOT AUTHORIZED TO GRANT DEFER-MENTS OR EXEMPTIONS. Also on the desk was a wooden box which read, WHEN EXCUSED FROM THE COURT-ROOM, PLEASE PLACE BALLOT IN THE BOX HERE.

I wondered what a ballot was. I strolled over and looked at the box. In it was one of the three-by-three stubs. My first clue as to how they would run my life.

At least those signs made sense. I found two others that didn't. On the wall near the coffee and candy machines was a sign, NO SMOKING, EATING, OR DRINKING IN THIS ROOM. There was also a garbage can with a sign, PLEASE PUT REFUSE IN CONTAINER. I looked at those for a while. What refuse? Obviously the refuse from the coffee and candy you were allowed to buy but weren't allowed to drink or eat.

At this point I realized I was *holding* a cup of coffee. Uh oh. Blown it already. Not even roll call and I'm already doing things wrong. What will they do to me? Probably some court officer will show up and haul me away.

I went out the back door into the hallway, where several people were sitting on benches, smoking and drinking coffee. Aha. The designated area. These peo-ple were also talking in small groups, but once again no one knew me. I stood, looked around and discov-ered another sign on the jury room door. On inspec-tion it proved to be a blowup of a sample summons with instructions as to how to fill it out, which im-mediately made me start wondering if I'd filled out

21

mine correctly, no help now since I'd already turned it in. On the bottom of the sign were the words GOOD MORNING JURORS, bordered by two yellow smiley-faced suns. Oh dear. Have a nice day.

I finished my coffee, deposited my cup in the proper receptacle and went back into the jury room. No court officers appeared to handcuff me and lead me away. Hot damn. I'd gotten away with it.

Just inside the door I found another sign. It said EVACUATION. That caught my attention. I went over and looked at it. It turned out to be a printed form with the appropriate information filled in in the blanks. In full it read:

EVACUATION
IN CASE OF FIRE OR OTHER EMERGENCY
USE STAIRWELL—C—
OR ALTERNATELY
USE STAIRWELL—D—
ROOM—362—

That was a hell of an ominous note. We were in an interior room with no stairwells whatsoever and no clues as to where they might conceivably be. Well, with luck the building wouldn't burn down in the next two weeks. If it did, I could envision people trampling over each other screaming, "Where's stairwell C, dammit?"

I looked around some more and discovered the most peculiar sign of all. It was on the wall behind the counter/desk. It read IN REAR OF ROOM ONLY.

I blinked. Surely that couldn't be the entire sign. I walked up, looked closer. Sure enough, it wasn't the entire sign. There was obviously a top part of the sign with other words on it. But here was the interesting thing. The top of the sign was not missing. Instead, it was covered up by a metal bar that had been screwed into the wall with four huge metal screws. The bar was just wide enough to cover up the top line of the sign. But the thing was, the metal bar had no conceivable purpose *except* to cover up the top line of the sign.

Good lord. What was it that was going on in the rear of this room that they didn't want us to know about? It couldn't be smoking and drinking coffee— that was well advertised and took place in the corridor outside. But in the rear of the room? Hmmm. The mind boggled.

I was not to find out. At that moment a young man in a suit and tie who looked like a college student stepped up the counter/desk, picked up a microphone which had been concealed behind it, and suddenly his voice boomed throughout the room. "All right, listen up, jurors. I am going to call the roll. When I call your name, please answer by saying 'here.' "

With that he picked up the stack of ballots, the three-by-three summons stubs, and began reading the names off of them and then placing them facedown in two piles, one for those present and one for those absent.

I glanced at the clock. It was ten after ten. Not bad.

I heard the name Stanley Hastings.

I answered, "Here."

Small beginnings.

Idle musings.

I wasn't sure what I expected next.

But I certainly never expected murder.

3.

THAT'S NOT REALLY TRUE. About my not expecting murder, I mean. Because after all, I'd been called as a juror, and it was certainly conceivable one of the trials they were assembling jurors for might be a murder trial.

But that's not what I meant. In that case, the murder would be a *fait accomplis*. Something that had happened in the past that we were now being asked to judge. What I mean is, I didn't expect a murder to *happen*.

Not that it happened right away. Nothing much happened right away.

Except we saw a movie. It was, naturally, about jury duty. It concerned the experiences of three jurors of predictably racially mixed backgrounds. All were serving jury duty for the first time. All began with certain reservations or doubts. All served on one form of jury or another—criminal, civil or grand. And— surprise, surprise—all emerged from the experience with a sense of pride, accomplishment and fulfillment at having done their civic duty.

To the best I could determine, none of them was the sole proprietor of their business.

day, it was six. Which meant maybe my two weeks here didn't have to be a total loss.

I went to the bank of pay phones, all of which were occupied by prospective jurors trying to establish contact with the outside world and straighten out their disrupted lives, waited my turn, and called Rosenberg and Stone.

Wendy/Janet answered the phone. Wendy and Janet were switchboard girls with identical voices, so it was impossible to ever know which one you were talking to.

"Rosenberg and Stone," Wendy/Janet said.

"Hi, it's Stanley," I said.

"Stanley," she said. "I thought you had jury duty."

"I do."

"Then why are you calling?"

"I found out it isn't going to take as much time as I thought. I may be able to handle some work.

"I don't understand."

That was not surprising. Between them, Wendy and Janet had the IQ of a tree stump. Explaining anything to one of them was never easy. I tried, but the end result was Wendy/Janet told me I would have to talk to Richard. That figured. The only decision Wendy/Janet was capable of making on her own was the decision to defer to Richard's judgment.

Richard wasn't particularly glad to hear from me.

"Yes?" he barked, in his familiar high-pitched nasal whine.

"Yeah, Richard. It's Stanley."

"Stanley. I thought you had jury duty."

"I do. I'm there now."

"Then why are you calling?"

"It turns out I'm gonna have more free time than I thought. I'm gonna be able to handle some cases."

"Hey, you got jury duty, you gotta be there. You can't be running out on 'em.''

"I know that, but it's a short day. I don't have to be there till ten. So I can do a signup first.''

"And get there by ten?''

"If it's in Manhattan, sure.''

"I don't like it.''

"Why not?''

"You're gonna be late.''

"No, I won't. Look, I'm uptown already. I can do a case in Harlem—there's always a case in Harlem, right? I can shoot up there, sign the guy up, I'm downtown by ten o'clock easy.''

"Oh yeah?'' Richard said. "What time you leave your house?''

"Eight o'clock.''

"For what, an eight-thirty appointment?''

"Sure.''

"You're gonna meet the guy at eight-thirty, sign him up and get downtown by ten o'clock. You're telling me you can do that?''

"Absolutely.''

"Oh yeah?'' Richard said. "Then you ought to look at your time sheets. Every signup you do in Harlem you put down two hours. Now you're telling me you can do the signup plus drive from Harlem all the way down to Centre Street in under two hours? I have to wonder what the hell you been billing me for.''

Jesus Christ, what a cheap prick. I mean he only paid me ten bucks an hour and thirty cents a mile, so twenty bucks for a whole signup didn't seem excessive.

But I realized I was on dangerous ground. "All right, so I make the appointment for eight o'clock, I leave the house at seven thirty. Christ, Richard, give

28

me a break. Every investigator charges two hours for a Harlem assignment. I should get paid less because I'm faster and more efficient? Hell, if I'm faster and more efficient, maybe I should get a raise.''

Richard sidestepped that issue neatly. ''It's not the money,'' he said, a ballsy remark, coming from him. ''I just don't want you showing up late for jury duty. I have to work in the system. It would be a real embarrassment to me to have you come late to jury duty, and then have them find out it was because you were out working for me.''

''That won't happen, Richard. I promise you.''

''Oh, all right. Christ. So that's all you called about? One lousy signup?''

''No. Two lousy signups. I can handle one in the afternoon too.''

''Oh yeah? How is that?''

''I can make a five o'clock appointment.''

''You don't get off till five o'clock.''

''Technically, yes. But I found out if nothing's doin', they let you off at four.''

''What if something's doin'?''

''Then they keep you later.''

''Then you can't have a five o'clock appointment.''

''Sure I can. In the first place, nothing's gonna be doin'. But if there was, there's a bank of phones here, I could call the client, tell him I'm gonna be a little late.''

''What if the client has no phone?''

''Then I'll call the office and tell Wendy/Janet I'm gonna be late, and when the client calls in to ask where I am, they can tell him.''

''How's the client gonna call in if he has no phone?''

''He'll go out to a pay phone, just like he did to make the appointment in the first place.''

"Yeah, well what if he's laid up in bed and can't get out to a phone?"

"Then he'll be there when I get there."

There was a moment of silence on the line.

Son of a bitch! I'd done it. I'd out-argued Richard Rosenberg, the master debater himself.

Richard sighed. "All right," he said. "You got your signups. Tell Wendy/Janet I said it was all right."

Now it was my turn to pause. "Well, listen, Richard, Wendy/Janet's not too keen on the idea. I think they'll have to hear it from you."

Richard was back in form. "Oh no you don't," he chuckled. "You want the job, you pay the price. You know if you tell 'em I said so, it will be all right. You want the job, *you* explain it to Wendy/Janet."

Still chuckling, Richard hung up the phone.

What a prince. The least he could have done was transfer me back. And that was my last quarter, too. Well, hell, this was company business. I used the Rosenberg and Stone calling card number.

"Rosenberg and Stone," came the voice of Wendy/Janet.

The worst part about dealing with Wendy/Janet was, if you have to refer to a previous conversation, you never know if you were dealing with her or the other one. And you can't really ask, because for some reason not recognizing their voices tends to piss them off immensely.

"Hi, it's Stanley."

"Stanley," she said. "I thought you had jury duty."

So. It was the other one. At least I knew that. Which didn't really help me. If I knew I was talking to Wendy, I could ask to talk to Janet. Or vice versa. But I couldn't just say, "Let me talk to the other one." Not if I wanted to stay in their good graces. And I certainly did. Wendy and Janet, as incompetent as they were, were responsible for handling all incoming calls and parceling out work assignments to the investigators. Which made me dependent upon them for my livelihood.

So I had to go through the whole spiel again. First I had to explain that I'd just been on the phone with Richard, since Wendy/Janet didn't know I'd been on the phone with Richard, since Wendy/Janet hadn't been the one who'd connected me.

By the time I got off the phone my head was spinning, but I had Wendy/Janet's solemn assurance that she understood the situation. On that, I would not have made book. But in more practical terms, she had given me a signup for eight-thirty the next morning, with a Lincoln Monroe Jackson of 109 West 129th Street, who had fallen in his building and broken his leg.

I hung up the phone went back and sat down. Well, hell, I'd done it now. The die was cast. I was up to my old tricks again, juggling my responsibilities.

Suddenly I felt like shit. Insecurity poured over me. The worst of it was that Lincoln Monroe Jackson had no phone. See, with Wendy/Janet I always like to call the client first and verify the address before going there, since Wendy/Janet are so likely to be wrong. And tomorrow morning I won't have time to cope with a wrong address, what with having to get downtown by ten o'clock for jury duty and everything. So by all rights, the Lincoln Monroe Jackson case had all the earmarks of being a potential total disaster.

Not so, quoth the schizophrenic. If the client is not at that address, then there is no way to verify what address he's really at, so you hang it up and wash it out and go downtown and serve your jury duty. And if Wendy/Janet ever straightens it out and you finish the assignment, you add on an hour's time for having gone to the wrong address.

Thinking along those lines made me feel a little better. Maybe it would work out. By rights, it *should* work out. After all, a guy named after three presidents wouldn't screw me, would he? Of course not. I'd do that signup and I'd get another one for the afternoon, and I'd get four hours for the day. At ten bucks an hour, that's forty bucks.

And hell, who said my afternoon signup only had to be two hours? So I get home late. Big deal. Maybe I could take an afternoon case out in Queens, get three hours plus some mileage. Hell yeah, no reason why I shouldn't do that. Maybe I should call Wendy/Janet back.

I'd just gotten into the phone booth to do that when I heard the squawk of the loud speaker. "All right, listen up, jurors. When I call your name answer 'Here,' take all your belongings and go out and wait in the corridor for the court officer."

I looked out of the booth. College Boy was at the microphone. He had set up a metal drum on the counter/desk, and as I watched he opened a flap, dropped the ballots in, closed it, turned a crank and gave the drum a spin. He looked as if he were raffling off a turkey at the county fair. He cranked the drum around a few times, opened the top, reached in and pulled out a ballot.

"Carla Feinbaum," he said.

A voice said, "Here," and an elderly woman got up from one of the chairs, gathered up her purse and her *Daily News* and shuffled up the aisle toward the back door.

Good lord. So this was how they chose jurors. It

She smiled helplessly, immediately belying the image. "I don't know. It's my first day."

A plump, middle-aged man with a rather jolly expression leaned in. "We wait here for the court officer. When they're ready, he'll come take us upstairs."

"I thought the criminal court was across the street."

"It is, but there's courtrooms here too. There's courtrooms all over."

"Have you done this already?"

He seemed pleased. "Oh yes. This is the fifth time I've been called."

"Fifth?"

"Yeah. It's my fifth case. They keep kicking me off." He seemed rather pleased by that, too.

So was I. An expert. "Oh yeah? How come?"

"Because I have a college education. A criminal case, they usually kick you off if you have a college education."

"Really?" the woman said. "And why is that?"

The guy shrugged. "I think it's 'cause the defendant's usually dumb. You're supposed to be tried by a jury of your peers. I think the defense attorneys figure educated people are going to be prejudiced against uneducated criminals."

"I suppose that makes sense," I said.

He shrugged again. "I don't know. All I know is, I been booted off four times."

I felt a glimmer of hope. I have a college education. Maybe I'd be booted off too. I sure hoped so. I had an appointment the next morning with Lincoln Monroe Jackson, and I had no time for this shit.

A young court officer pushed his way through the crowd. He wore a white shirt and dark pants, standard court officer uniform. He also wore a gun, which I hoped was utterly superfluous and just for show. I couldn't imagine a shootout in this building.

"All right, listen up, jurors," he said. "We're going to part 24 on the sixth floor. When you get up to the sixth floor, just wait in the corridor for further instructions."

He turned and led us down the corridor to the elevators. We couldn't all fit in one elevator, of course. When the first one arrived, the court officer shoved in as many jurors as he could, pressed the button and sent them up. He immediately rang for another elevator. There were six in the bank, so it wasn't that long before we got one. In fact, we got two, almost simultaneously. I got shoved into the first one of those, and we rumbled up to six.

I got out and stood around looking stupid, waiting for the other elevators to arrive. The last one did and the court officer emerged and herded us all down the corridor and around the corner, and stopped us in front of a door that read PART 24.

"All right. Wait here," he said.

He opened the door and slid inside, closing the door behind him.

I stood there in mounting distress. Good lord. When they called fifty names I figured they were calling jurors for at least two separate trials. But no, they'd all come here. What was going on that was so important they needed fifty jurors? Whatever it was, I sure didn't want to be part of it. Could I really count on my college education to keep me out? If so, it would be the first concrete thing my liberal arts degree had ever done for me.

The door opened again and the court officer came out.

JUROR

"All right, jurors. Please file in quietly and take your seats."

He stepped aside and ushered us in.

I filed in quietly.

It was a small, contemporary courtroom, the type you see on TV. We were filing in from a door in the middle of the back. Directly in front of us were three rows of benches for the spectators, and this was where the court officer was indicating for us to sit. Ahead of them was a rail and a gate, leading to the rest of the courtroom. Directly ahead of us, in the middle of the back wall, was the judge's bench, raised and regal. Behind it sat an elderly judge, white-haired, bespectacled, solemn and dignified in his judicial black robe.

To his left, on the side wall, was the jury box. To his right, on the other side wall, was the bailiff's desk. To his immediate left, higher than the jury box but lower than his bench, was the witness stand.

In front of the judge's bench were two tables. At the table to his right sat two middle-aged men in suits and ties. Clean cut, clean shaven, impeccably and conservatively dressed. One fat and one thin, but otherwise absolutely identical. Obviously the prosecutor and his assistant, though which was which I couldn't tell.

At the other table sat a slightly older attorney. Slightly seedier, slightly tweedier, slightly more folksy, but still with an air of practical, down to earth respectability. Next to him sat a young black man about twenty years of age, who, despite being dressed in a new suit, and despite, I was sure, countless hours of coaching by his attorney, could not somehow help looking tough.

I sank into my seat on the bench with a hollow feeling in the pit of my stomach that simply would not go away. Jesus Christ. Oh my god. Jesus fucking Christ.

When we were all seated the judge said, "Good afternoon, jurors. I'm Judge Coles. We will be selecting jurors this afternoon. This is a criminal case, so we need twelve jurors and four alternates. We have already chosen ten jurors, so we are looking for two more and four alternates. Bailiff, would you please fill the box."

It was another turkey raffle. The court officer handed our ballots to the bailiff, who dropped them into another tin drum, cranked it up, and began pulling out ballots and reading off names.

I was the sixth name drawn. Wouldn't you know it. I never win anything. And here I am, two for two.

I marched through the gate as if I were the one who was on trial, and seated myself in the juror box in seat number six.

I did so as if in a daze. Here it was, my worst nightmare. The judge's words kept ringing in my ears like a death knell. "We've already selected ten jurors." I mean, good lord. The fifty of us had not been brought here to form a jury. Jury selection had already been going on, obviously for some time. All of us had been brought here to find two real jurors and four alternate jurors, a grand total of six people still needed to judge this case.

Which meant it was the thing I dreaded most. A big case. A murder case. Here I was called into the box, and I knew as sure as I was sitting here, that my college education not withstanding, I was going to be chosen. I would be put on the jury and the case would last for months. That's what happened in murder trials. Christ, the Larry Davis trial had gone on for months, hadn't it? And then there was the deliberation. Jesus Christ, the deliberation! That alone could last for weeks. And, oh shit, they'd sequester us. That's what they did in murder trials. Put up in a hotel and not allowed to go home, and not allowed any contact with the outside world. Not allowed to do anything until we hammered out a verdict.

A verdict that would never come because we couldn't agree. And, Christ, what if it's the worst? What if it's like *Twelve Angry Men?* What if it's eleven against one, and I'm the only holdout? What a moral dilemma. How strong am I? Can I hold out in the face of those odds? And if not, can I live with myself if I send a man to prison just because I'm tired and I want to go home? Jesus Christ, oh god, oh damn it to fucking shit hell.

When the box had been filled, Judge Coles said, "All right, jurors. As I said, this is a criminal trial. This is the case of the people of the state of New York versus Raheem Smith. It is a case of petty theft arising from a chain snatching that occurred on the 66th Street Broadway IRT line. Mr. Smith is represented by his attorney, Mr. Franklin. The People are represented by Assistant District Attorney Blaire and Assistant District Attorney Maxwell. Now first of all, I am going to ask if any of you know any of the parties involved. Then I am going to ask if any of you have ever been personally involved in a chain snatching incident. Then . . ."

He went on, but I had stopped listening. My head was spinning. Good lord. This wasn't a murder case. This was a simple chain snatch. All these people, the attorneys, the judge, the bailiff, the court officers, the court reporter, and the hundreds of prospective jurors who must have paraded through this room—all that time, effort and money was being expended because some punk snatched someone's gold chain.

It had never occurred to me before, but now I realized, if this was what it took to try some punk chain snatcher, no wonder our court system was so backed up. No wonder crime flourished in our city. No wonder the police couldn't seem to do anything about it. Sure, every man's entitled to a day in court. Every man's entitled to a trial by jury. Yes, I'm a liberal and I believe in civil rights.

But Jesus Christ.

I looked at the attorney sitting beside the defendant, and then at the two prosecutors, and wondered why in the world they hadn't plea-bargained this case. To me, there was only one explanation. The defendant must have had prior convictions. He was probably out on parole now, and a conviction of any kind would violate that and send him back to jail. That was why his lawyer wouldn't cop a plea. Yeah, that had to be it.

It suddenly hit me in the face. You mealy-mouthed, hypocritical, liberal asshole. Do you hear what you're thinking? Never once did it cross your mind, never once did it occur to you that this defendant might be *innocent*. Maybe that was why he wouldn't cop a plea. Maybe that was why he was fighting the case.

Realizing that made me feel pretty bad.

What made me feel worse was realizing I didn't care. Some solid citizen. Some prospective juror. But to be honest, that was the case. I didn't care if the man was innocent or if the man was guilty. And I didn't want the responsibility of making that determination. I had my own problems, and my own totally selfish motives. And they had nothing to do with the man in that courtroom. All I knew was, guilty as it made me feel, more than anything else in the world, I wanted to be off that jury.

That jury I knew they were going to put me on.

5.

THEY DIDN'T.
They kicked me off. It took them all day to do it, but in the end they let me go. The judge interrogated us for an hour and then set us to lunch, and when we came back the attorneys interrogated us for a couple more hours, and the end result was, of the sixteen prospective jurors they booted fourteen of us and kept only two. The kicker was, just before we went home the guy who'd been booted off four juries already because of his college education came downstairs grinning from ear to ear and announced the judge had just booted *everyone* because the attorneys had finally plea-bargained the case.

Somehow, that did not restore my faith in the judicial process.

But it did leave me free to handle the Lincoln Monroe Jackson case, and eight o'clock the next morning I dropped my son Tommie off at the East Side Day School, and headed uptown for my eight-thirty appointment in Harlem.

Lincoln Monroe Jackson lived in one of those projects I see in my dreams, and I don't happen to sleep well. The glass in the foreboding bleak metal door had been kicked in, and the doorknob was missing. The lobby was dark, was scrawled with horrid graffiti, and stank. It was also occupied by a very strung-out looking black man who might have been any age from twenty to sixty. He had his hands deep in the pockets of his grungy army jacket. The temperature was close to eighty and rising fast, so the only reasons I could think of for him to wear it was because he had no place to leave it, or because he didn't even notice it was warm out, or because he needed some place to carry his gun. Speculating on that did not cheer me, nor did the fact he was staring at me fixedly, as if trying to make up his mind whether I was a cop or a moron—any white man in a suit and tie in that building had to be either one or the other.

There were two elevators in the lobby, and one of them might have been functioning, but I didn't feel like hanging around to find out. There was a metal door to a stairwell to the right of them, and I headed for that, even though Lincoln Monroe Jackson lived on the seventh floor. Seven floors was nothing. In buildings like this, rather than wait for the elevator, I'd often climbed as high as twelve.

I reached the seventh floor, went through the usual bullshit of locating the apartment among doors on which the numbers had long since fallen off, and finally located Lincoln Monroe Jackson.

He was a cheerful cripple, an amiable black man of about forty, who seemed perfectly pleased with everything, including the cast on his leg. Which was actually not that surprising—after all, he expected it to make him money. But he was also cooperative, direct and succinct, which was a great relief to me, seeing as how I had to get downtown by ten o'clock.

I filled out the fact sheet in no time, Lincoln Mon

roe Jackson supplying me with all his vital statistics, as well as all the details of his accident, which had occurred in his building. The hardest part of the fact sheet is the blank marked HISTORY, on which I was supposed to record a description of the accident. Some of these can be long, complicated and meandering. Lincoln Monroe Jackson's said simply, "SLIPPED IN URINE."

That did not, as you might think, make him unique. Sadly enough, with poor people in poor neighborhoods, I had had occasion to write the words SLIPPED IN URINE before.

Lincoln Monroe Jackson's accident had occurred in the stairwell from the eighth to the seventh floor. He had been going down the stairs, slipped in a pool of urine, fallen down and broken his leg. For this, he was attempting to sue the City of New York. At first glance, that might appear strange. I mean, after all, how could you hold the City responsible unless someone from the mayor's office had come down and pissed in the stairwell? But as it turned out, in my humble opinion, which of course counts for nothing, Lincoln Monroe Jackson actually had a case. You see, the project had odd/even elevators, which has to be the greatest technological advancement since the Edsel. I'm no genius, but even I know odd/even elevators don't belong in a project. Things break down fast in projects. The arrival of an elevator in a project lobby is a fortuitous event. When it occurs, no matter what the floor they're going to, everyone gets in, rendering the concept for which odd/even elevators were originally designed absolutely worthless. So people ride to floors they don't want to go to, and have to use the stairwells.

The day of Lincoln Monroe Jackson's accident, the odd elevator had in fact been broken. So he had been forced to ride the even elevator to eight, and walk down the stairs to seven, thereby slipping in the urine. As far as I was concerned, that made the City of New York responsible, the New York Housing Authority responsible, and the stupid architect who had designed the odd/even elevators responsible, and made me feel damn good that this innate stupidity was getting its deserved comeuppance.

I got out of the building by nine, hit only moderately bad traffic jams, and got down to Centre Street by ten of ten. That would have been fine if I hadn't been in my car. I'd driven down, of course, rather than take the subway since I was planning on doing another sign-up at five o'clock. And a car in Manhattan is a great blessing unless you're trying to park it. The municipal lot was jammed and two cars were circling. I joined in and made three, and was lucky enough to get a meter ten minutes later.

The meters were good in that they were two-hour meters, and bad in that a quarter got you a whopping twelve minutes. I'd scouted the lot the day before, so I was prepared, having ripped off my wife Alice's laundry money. I fed ten quarters into the meter, giving me a cool two hours, and hustled up to 111 Centre Street quick like a bunny, telling myself not to worry, these things never started on time anyway, and, wouldn't you know it, when I got there College Boy was already calling the roll. And since he did it from the stack of ballots rather than alphabetically, I had no way of knowing whether he'd already gotten to me or not.

I stood in the back by the doorway, listening for my name, which of course never came. Before I had time to wonder what I should do about that, College Boy said, "Anyone whose name I didn't call, please come up to the desk."

So. College Boy thought the counter was a desk too. Maybe it was. I walked up to it, stood in line behind four other people. When it was my turn he said, "Name?" and I said, "Stanley Hastings."

There were two stacks of ballots on the counter/ desk, one large and one small. College Boy picked up the small stack, riffled through it, pulled out a ballot, said, "Stanley Hastings?" When I said, "Yes," he put it on top of the large stack and turned to the next person in line.

And that was it. No reprimands. No, "You're a naughty boy, and if you do it again you'll be kept after court." If you missed roll call, you just told College Boy and he found your ballot. Knowing that made me feel a lot better about the parking lot.

As I turned away from the desk, I heard a voice say, "Hey, what's with you?"

I looked up to see my buddy, the old man from the day before. "Hi," I said, "how you doing?"

"Terrible," he said. "I ain't been called. So what's with you?"

"What do you mean?"

He pointed. "Yesterday you were dressed like a shlump, today a suit and tie."

"Oh," I said. I'd forgotten I was wearing my suit. I mean, I knew I was wearing it, but I hadn't really thought about it. I was wearing it, of course, because I'd done a signup in the morning and was hoping to do one in the afternoon. "Oh yeah," I said. "Well, I'm working today."

"Today?"

"Well, I did a job before I came here. There wasn't time to change."

"Well," he said, "maybe it's a good idea."

"Oh?"

"Yeah. Dress for success. Maybe they'll choose you if you look more respectable."

That was a disturbing thought, and one that hadn't occurred to me. Shit, wouldn't that be just my luck, to be chosen for my suit.

But there was no sense explaining all that to my buddy. I just smiled and nodded. "Excuse me. I have to make a phone call."

So did half the room. All five phones were filled, and there was a line of six people waiting. I stood in it fifteen minutes and finally got a booth and called the office.

"Rosenberg and Stone," said Wendy/Janet.

"It's Stanley."

I half expected her to say, "Stanley? I thought you had jury duty," but she didn't. "Hi," she said. "Did you do the signup?"

"It's taken care of. But I need another one for this afternoon and one for tomorrow morning."

"Nothing's come in yet."

"Okay. When it does, beep me."

"You're on the beeper?"

"Yeah, but I may be tied up, so don't go nuts if I don't call in right away. Just assume I've heard it and I'll call in first chance I get."

That was a half-truth. The whole truth was, if she beeped me, I wouldn't call in right away because I wouldn't hear it. That's because there were a whole bunch of signs in the lobby about no electronic equipment allowed in the courtrooms. So I figured my beeper was a no-no. I was wearing it on the side of my belt, hidden by my suit jacket, and I had the silent switch on. When that's on, if you get beeped it makes no noise and you don't know it. But when you slide the switch from silent to on, if you've been beeped any time since you set it, it will start beeping then, and if you haven't, it won't. In the course of my regular work I use the silent switch mainly for going into hospitals. There, I'd set it when I went in, and check it when I came out. Here, I figured I could duck into the men's room every half-hour or so to see if the office wanted me.

I didn't want to explain that to Wendy/Janet. Because if she knew I wasn't supposed to have a beeper, maybe she'd decide I shouldn't have one and she shouldn't beep me. And if she got that idea, I'd never talk her out of it. She'd wind up taking the matter up with Richard, and I had no idea how he'd feel about it. Besides, explaining anything to Wendy/Janet was tough sledding anyway. Hence the half-truth.

While I was still in the phone booth, College Boy said something that I couldn't make out with the door shut. But I could see him setting up the metal drum again, so I bid a fond farewell to Wendy/Janet, and came out to see what was going on.

It was, of course, another turkey raffle. The only difference was when he called their names, the people were now taking all their belongings and shuffling up the corridor to the right of the counter/desk. I had no idea where they were going, but when he called the name Stanley Hastings, I muttered some remark about College Boy's parentage, and shuffled up the corridor behind.

The destination turned out to be a room three doors down the corridor to the right. It was a small room with two rows of chairs, six in the front, and maybe eight or ten in the back. The front row was already filled and the back row was filling up fast, so I slid into the row and helped fill it.

In the front of the room, close enough so that the people in the front row could reach out and touch them, were two attorneys sitting on chairs. One was young, clean cut and plump, with a baby-fat face that seemed to smile a lot, but hard eyes. The other looked as if when the first courthouse was built, he'd held the hammer. Emaciated, with a few wisps of stringy white hair, and a pair of pince-nez that seemed in danger of sliding off the point of his nose, he somehow gave the impression that it had taken all his energy just to get there, and we shouldn't really expect anything more from him.

When the room had filled up with about sixteen jurors, one of whom was my buddy who gave me a triumphant thumbs-up sign, the court officer came in holding the ballots and conferred with the attorneys. They talked together in low tones, seemed in agreement, and then the plump one said, "All right, let's fill the seats."

The court officer took the ballots, shuffled them up, and began selecting jurors. The fact that he did this without the aid of a metal drum, somehow made this case seem of less importance. So did the fact there were only sixteen of us called instead of fifty. So did the fact we were in this tiny room with no judge and no defendant.

All this was enough to make even one as slow on the uptake as I to suspect this was not a criminal case but a civil suit.

It was. When the first six names had been called, mine, of course, being one (Jesus Christ, how come I never win the fucking lottery? Perhaps because I never play), and we had a fun game of musical chairs, moving the six people who had been called into the front six seats, and the people who had been occupying them into the back, the plump attorney said, "All right, ladies and gentleman. This is a civil suit. We will be selecting six jurors and two alternates. I'm Mr. Kleinbaum, and I'm an attorney for the City of New York." Indicating the elderly man, "This is Mr. Feldergrad, who is representing Ernestina Felicio. Mrs. Felicio is the plaintiff in this action. She claims she tripped on a crack in the sidewalk, fell down and broke her hip, and she is suing the City of New York."

I almost burst out laughing. Good lord. A trip-and-fall. Over fifty percent of the cases I handled were trip-and-falls. Hell, I'd handled one this morning. There was no way in hell they were going to want me on this case.

When the two attorneys had each put their two cents in about the matter at hand, they began examining the jurors.

When they got to me, I caused a minor splash by admitting to being a private detective. I went on to explain that a lot of the cases I handled were a lot like this one.

But they didn't let me go. The venerable Mr. Feldergrad merely peered down over his pince-nez and said, "And would your previous experience prevent you in any way from being fair and impartial in this particular case?"

I should have just said, "Yes." But I didn't really want to admit to being a prejudiced moron. And damn it, it was unfair of them to make me evaluate what effect my experience might have had on me. Why couldn't they take it at face value that having done the work was bound to influence me, and they should just let me go? But no, they left it up to me. Which just didn't seem fair.

So I waffled. "Well," I said, "I would of course try to judge the case on its own merits. But I think anyone's opinion has to be colored by their experience."

I figured that would do it. But Mr. Feldergrad merely nodded and said, "But you would still try to be fair?"

I gritted my teeth. "I would certainly try to be fair. Whether or not it would be possible under the circumstances, I leave up to you."

He nodded again. "Tell me, in any of these cases you investigated, were you ever called upon to testify?"

My heart sank. Good lord. This moron was actually going to put me on the jury. "No, I haven't," I said.

"If you were called upon to serve, you say that you would put aside your previous cases, and make every effort to be fair?"

I'm afraid I snapped. I tried to keep the anger out of my voice, but I'm afraid the exasperation showed through. "Yes," I said. "I would certainly make every effort to be fair. But I must point out, it is impossible to have done the job I've done without forming opinions about it. Without becoming slightly jaded. And I cannot let you put me on this jury without knowing, however fair and impartial I might try to be, in over half the trip-and-falls I handle, my personal opinion is that the client fell down because he was too dumb to look where he was going."

There was a moment's stunned silence. Then Mr. Feldergrad's eyes blazed. He straightened in his chair, rammed the pince-nez back on his nose, and launched into as eloquent a diatribe as his reedy voice would allow, about how the laws of the land didn't require people to walk around with their heads down looking at their feet all the time in case the pavement might be broken, and how everyone had a right to walk the sidewalks and expect the sidewalks to be maintained and free from hazard, and he went on and on and on until he finally sputtered and ran out of steam. At which point the plump attorney from the city tapped him on the shoulder and suggested they confer in the corridor.

When that happened, I knew I'd won. I wasn't pleased at having had to go so far. I was sorry to have upset the old attorney, and damn glad he hadn't had a stroke, which had seemed highly likely, but at least I knew I had accomplished my purpose. I knew damn well when the lawyers came back they were gonna throw me out.

They did.

And not just me.

They threw out the entire room.

6.

HIGHLIGHTS of a week in hell.
After that, everything was a mish-mosh. A confused jumble of images, thoughts and feelings which are all blurred together in my mind. I spent the week racing around like a madman, signing up clients in Harlem in the mornings, bucking traffic jams, sometimes missing roll call and sometimes making it, rushing out every two hours to feed an endless succession of quarters into parking meters, sneaking into the bathroom every half-hour to check my beeper, calling the office, making appointments, changing appointments, winning turkey raffles, getting put on juries, booted off juries and just generally having a lousy time.

And coloring all this was the overriding knowledge that I had betrayed a friend. The friend, of course, was my buddy, the old man whose one dream was to do a quick civil case and get out of there. For him, the Ernestina Felicio case must have seemed like a godsend, a simple trip-and-fall, quick, easy and over. But thanks to my irresponsible statement, he, of course, had been booted out with everybody else.

Judas. Betrayer. Backstabber. He said none of those things to me. In fact, he said nothing to me. When I came up to him afterwards to apologize, he turned away. So it was not as if I had to put up with him berating me. With him whining, complaining, bitching, moaning, telling me what an asshole I am. In point of fact, he never spoke to me again.

But he was always there, slumped in his seat, which was always the same one, smack dab in the middle of the Juror Assembly Room, his sour, hostile eyes smoldering, an odious, malevolent presence I never failed to see. A nagging conscience from which there was no escape. A constant reminder, as if I really needed one, that I was indeed a stupid asshole.

I prayed that he would be called, get put on a case and leave. I wanted it as much for his sake as for mine. And I must say, I sure wanted it for me. And every time College Boy set up the steel drum, I crossed my fingers and thought, "Hey, you sour old codger, this one's for you."

But, of course, it never was. Wouldn't you know it. While I was there, he was never called again.

I was called all the fucking time.

I don't know what it was, after a while I got to wondering if there must be some stickum on my ballot or something, but it sure seemed like every time College Boy stuck his hand in the metal drum, out it came.

I got booted off four or five more juries, I'm not sure, after a while they tend to blend into one another. I know I was called for another criminal case, sent upstairs with a bunch of fifty people, sat through two complete interrogations, was never called into the box, and was sent downstairs again because the jury was finally filled. And I know I was called for another civil case that had something to do with a bunch of gold rings that were bought and never paid for. I was glad not to get put on that—it would have been boring as hell. And I was called once for car theft and once for sale of narcotics, though one of those may have been the one I already mentioned, the one I never got put in the box, as I say, it's all kind of a blur.

A few isolated incidents stood out.

One was when I forgot to set my beeper on silent switch and it suddenly went off when I was sitting in the Juror Assembly Room. Thank god it wasn't during roll call or a turkey raffle or anything like that, and thank god there were no court officers around but still the room was pretty crowded, and every head in the place turned. I switched the thing off as quickly and unobtrusively as I could, and started looking around myself, as if trying to figure out where the noise had come from, but I don't think I fooled anybody really, because after that I kept noticing people looking at me kind of strange. Of course, that might also have just been because I was constantly looking over my shoulder to see if a court officer was bearing down on me to whisk me away. Of course, none ever did.

Another time was when I was sitting in the room and suddenly there came a crash and a scream from out in the hall. Naturally, we all got up and went out to see what had happened. We found a man the size of a small whale lying on the floor beside a bench, moaning and holding his left arm. There was a piece of wood on the floor next to him, which on closer inspection proved to be the arm of the bench the man had previously been sitting on. He'd leaned on it, it had snapped under his weight, and he had fallen to the floor.

We all crowded around, jabbering and being particularly unhelpful. Finally someone went to get a court officer to call a medic, but that was the extent of what anybody knew what to do. The guy was obviously in serious pain, and kept moaning and holding his arm, and the whole situation was real tense and uncomfortable until someone in the crowd deadpanned, "Is there a negligence lawyer in the house?" Which, of course, cracked everybody up, and I have to admit I laughed too, which would have made me feel bad if the whale on the floor hadn't also found it funny.

But even as I laughed, I couldn't help thinking Richard paid a bonus for anyone who brought him in a negligence case, and if I could just sign this guy up, I could make a hundred and fifty bucks. It was a very fleeting thought, and one I pushed right out of my mind, having long ago found that kind of ambulance chasing distasteful. But I still couldn't help thinking it.

Another highlight wasn't really a highlight, just a wild idea. I'd just been kicked off one jury or another, and the court officer had given me back my ballot and told me to report back to the Juror Assembly Room, and it suddenly occurred to me, *I had my ballot*. And if I didn't turn it in to College Boy, if I just kept it in my pocket, *they couldn't call me*. I could wander around, go out to the movies, go do a signup or a photo assignment, and no one would ever know. Of course, I didn't do that, I turned in my ballot like a good boy, but what a great idea.

The last highlight was the best. It was getting on toward the end of the week, I'd just won yet another turkey raffle, and as I followed the parade down the corridor to the right of the counter/desk, I was very apprehensive. Please, whatever it is, don't put me on it.

I walked into the juror examination room, took one look, stopped short, and burst out laughing.

The attorney for the plaintiff was Richard Rosenberg.

7.

DISASTER.
 No, don't get me wrong. The disaster wasn't Richard Rosenberg—that was a piece of cake. Richard just stated that he knew me and that we had a business relationship, and he and the other attorney excused me by mutual consent. No, the disaster came much later, and in a wholly unexpected manner.

It was Tuesday, the second day of the second week of my incarceration, my seventh day overall. By then things were looking up. I'd weathered the worst of it. And I'd totalled enough jobs before and after jury duty that I wasn't really taking it on the chin. And I'd augmented it by doing signups on Saturday, something I don't usually do, but which I'd done this time just to make me feel better. I'd done three of 'em, and while I still wasn't close to breaking even, I'd at least cut my losses by more than fifty percent.

Plus, it was my buddy's ninth day. He still hadn't been called, but by now that no longer mattered. By the end of tomorrow he'd be gone. In fact, from what I could gather by chatting with some of the other jurors, if he hadn't been called by the end of the day, they'd probably just give him his ballot and send him home. Because even if he got called, it wouldn't be fair to start him on something on his tenth day. That made pretty good sense to me, and I was praying it was true, because I couldn't wait to be rid of his malevolent presence.

And I was feeling pretty good because I was in the second week of service myself, and while I wasn't as far along as my buddy, it was still as if I could almost see the light at the end of the tunnel.

It was 11:30 Tuesday morning. I know because I'd just been in the men's room to check my beeper, and was now looking forward to sneaking out at twelve o'clock to feed ten quarters into the parking meter. Having responsibilities gives you a good sense of time. I hadn't been beeped, but I was thinking of calling the office anyway, because I didn't have a job for this afternoon yet, and I was going to tell Wendy/Janet it doesn't have to be Manhattan, give me one for Brooklyn, Queens, New Jersey, the Bronx, hell, I don't care.

I was on my way to the phone booth to call the office when College Boy held another turkey raffle, and guess who won? No, it wasn't my buddy, thank god for that. I'd have felt terrible if he won one now. Much better they ignore him and send him home. But luckily he didn't win.

I did.

I took all by belongings (none), and followed the procession past the counter/desk and down the corridor into a jury examination room. I was an old hand at the game by now, so I knew that this meant a civil case.

That didn't please me. I figured the odds of me getting put on a civil jury were slightly higher than getting put on a criminal one. Which still wasn't that bad, since I figured my odds of getting put on a criminal case at zero. But even so, it made me apprehensive, being in my second week and all.

I was one of the last names called, so the room was crowded by the time I got in.

Very crowded.

In addition to the sixteen jurors, there were four, count them, four lawyers.

This was something new. I frowned. Shit. Maybe this was a bigger case than usual.

If this had been a tag-team wrestling match, it wouldn't have been fair. It also would have been fixed, but that's beside the point. At any rate, what I mean is, it wouldn't have been two-on-two. Three attorneys were sitting on one side of the room, and one on the other.

The three attorneys sitting together were two men and a woman. The men appeared to be somewhere in their forties. They were completely bald on top, but the hair on the sides of their heads was still dark. And the shorter of the two had a dark moustache.

The woman seemed slightly younger. She had straight blonde hair, cut in bangs. She sat between the two men.

The grouping was unfortunate. I knew they were lawyers, but all I could think of was Peter, Paul and Mary.

The attorney sitting alone was something else. He looked slightly older than the other two men, but that might just have been his hair. He had more of it than the two of them combined, but what he had was all gray. And it was groomed. It swept back from his forehead in flowing waves. It wasn't held in place with grease or hairspray, but it wasn't dry and brittle, either. Just sleek, flowing, silver hair. Topping the effect were razor-cut silver sideburns, fashioned to a point.

The face wasn't bad, either. A silver moustache and goatee, cut short and severe, surrounded the firm line of the mouth. Straight nose, broad face, aggressive chin out and slightly up. And piercing sky blue eyes, completing the image, told you this was a person to be reckoned with. Intelligent, alert, sly, cunning—that was the picture I got. I didn't know who he was, but I immediately dubbed him the Silver Fox.

I also immediately revised my initial estimate upward. If he were involved in this case, it must be even bigger than I thought.

It wasn't.

When we were all assembled, Peter spoke first. Or maybe it was Paul. I must confess, with Peter, Paul and Mary, I'm not sure which is which. I know which one is Mary. It's the other two I'm not sure of. Now I'm sure this wouldn't please them, and it is with all due apologies that I confess my ignorance, but at any rate, the short one with the moustache spoke first, and whether that's Peter or Paul, you got me.

"Ladies and gentlemen," he said. "This is a case involving a rather large sum of money. When you hear the case, it may sound rather boring and trivial. But with a large sum of money involved, the outcome is quite important to the various parties.

"Let me introduce those parties to you now.

"The plaintiff in this action, Dumar Electronics, is represented by Mr. Pendergas."

He indicated the Silver Fox. Mr. Pendergas nodded and smiled, but those ice blue eyes remained hard.

Peter/Paul went on. "The defendants in this action are Veliko Tool and Die, represented by Mr. Wessingham."

Here, if he was Peter, he indicated Paul, and if Paul, Peter.

"The City of New York, represented by Ms. Cunningham."

Indicating Mary.

"And Delvecchio Realty, which I represent. I'm Mr. Feingarten."

He took a breath. "Now, this is a case involving a fire."

Well. That sounded more interesting than a sum of money.

He went on. "Now, you must understand, this is not involving a death, or any personal injury. We are concerned here only with property damage."

Wrong again. It *is* dull as dishwater.

As if he were reading my mind, Feingarten said, "But please don't think this is a dull case, and therefore unimportant. There is, as I said, a large sum of money involved. So I ask you to treat this case with just as much diligence as you would one involving a serious personal injury.

"And, it is of no less importance just because it happens to be eight years old."

Good lord. Peter/Paul Feingarten must be one hell of a lawyer. If he couldn't make a better presentation than this when he got into court, his client was sunk. There were audible groans in the room when he said eight years. Plus his harping on the fact that the case wasn't unimportant, had the effect of convincing every juror in the room that it was exactly that.

Not that he could really help it. You take a property damage case that had been dragging on for eight years, and probably the best lawyer in the world couldn't make it sound interesting.

Feingarten went on. "We have been selecting jurors for some time now."

Here he shot a look at the Silver Fox, who rolled

his eyes to the ceiling, which I thought was a good move, probably ingratiating him with most of the jurors who were thinking the same thing.

"And so far," Feingarten said, "we've selected six jurors. We are looking for two alternates."

He turned to the court officer, who was holding the ballots. "So let's call two names here, and maybe we'll get lucky."

They called two names, and guess who got lucky? Me, and a black woman about sixty, whom I could tell was plump when she stood up, and could tell wore too much perfume when she sat down, seeing as how she sat down next to me.

The attorneys then proceeded to interrogate us. Which was short, because there were only two of us, and long, because there were four of them. Of course, each one of them had to have his say. Or her say, in the case of Mary. Who was, incidentally, sharp as a tack, and asked what I felt were the most pertinent questions regarding my detective work.

Which was no mean feat, because the Silver Fox was no slouch either. I actually felt uncomfortable being interrogated by him. Which was silly, because I wasn't on trial. But those blue eyes seemed to bore right through me, and I actually found myself defensive and apologetic about my answers, such as, "No, I never carry a gun," or "No, I never worked for an insurance company, it was always for the other side," and, "Yes, I have photographed fire scenes, though the primary reason was for showing the cause of personal injury."

As I said, I felt uncomfortable answering his questions, but I was also happy to be answering them, because they all seemed good reasons why I shouldn't be put on that jury.

All in all, the black woman handled her questioning better. She was calm, unruffled and completely self-assured. It turned out she was a token clerk for the Metropolitan Transit Authority, and she fielded questions such as, ''Would the fact that you happen to be employed by the City of New York in any way affect your ability to judge a case in which one of the defendants happens to *be* The City of New York?'' by answering matter of factly that she didn't see why one thing had anything to do with the other.

So, all in all, the questioning went pretty smoothly, but what with there being four lawyers and all, by the time they were finished it was a quarter to one, so they broke and told us all to come back after lunch.

That didn't please me. I would have been happier to have been dismissed then and there. But I wasn't really worried, because after the attorneys left, the prospective jurors all started talking, and the general consensus of everybody in the room was that when we got back from lunch they'd take the woman and reject me.

They didn't.

They took both of us.

8.

I WAS DEVASTATED. It was hard to believe. I mean, yeah, I'd been winning turkey raffles, but this was like winning the lottery. The odds were astronomical. There was no way they should have taken me. I should have been out the door, scot-free. But no, for some perverse reason which I couldn't possibly fathom, a sixties folk-rock trio and an aging matinee idol had elected to throw reason to the winds, and make a decision that on the surface made no sense.

My head was spinning. How could they have been that stupid? Maybe it was like Peter/Paul said. Maybe they'd been selecting jurors for some time now and, weary of the whole process, they just wanted to get it over with. If so, it was pretty shoddy practice. Surely their clients deserved better. Maybe the bar association should hear about this.

I sat there stunned, thinking all this and watching my life rush before my eyes, a drowning man going down for the third time, while around me, everything was a flurry of activity. The other jurors, delighted they hadn't been picked, were chatting and laughing and making their way out, and the lawyers, happy as clams that the selection process was finally over, were packing up their briefcases and saying something about hunting up the judge and getting going this afternoon, and before you knew it, all the jurors had filed out with the lawyers hot on their heels, leaving the two winners, the black woman and me, sitting alone and forgotten in the empty room.

We looked at each other. I must have looked terrible, because she said, "Are you all right?"

I blinked. "I guess so. I'm just . . . I mean, they *took* me."

She smiled. "Yeah. Wasn't that a surprise?"

"I'll say."

"Nobody thought they'd take you, you bein' a detective and all. Now me, I thought they'd take me."

"Yeah."

"I'm lucky. This is only my second day."

"It's my second *week.*"

"Oh? Bet you thought you'd never be called."

"Yeah." I sighed. "So what do we do now?"

"Didn't you hear? They said to wait for the court officer."

I hadn't heard. I'd been in my own little world. They could have told me to stand naked on a chair and recite the Gettysburg Address and it still wouldn't have registered. All my plans, all my schemes down the drain. Put on a case, and what a case. Besides being totally dull, with four lawyers on the case it could last forever. After all, it had been eight years already, what's a few more months? Another year, even.

I was saved from further musings by the arrival of the court officer.

Now let me say, in the seven days I'd been led around all over the building by them, I had found the court officers to be a most genial group of people. Despite the fact they wore uniforms and carried guns, they were in no way intimidating. They were more like grownup Boy Scouts, trustworthy, loyal, helpful, friendly, courteous, kind, and all that. Or is that Cub Scouts? At any rate, if I had to point to one bright spot in my first week of jury duty experience, I would have to say it was the attitude of the court officers.

Which is why this one was such a shock. I'd never seen him before. I was sure. If I had, I'd have remembered him. He was a sour-faced little man with no neck, who looked as if he wanted to bite someone. A rather pissed-off bulldog.

He came in carrying two ballots. He eyed us suspiciously, looked at the ballots and said, "Hastings and Abernathy?"

We each said, "Yes."

"Let's go," he growled, and turned and walked out the door.

Mrs. Abernathy and I looked at each other. She smiled, shrugged and got up, no mean feat, being so large. After a moment I got up and followed her out.

The sour court officer was standing in the hall. He had his arms folded and was glaring at us. He was not tapping his foot impatiently, but he might as well have been. He certainly gave that impression.

As soon as we were out the door he turned and marched down the hallway and back through the Juror Assembly Room. Mrs. Abernathy waddled after him, but there was no way she could keep up, and by the time he reached the corridor we had fallen way behind. He stood there, just outside the doorway, arms folded, watching us come up the aisle. This time he *did* tap his foot. As soon as we cleared the doorway he stamped off down the corridor to the elevators. By the time we got there he had already rung the bell, caught an elevator, and was holding the door open despite the protests of some of the people in it.

"Court business," he snapped. "Hold your talk. Jurors entering."

Mrs. Abernathy and I stepped in, he released the door and we rode up to four.

"Out," he said, and held the door once again, making sure we got off. When we did, he released the door and said, "Follow me."

Instead of leading us to the main corridor, he turned and marched to a door in the far wall between the two elevator banks. He pulled out a key from a chain on his belt, unlocked the door and held it open. His having to unlock the door gave us time to catch up. We went through it and he closed it behind us, making sure it was locked.

We were now in a narrow back hallway. He led us down it, turned a corner, led us down another narrow hallway past several doors, all of which were closed, turned another corner and stopped in front of a door. He pushed it open, said, "In here," and stood aside to let us pass.

Mrs. Abernathy and I went in. It was a small room with a long table in the center with a dozen chairs around it. Six people sat at the table. The court officer pointed to it and said, "Sit down."

Mrs. Abernathy plopped into the nearest chair available. The one next to it was vacant, but remembering the perfume, I opted for the one at the far end of the table instead.

The court officer watched impatiently, tapping his hands together, as if to say, "Christ, can't people just sit down?" When we were settled to his satisfaction, he said, "All right, now listen up. Take out a pencil and paper and take this down. I am your court officer. My name is Ralph. Write that down.''

There was a pause while we all fumbled for pens, pencils, papers, notebooks, whatever, and wrote down the name Ralph.

"All right," he said. "Get this and get this clear. Up till now you have been responsible to the Juror Assembly Room. That is no longer true. From this point on, you are responsible only to me. You will report to me, you will listen to me, you will do what I tell you.

"When you report in the morning, you will not, I repeat, *not,* report to the Juror Assembly Room. We are now on the fourth floor. When you arrive in the morning and when you return after lunch, you will wait on this floor in the corridor by the elevators for me to come and get you. You will be on time. If you are told to report at ten o'clock, you will not show up at five minutes *after* ten, you will show up at the latest at five minutes *before* ten, so at ten o'clock when *I* am here, *you* are here. And the *only* place that you will be is in the corridor next to the elevator. I will pick you up there and bring you back to this jury room. And don't think you can arrive late and find the jury room yourself. The door is locked. You can't get here. The only way you can get here is if I bring you.

"If for any unforeseen reason you are going to be late—and this should *not* happen—you will call me and you will tell me, so I can make arrangements to have you brought in. And do *not* call me at five minutes of ten and say, "Oh, I'm going to be late." At ten o'clock we will have the judge and the lawyers and the witnesses waiting on you. If you are going to be late, you call me well in advance and you have a damn good reason why you are going to be late, or you will be in serious trouble. Is that clear?''

No one said a word.

"Fine. Take down this number.''

He repeated the number twice and we all dutifully copied it down. He then repeated it again to make sure we'd gotten it right.

"All right," he said. "While you are in this room you are in my charge. You will not leave this room unless I leave with you. You will not poke your head out into the hall. If you want something and I'm not here, you will simply wait until I *am* here.

"And there is no reason why you *have* to go out.'' He pointed to a door behind me in the back wall. "That is a bathroom. If you want coffee or rolls or whatever, that is fine. But *bring them with you*. Once you are here, you may *not* go out again to get them.

"If you need to make phone calls, make them *before* you get here, and *after* you are dismissed. There is no phone in the room, and you may *not* go out to use a phone. There are no exceptions. Plan your life accordingly. Is that clear?''

He glared at us. No one said a word.

"Good," Ralph said. "In case you missed it the first time around, your job now is to stay here. You are *not* to leave this room for any reason. When the judge is ready for you, I will come and get you.''

With that he turned on his heel and stalked out, slamming the door behind him.

9.

LEAVING ME ALONE with my fellow jurors. It was
the first time I'd got a good look at them. Up till
that point I'd been too overawed by Ralph. Now
I looked around the table at the people I'd been dorked
into spending some time with.

Mrs. Abernathy and I were just the alternates, the
new kids on the block. The other six were the regu-
lars, the first team, the old hands at the game. The
minute the door was closed they all looked at each
other with expressions that commented on Ralph's exit,
such as smiling, shaking heads, rolling eyes to the
ceiling, giggling and laughing outright. Apparently
Ralph was already a known quantity and an object of
derision.

After that they all introduced themselves to Mrs.
Abernathy and me, which in my case was less than
helpful. I'm poor at names, and have trouble remembering even one person I'm introduced to. Throw six
at me and I'm lost. I needed to sort the people out
first before any of the names began to stick.

Going around the table clockwise, the first person
on my left was an older man in a sweater and tweed
jacket, which seemed a bit excessive for the warm

weather and gave me the impression the man was either a college professor or wanted to look like one.

Next to him was a young Hispanic woman with hoop earrings. She had a pleasant enough plumpish face, with perhaps a bit too much makeup.

Next to her was a woman I'd have voted hands down the juror I'd most like to be stranded on a desert island with. She was about thirty, with long, curly blonde hair framing an attractive, girlish face. She was wearing a blue sleeveless pullover and, in my humble sexist opinion, was not wearing a bra. Under different circumstances it might have been pleasant to be part of a group she was in.

The chair at the end of the table opposite me was vacant. Around the corner from that, sitting directly opposite the blonde was a young man who looked like a college student. If so, he was a cocky, jock type, and I wondered if he was sitting opposite Blondie on purpose, and if by the end of the trial perhaps they'd become an item.

Next to him sat Mrs. Abernathy. Next to her was the vacant chair I'd passed up. Next to that was a sharp-looking woman in a business suit. She had short hair and a rather severe look, the type of woman I wouldn't want to argue with. The type of woman who'd make me feel like she was the grownup, and I was a little boy. It was a shock to realize she must be younger than I was.

Next to her was a young black man who might have been quite handsome, but who had elected to give himself one of those haircuts that for some reason had become popular among blacks, with the hair shaved off around the head and sculpted into a tall cylinder on top. It might have been the height of fashion, but, unfortunately, in his case it made his head look like the eraser on a pencil.

After the introductions which whizzed by me to no avail, Eraserhead spoke first. He looked at me and grinned. "So you're the one, right? You're the private detective?"

"Yeah. That's right."

"Yeah, that's what Chuckles said."

"Chuckles?"

The businesswoman jerked her thumb at the door and smiled, which made her look much less severe. "Yeah. Ralphie. We call him Chuckles."

"Not to his face," the professor put in, and everyone laughed.

Eraserhead explained, "Chuckles told us to stand by after lunch because we might be getting a jury. But he said they might not, 'cause they probably wouldn't take the detective."

I sighed. "Oh."

The Hispanic woman with the hoop earrings said, "You're really a detective?" Her face was lit up like a Christmas tree and she was smiling a mouthful of white teeth. "I never met a detective before."

"Down girl," College Boy said. The new College Boy, not the one who ran the turkey raffles. It was an attempt at humor that didn't go over, leaving him looking miffed and young.

Hoop Earrings took no notice. "You shoot people?" she said.

"That's just on television."

"But you're really a detective?" Business Woman said.

I don't know why people find that so hard to believe. I mean, all right, I don't look like a private detective, but then who does? I guess in the normal course of their lives, most people never see one outside of TV.

"So what do you do?" Eraserhead said. "Stake out places and follow people?"

"Nothing that glamorous," I said, and went on to explain how my business was largely personal injury work and consisted of nothing more exciting than photographing cracks in the sidewalk. Even so, I was clearly the shining star on that jury, which I might have found gratifying if I'd been in a better mood.

Which I wasn't. The worst had happened, and as far as I was concerned, things couldn't have looked blacker. Not only had I been put on a jury, but here I was locked in a room with no telephone, so I couldn't call the office. Worse than that, I couldn't even check my beeper. There was a bathroom, but it was right by the head of the table, and when College Boy went in to use it we could hear him piss. My beeper would fill the room like a police siren. Unless I wanted to take seven strangers in on my guilty secret, which I sure as hell didn't, I was out of luck. So I just had to sit there chatting amiably with a group of people who were annoyingly glad to have me.

All except Blondie, who seemed preoccupied with her crotch. I must say that fascinated me. I mean, here was a group of people, all joking and talking animatedly, and here was the most attractive person in the room oblivious to it all, staring down at her crotch.

It was very distracting. I found my eyes kept coming back to her like a moth to a flame. And every time, there she was, head down. Occasionally she'd raise her head, but not to look at anyone. Instead she'd stare blankly over the head of College Boy at some spot on the wall midway between the floor and the ceiling.

When she did this, I noticed her lips moving slightly. After a moment she'd look at her crotch again.

I was intrigued enough by this phenomenon to be considering whether I should get up, wander over there and look at her crotch too, when she sighed, raised her hands from under the table, and the mystery was solved.

She was holding a book. She'd been reading it in her lap.

I recognized the book at once. It was a paperback, thinner than a pocketbook, but slightly wider, with a plain, dull paper cover rather than a colorful glossy one. I knew what it was from my days back in summer stock. I couldn't tell what play it was, but it was either a Samuel French or Dramatists Play Service script.

Which explained her strange behavior. Blondie was an actress and she was memorizing her lines.

I resented that too. I guess I was just in a particularly foul mood. But in New York City, where there are thousands of actresses, it would have been much more interesting to meet a beautiful woman who just happened to be fascinated with her crotch.

We sat there for what seemed like hours. There was no clock in the room and I didn't have a watch. During that time, Blondie kept reading, and the others kept talking. After they'd exhausted the subject of my detective work, they moved on to the case and how dull it sounded, which did not cheer me. Business Woman referred to Pendergas as Pretty Boy, which appeared to have been accepted as his nickname. That seemed inadequate to me. I wasn't about to argue, but I knew I'd always think of him as the Silver Fox.

They referred to the other lawyers as Peter, Paul and Mary. I guess that wasn't such a clever observation on my part. I guess it was totally obvious. To my amusement, when I asked, no one was sure which was Peter and which was Paul.

Finally the door opened and Ralph came in.

"All right, jurors, let's go. Court's waiting."

It was remarkable. I don't know how he did it, but somehow Ralph managed to give the impression that we'd all been slacking off and holding everyone up.

"Let's go, let's go," he said. "Line up in reverse order."

"Reverse order?" I blurted.

"Yes, yes," he said impatiently. "You were last, so you're first. Right here by the door, everyone line up behind him. Remember your number. Don't make me remember it for you."

We lined up by the door. I was first. Then Mrs. Abernathy. Then the Professor. Then Hoop Earrings. Then Business Woman. Then Blondie. Then College Boy. Then Eraserhead.

"All right. When you file into court there is no talking. Sit down, pay attention, do as you're told.

"Now, when you file in, sit in this order. You two," he said, indicating Mrs. Abernathy and me, "sit in the first two chairs in the first row. The rest of you, sit in the first six chairs in the second row. Do not, I repeat, do *not* climb over each other. You may think it stupid of me to say it, but I've had morons do it.

"You," he said, pointing to the Professor, "do not sit in the first chair you come to, you walk in counting to the sixth chair in the row. You sit there.

"You," he said, pointing to Hoop Earrings, "follow him and sit in the chair next to him, five. *Not* the chair on the far side of him, the chair on the near side of him. You file in in a line, you sit in a line. Is that clear?"

Eraserhead said, "I'm the last one in, so I sit in the chair closest to the door, right?"

Ralph gave him a withering look. "Brilliant. A Harvard man. I knew this jury was smart. All right. Let's go."

Ralph opened the door and let us out. Straight across the hall was another door. Ralph banged on it, pushed it open a crack, called, "Jury entering," and threw the door wide open.

And there was the courtroom. We were entering from the side of the front wall, so the jury box was right in front of us, two rows of seats stretching out along the side wall.

Ralph, convinced that he was dealing with morons, pointed to the front row, in case I couldn't tell which one that was. I filed into it dutifully, counted the seats skillfully up to two. I looked behind me to see the rest of the jury filing docilely into the second row. The Professor counted up to six, no problem, Hoop Earrings did not climb over him, the rest filed in behind them, and, as if on cue, we all sat down.

Ralph smiled triumphantly as if he had performed a small miracle, stepped off to the side, leaned against the wall and folded his arms.

I looked around the courtroom. The lawyers were at their tables. Peter, Paul and Mary were at the far table, and the Silver Fox was at the near one, the one right in front of the jury box.

The judge was at his bench. Or I should say, her bench. The judge was a woman.

My first thought was, wow, the judge is a woman. My second thought was, gee, the Silver Fox was really gonna sweep her off her feet. My third thought was, boy were those horribly sexist thoughts. But that didn't stop me from having them.

She was attractive too, which floored me. Somehow I don't think of a judge as being attractive. And, as with Business Woman, it was a shock to realize she was probably younger than I was.

She looked down at us and smiled. "Good afternoon, jurors. I'm Judge Davis. I'm presiding over the case of Dumar Electronics vs. Veliko Tool and Die, Delvecchio Realty, and the City of New York."

She went on to give us instructions as to what we could and couldn't do. We could take notes if we wanted. We could not talk. We could not raise our hands and ask questions. Any communications we wanted to make with the court could be made only through the court officer, and we could communicate with him only when we were in the jury deliberation room, which was of course the room we had just left. But there was no foreseeable reason for us to communicate with the court until we had actually begun our deliberations.

We were also not to communicate with any of the lawyers or witnesses in any way. Not even to say good morning. If we should run into them in the hall or the elevator, we should pass by without speaking, nodding, or making any sign of recognition of their presence. Judge Davis assured us that, while this might be hard at first, the lawyers understood and would not think us rude.

And—Judge Davis stressed this several times—we were not to discuss the case with anyone, including friends, spouses, employers, what have you, while the case was pending. Moreover—and this surprised me—we were not to discuss it among ourselves. Not until we had heard all the evidence and were instructed by her to begin our deliberations. Until that time, we were not to discuss the case among ourselves in any way.

There was a clock in the courtroom, and by the time

she finished giving us our instructions it was ten to four. I hoped that meant she was planning to break for the day, but she wasn't. She moved right on to the opening arguments.

First up was Pendergas, Pretty Boy, the Silver Fox. That was good. I figured he'd at least be interesting.

He wasn't. His summary was dry.

His client, Dumar Electronics, ran a business on the fourth floor of a building on West 26th Street. On the night of February 15, 1982, fire had broken out in Veliko Tool and Die, which was a business on the third floor of that building. The fire had spread to the fourth floor, causing damage to Dumar Electronics stock estimated at two hundred and twenty-five thousand dollars. The damage had been so great because the sprinkler system in the building did not work.

Veliko Tool and Die was negligent for starting the fire. Delvecchio Realty, the landlord of the building, was negligent for not maintaining an adequate sprinkler system. And the City of New York was negligent because the fire inspector had inspected the building the previous January and had failed to notice that the sprinkler system did not work.

I must say I was disappointed with the Silver Fox. I'd expected him to be flashy and dramatic, to make the story interesting. But he wasn't and it wasn't. He was calm and matter-of-fact, and the story was simple and straightforward. Which surprised me. I'd really expected him to be good.

Then it hit me. Damn, he *was* good. If I thought the case was simple and straightforward, then he'd accomplished his purpose. By being calm and matter-of-fact, he'd convinced me this was a very simple case. In fact, he'd sold me a bill of goods. But even knowing that didn't diminish the effect he'd created.

The other lawyers came next, and when they did, they were on the defensive. I knew what happened, and if they wanted to prove different, they'd have to show me. And for the most part, they didn't.

Peter/Paul (the tall one) for Veliko Tool and Die, argued that we must keep an open mind, that it was yet to be shown that the fire had actually started there and spread upstairs and not the other way around. And if it *had* started there, it was yet to be proved whether it had started there because Veliko Tool and Die had been negligent, or whether that negligence might be attributable to one or more of the other defendants.

Mary went next. Her argument was that it was up to the Silver Fox to prove that the City of New York had been negligent in its inspection. She pointed out that for obvious reasons, no fire inspector ever activates a sprinkler system to see if it is working, which seemed a valid point.

Last was Peter/Paul (the short one with the moustache), who pointed out that the landlord for the building couldn't be held responsible for a sprinkler system that the City of New York had approved. Nor could he be responsible for a fire resulting from the negligence of one of his tenants.

In short, all three defense attorneys, while refusing to concede that any negligence had, in fact, occurred, maintained that if it indeed had, it had been the responsibility of someone else.

All of which was less than conclusive.

And all of which was also time-consuming. By the time the second Peter/Paul sat down it was close to five and I was going bonkers.

Judge Davis announced that we would adjourn until ten o'clock tomorrow morning, admonished us once more not to discuss the case with anyone, and we were dismissed.

Ralph jerked the door open, said, "Let's go," and we filed out. Once in the hall he jerked out his keys and opened the door to the jury deliberation room, which had been locked to protect our belongings. Since I had none, I didn't have to go in, and since Ralph informed us we were allowed to leave without escort, I immediately hotfooted it down the corridor and out the door.

There was a men's room beside the elevator bank. I ducked into it and checked my beeper. Sure enough, it was beeping like crazy. I shut it off, went out, found a bank of phones in the corridor and called the office.

Wendy/Janet answered the phone.

"Rosenberg and Stone."

"Hi. It's Stanley."

"Stanley. Where are you? I must have beeped you five times."

"I got tied up," I said. I didn't want to tell Wendy/Janet I'd been put on a jury. She might figure that was a reason to stop giving me work. "You got a case?"

"I got nothing for tonight, thank god, 'cause you wouldn't have made it. But I got one for tomorrow morning."

Under the circumstances, things couldn't have been better. It had been a long, hard day, and I didn't feel like going out on a case now, even if she'd had one. I took down the information, and told her once more not to get excited if I was slow answering the beeper, that I'd be sure to call in.

I hung up and walked down the corridor to the elevator. There were a bunch of people waiting, what with it being rush hour and all. I was preoccupied with my thoughts, and I didn't really notice anybody until a voice behind me said, "Hi."

I turned around.

It was Blondie.

10.

"**I** DON'T THINK I caught your name."

I was glad she said that. I hadn't caught hers, and I'm shy about asking.

"Stanley Hastings. And yours?"

"Sherry Fontaine."

"Oh?"

She smiled. "You sound as if you don't believe me."

"No, it's just . . . Is that your real name, or your stage name?"

"Stage name? Oh, the script. No, it's my real name. I didn't have to change it."

The elevator arrived and we stepped in. So did a bunch of other people. And the elevator had been crowded to begin with. I found myself rather close to Sherry Fontaine, whom I was even more convinced was not wearing a bra.

Carrying on a conversation in the midst of a lot of other people makes me uncomfortable, but it didn't seem to bother her.

"Well," she said, "pretty dull case, huh?"

I frowned. We'd been instructed not to talk about

the case. But surely that meant the specifics of the case. Whether it was dull or not didn't really count.

"Dull is the operative word," I said.

The elevator stopped on three and more people tried to pile in.

"Any closer and you'll have to marry me," Sherry said.

I grimaced. "I'm already married."

She smiled. "That's your loss."

It was not the type of conversation I wanted to have in an elevator. People around us were picking up on it and grinning at us. I felt in serious danger of blushing, which wouldn't have done at all.

My beeper picked that moment to go off. I'd forgotten to put it back on silent after I'd checked it in the men's room. In the crowded elevator it sounded like an air raid siren. I fumbled under my jacket to shut it off.

"What the hell was that?" Sherry said.

I didn't want to say. With my luck, there was a court officer somewhere in the crush who would grab me and impound the damn thing. "My beeper," I said out of the side of my mouth. "I gotta call my office."

"Why are you talking like a gangster?"

The elevator arrived at the ground floor and people piled out. I crossed the lobby, found a pay phone, and called the office, hoping like hell it wasn't a case for tonight. As I said, I just wasn't up to it.

It wasn't. It was for tomorrow night in Harlem if I wanted to take it, which I sure as hell did. Despite being on a jury and getting out at five, I needed the money.

For once I was lucky. The client had a phone. So even though the appointment was made for five, if I didn't get out of court till five, I could always call the client and just say I was gonna be late. Piece of cake.

I hung up the phone and turned around to find Sherry Fontaine standing there. I must say that surprised me.

"So?" she said.

I put my notebook and pen back in my jacket pocket. "I got a case in Harlem."

"Oh? For tonight?"

"No. Tomorrow night. After court."

She nodded. "So where you heading?"

"Home."

"Where you live?"

"Upper West Side."

"Me too. Wanna catch the subway?"

"I got a car."

"You got a *car?*"

It was only natural to offer her a ride. She turned out to live on West End Avenue in the eighties and I go right by there.

We went out and walked down to the parking lot.

And discovered I'd gotten a ticket. Shit. Of course I had. I'd fed ten quarters into the meter at two o'clock, just before I'd returned from lunch, but at four o'clock when the meter ran out I'd been sitting in court. And wouldn't you know it, the meter maid came around.

I pulled it off the windshield to inspect the damage. Overtime parking. Thirty-five bucks. Which more than knocked out this morning's signup, making the day a total washout.

I unlocked the car, hopped in and switched off the code alarm. I reached over and unlocked the passenger door, and Sherry Fontaine got in. I fired up the ancient Toyota, pulled out of the lot, and began fighting my way through rush hour traffic.

While I drove, we made small talk. Sherry had a

pleasant voice along with everything else. It was cultured and refined, with an occasional hint of southern drawl. I figured that to be an affectation, part of her theatrical image.

Sherry said, "So you're a private detective?"

"Yeah."

"You do trip-and-falls and stuff like that?"

"You heard that? I thought you weren't listening."

"I was working on my lines, but I heard what you were saying."

"You got a show?"

She grimaced. "I got a showcase. No money, but it's a chance to be seen."

I knew about that from my days as an actor. Showcases were no pay, hard work, and despite the premise, usually nobody important ever came to see them. Nonetheless, there were always hundreds of actors willing to kill to get in one.

"So when do rehearsals start?"

"We're rehearsing now. I gotta go home, change and get over there."

"They rehearse at night?"

"Yeah. You take a showcase, everyone in it's doing it for free, they got other jobs."

"I know. I used to be an actor."

"Oh yeah? Why'd you quit?"

"No work. I couldn't make a living."

"Yeah? Tell me about it."

"You get work?"

"Now and then. In between I waitress."

"Right."

"Oh? You wait tables too?"

"No, I never did. I've done a lot of other job-jobs. My detective work is a job-job."

"Oh? You still try to act?"

"No, now I try to write."

"Any luck?"

"About as much as with acting."

"Yeah." She looked at me. "You shouldn't have given it up. You're not a bad-looking guy. I bet you could still get work."

Let me say right here that I'm a happily married man, I don't cheat on my wife and I had no sexual designs on Sherry Fontaine. It just isn't in my nature, and wouldn't be, even without the threat of AIDS. But despite that, I'm human. And I couldn't help responding to and being pleased by the fact that this very good-looking young woman seemed to find me attractive. I mean, she'd waited for me, sought me out, inveigled a ride, and now she was coming on to me. And while I had no intention of acting on it, it was doing wonderful things for my ego. This very desirable woman was *interested*.

"So," she said, "your detective work is a job-job?"

"Yeah."

"You do it full-time?"

"More or less. I get cases through a law office. When there's work, they beep me. Like in the elevator. I do as many cases as I can. Sometimes it's an eight-hour day. Sometimes it's more. Some days are slow and it's less. I try to fill those days with photo assignments left over from other jobs. But the point is, it's flexible. I make my own hours so I can do other things."

"Like writing?"

"Yeah."

She nodded. "I see. So anyway, your detective work—you do a lot of trip-and-falls, right?"

"Yeah. Why?"

"My girlfriend, Velma—back in Cincinnati—she

had a case like that. Maybe ten years ago. She got hit by a car. Hit-and-run. Never got the driver. But she went to an attorney, and it turns out you can sue anyway."

"Right, it's a no-fault claim."

"That's right. No-fault. The attorney tells her they don't have to catch the driver, they can still sue.

"Only thing was, she wasn't really hurt. Just a few scrapes and bruises. But it turns out she had broken her leg in a skiing accident two years before."

My eyes widened. "You're kidding."

"No, I'm not," she said. "Isn't it great? The attorney got ahold of the X-rays of her broken leg, filed a no-fault claim, and she wound up getting thirty thousand dollars."

"Jesus Christ."

"Yeah. Isn't that clever?"

"Clever isn't the word for it."

"Hey look, it's just an insurance company and they got millions."

"Yeah, sure, but—"

"But what? I think it's really clever. And everyone always bilks insurance companies. I mean, hey, the lawyer you work for—I bet he does stuff like that."

"No, he doesn't," I said.

That was a half-truth. I mean, I'm sure Richard Rosenberg bilks insurance companies out of millions, but *not* with phony X-rays.

"Yeah, but he could," she said. "And he wouldn't even have to know."

"What?"

"Look," she said. "I broke my arm a few years back, and I never did anything about it. Suing, I mean. It wouldn't have worked anyway. There wasn't any liability. But I have the X-rays, and—"

"Forget it," I said. "Richard wouldn't touch it."

"Yeah, but like I said, he'd wouldn't have to know. You investigate for him, right? So you just sign me up as a client, fill out all the papers. Treat it as a trip-and-fall. Find some great crack in the sidewalk, take pictures of that. I give you the X-rays, you turn it in with the rest of the case, and who's to know?"

"It wouldn't work."

"Why not?"

"They're old X-rays."

"So what?"

"There are tests that can determine that."

"Who's gonna test them?"

"The defense attorney might."

"So? So, you dupe the negatives. Then they're new negatives."

I shook my head. "You don't understand."

"What's to understand?"

"Look, when I sign up a client, I fill out a fact sheet. The fact sheet asks, 'Was there a police report? Did an ambulance come?' "

"And if not, there's no case?"

"Not necessarily, but—"

"But what? So the police weren't called. So there wasn't an ambulance."

"With a broken arm, you have to go to a hospital."

"I could have gone to a private doctor."

"Then they'd want the doctor's name and his records."

"Oh."

I was getting angry. Not at her, I was getting angry at myself. I was angry because I wasn't saying, "No, I won't do it." What she was proposing was illegal and wrong and something I wouldn't do. But I wasn't saying that. I wasn't *refusing* to do it. Instead I was explaining *why it wouldn't work.* And the only reason I could be doing that was because I didn't want this beautiful woman to think I was a straight arrow stick in the mud.

Which was ridiculous. Because, as I said, I had no sexual designs on her. She was someone I just met, someone who couldn't matter in my life one whit, and yet here I was fumphering around not saying what I really felt, just because I didn't want to fall in her estimation, fail in her eyes, seem unhip, uncool, or whatever the hell her generation would use to refer to the socially unacceptable.

Generation. Maybe that was it. Or at least partly it. Maybe I didn't want to be an old fogy.

At any rate, at least the bit about the doctor's records slowed her down. She pursed her lips, pouted a bit, lapsed into silence.

I fought my way crosstown, got on the West Side Highway.

After a bit she said, "I have friend who's a doctor. Maybe I'll talk to him."

I said nothing, hoping she'd drop the subject.

She did. Once we got on the West Side Highway traffic got really jammed up and now we weren't moving. "Christ," she said. "This is awful."

"Yeah."

"If this doesn't clear up, I'm gonna be late for rehearsal."

"It'll clear up, but it's always slow."

"Damn. If it's like this, I should have taken the subway."

Maybe it was just that she had already gotten me in a bad mood. But now I felt on the defensive. Like she was blaming me for making her late to rehearsal. Like it was my fault for offering her a ride.

I said nothing, looked straight ahead.

As if she read my mind she laughed and said, "Hey, don't look so pouty. It's not your fault. I'm not blaming you."

"Uh huh."

"And I'd much rather ride in a car than the stinking subway. Say, you driving down tomorrow too?"

"Well, not directly. I got a job in Harlem first."

"Harlem?"

"Yeah."

"Then you're driving down?"

"Right."

"It's right on the way. You have to go right by me to get downtown. Could you pick me up?"

"It's a close thing getting there on time."

"Hey, I got to be there same time you do. Just tell me when you're going by, I'll be standing out on the street. I hate the subway."

I could have just said no. But it's hard to refuse a ride to someone when you're going their way. And should I really turn her down just because she made me uncomfortable about wanting to pull an insurance scam?

And if I had, would that have been the real reason? Or would it have just been that she made me uncomfortable by being an attractive woman.

Damn.

At any rate, I said I would.

Traffic thinned out, and we began to move up on the West Side Highway. Things relaxed somewhat, and Sherry got expansive and started talking about her acting career. It turned out it was no great shakes, in fact not much more successful than mine. She'd done some summer stock, some regional theatre, but virtually no work in New York outside of extra work in movies.

Which was why the showcase was important. Why she had her feelers out all the time.

She had an agent, which was more than I'd ever done, and he was starting to get her things. Not work, but auditions. Auditions were important even if you didn't get the work because you learned from them, you got better from them and, hey, maybe one day one of them would pan out.

The conversation was basically a monologue, during which I occasionally muttered brief noncommittal words of encouragement. Though frankly, the whole audition syndrome was a familiar and depressing one.

There was a pause and I glanced over. She wasn't looking at me, she was looking out the front window at the traffic, but she wasn't really seeing it. There was a look in her eye, and I recognized it. It was the same look she'd had just before she started in on the insurance scam pitch. I wondered if I was imagining it.

I wasn't.

She said, "Yeah, auditions are real important. You know, my agent got one set up for tomorrow afternoon, but I can't do it, 'cause I'm on a jury. If they hadn't put me on a jury, I'd planned on going and then just reporting late. I'm sure that would have worked. They'd just give me a slap on the wrist. But now I'm on this case."

"Yeah. Too bad," I said.

"Yeah, but I was thinking . . ."

"What?"

"You're a real private detective. Work for a law office. Couldn't the lawyer there call over to the court, say something big came up, he needed you in the afternoon? I mean, he might even know the other lawyers. Surely there's some sort of thing as professional courtesy, right? So you get excused for the afternoon so they can't have court, so they knock off at lunch-time.''

Jesus Christ.

Revelation, déjà vu, blast from the past, flashback, what have you.

I have to apologize for being a sexist pig again, but this is something that women just won't quite understand, but men will get right away. So pardon me, but this is really just for the guys.

Remember when you were back in high school, there was always some girl who, on the one hand you knew you were never gonna get into her pants, but on the other hand you just couldn't keep away from? And never mind getting into her pants—you were never even gonna get her bra unhooked, and you knew that, but you stuck around anyway.

Worse than that, she always wanted to do things you didn't want to do. Things you knew you *shouldn't* do. But you did them anyway. Like you'd be talking to her, and suddenly you'd realize, hey, we gotta get to class, and you'd tell her that, and she'd just laugh and put you down and tell you not to worry. And you'd know you ought to leave her and go to class, but somehow you just couldn't do that. So you'd stay, and it would get closer and closer to class time, and you'd get more and more anxious, but she simply wouldn't be hurried. By the time you did get her ass in gear, it would be too late, you'd only be halfway down the hill to the class house when you'd hear the bell ring. And even then she couldn't be hurried, she'd just smile and keep on talking.

And then you *would* leave her. You'd say, ''Come on!'' to which she would not respond, and you'd turn and sprint off down the hill with your books, run full-tilt to the class house, and come bursting in the door panting and out of breath, just in time to interrupt the teacher, who had just begun his lecture.

And the killer was, while he was bawling you out for disturbing the class, and sending you to Friday night detention study hall for coming late, she would calmly walk in the door and sit down at her desk, and the teacher wouldn't even notice.

'Cause that's the way it worked. That's the way it went. It was always her fault. It was always something *she* wanted to do. But whenever you did it, she never got caught and you always did.

And on those few rare occasions when she *did* get caught, when you had the secret satisfaction of knowing, well, I did get caught but at least this time she's getting her comeuppance too, when you showed up for Friday night detention study hall, *she* wouldn't be there. She'd have gotten out of it.

And as you sat there, too upset to do your homework, as you were supposed to do, all you could think of the whole night was, she must have gone to the headmaster's office and shown him her tits so he'd excuse her. Shown him her tits was the extent of it. You couldn't believe she'd fucked him. That was beyond comprehension, beyond your wildest imagination. Even showing him her tits was a fantasy you couldn't really believe. Still, it was a thought you could not get out of your head. It seemed the only explanation.

Because you never got any other explanation. If you asked her about it later, she'd just say, "Oh, the headmaster excused me," as if that were a perfectly logical thing. But it wasn't, and she'd never explain why. Which, of course, only added fuel to the fantasy. And how were you ever gonna find out why? God knows, you couldn't ask *him*.

Which of course, only served to make her more intriguing. And the next time she asked you to do something you knew was stupid, damned if you didn't wind up doing it again.

And there was a name for girls like her. And you knew it, and you knew it fit her. But even knowing that didn't help. And all the firm resolves you made when you were alone evaporated when you were with her, and you would find yourself a poor helpless fool, dancing to her tune, playing her game, doing yet another thing you didn't want to do, while in your heart of hearts you knew it was hopeless, you knew you were never going to get anywhere, and you knew exactly what she was.

She was Trouble.

11.

WHEN I GOT HOME Tommie was in the living room watching "Square One" on PBS and Alice was in the kitchen talking on the phone, so I was treated to living stereo as I plunked my briefcase down in the foyer. Usually when Alice gets on the phone it takes a natural disaster or an Act of Congress to get her off, but this time I heard her say, "Oh, my husband's home, I gotta go," and she came marching out of the kitchen to meet me.

"You're home early," she said. "Didn't you get a case?"

"No."

She looked at me. "What's wrong?"

I sighed. "They put me on a jury."

Her eyes widened. "You're kidding? Oh, no. In your second week?"

"Yeah."

"It's not fair."

"No."

"What's the case?"

"You wouldn't believe. Listen, I gotta get out of these clothes."

She followed me into the bedroom. I hung up my

suit, pulled on a pair of jeans, and told her about the case.

I told her everything, about Peter, Paul and Mary, and the Silver Fox, and the eight-year-old fire damage, and how nobody expected them to take me but they did, and now I was totally fucked and god knows how long this thing was gonna last.

Alice was predictably sympathetic, understanding and supportive. She regretted it had happened, but it had, so I should just accept it and go along with it and do it and get it over with. And if it meant longer hours and I couldn't do evening signups, I shouldn't worry about it, it was just for a little while, and besides she was pulling in money now to make up for it.

Which was true. Alice was making money on our computer now. After a few unsuccessful fits and starts at printing resumés and letterheads for people, and designing and selling computer programs, neither of which had brought in a dime, Alice had finally found a practical use for the damn thing. By using it simply as a word processor, Alice was now selling her services to people who had essays, term papers, book reports, screenplays, manuscripts and dissertations they needed typed. And it turned out to be an amazingly lucrative business. Alice was charging up to five bucks a page, depending on the length of the manuscript. And the reason people were willing to pay it was because, not only did they get a beautifully typed, letter-quality printout of their work, they also got a floppy disk with the manuscript on it. Which meant any time they needed to edit, revise or rewrite their work, all they'd have to do was find an IBM compatible computer, stick the disk in and call up their manuscript. This was an appealing proposition to people, particularly people too lazy to type their own stuff, and Alice was doing fine.

I knew all that, of course, but somehow it didn't make me feel any better. The whole time I was talking to Alice, I just felt more frustrated, helpless and uncomfortable.

Because, you see, I was preoccupied with something. As Alice and I were talking about the day and what had happened and how I felt about it, the only thing I *wasn't* talking about was driving Sherry Fontaine home.

Now don't get me wrong. I didn't want to *keep it* from Alice. Driving Sherry Fontaine home wasn't some dark, ugly secret I didn't want her to know about. No, it was simply that it was a minor thing, it wasn't important. Not in the face of my getting put on a jury, which was what the day was all about. And I didn't want to make it *seem* important by talking about it. I mean, "What happened today?" "Well, I drove a woman home." "You got put on a jury and all you can talk about is you drove a woman home?"

So I didn't want to talk about Sherry Fontaine. On the other hand, I didn't want to *not* talk about Sherry Fontaine. That would be awful. To be driving this woman, and have Alice not know about it. Then I *would* feel bad about it, even though it didn't mean anything. So I was preoccupied with the thought of, how can I bring up driving Sherry Fontaine home without making it seem more than it actually was?

I realized I couldn't, that it was a no-win situation, that any way I played it would simply be wrong. Which just made me more frustrated and angry. I mean, Jesus Christ, this is not adultery you're confessing to. This is just giving a ride to a juror who happens to make you uncomfortable.

At any rate, I continued my conversation about my day of jury duty, looking for a convenient opening to casually slip in the bit about driving Sherry Fontaine home, and the opening never came, and the conversation finally ground to a halt.

Alice said, "What's the matter?"

"What?"

"Something's bothering you. What is it?"

Which of course made it ten times worse. Now I had to tell her about driving Sherry Fontaine as if it was a big deal that was bothering me. Why didn't I get it into the conversation sooner? Why am I such a schmuck? Do all husbands have these problems? Damn.

Still, I was glad she'd asked. Now we could talk about Sherry Fontaine and get it over with, and then I could stop worrying about it. Christ, was I right about her—Trouble. I mean, I didn't agree to any of her schemes, I didn't do anything she wanted, and I'm *still* in trouble.

Asshole. Alice is a smart, intelligent woman. And Alice knows you. You have a good relationship, and this is not threatening it. It is, if anything, amusing. You're a good man, you didn't do anything wrong, and Alice will understand.

I sighed. "Well," I said. "I drove one of the jurors home."

Alice understood.

"Who is she?"

12.

I TOLD ALICE the whole shmear. I told her everything—about Sherry trying to con me into faking
a trip-and-fall, and trying to get me to get Richard
to get court called off so she could go to an audition,
and how I felt about all that.

Not exactly how I felt about all that. I didn't go into
the whole parallel about the girl in high school. That
was kind of abstract and personal and hard to explain,
and it was a male observation anyway, that Alice probably wouldn't relate to. But even without that analogy,
I think I covered the situation pretty well.

Alice shook her head. "If the woman's so obnoxious, why are you driving her?"

"She's not obnoxious."

"She sounds obnoxious to me."

"She just has wild ideas. I don't have to go along
with them."

"Go along with them? You wouldn't even consider
them."

"That's right."

"Did you make that clear?"

Damn. I hadn't made it clear. I'd just harumphed
and pointed out the flaws in her plan.

"Well, I . . ."

"You didn't make it clear? You didn't tell her no?"

"Not in so many words. I just told her she was way off base, and pointed out why it was a stupid idea."

Alice shook her head. "Men."

I don't know why, when women feel their husband's being stupid, they take it as a reflection on the entire male sex. But on the other hand, when Alice is confounding me with some irrefutable logic that makes sense only to her, but which I am at a loss to combat, I often think, women. Viva la différence.

Alice said, "You're driving her tomorrow morning?"

"Yes."

"You have a case first?"

"I got a case in the morning and one at night."

"Where?"

"Harlem."

"Both of 'em?"

"Yeah."

Alice frowned, pursed her lips. "You know, you could take the subway."

"Huh?"

"If they're only Harlem, you could take the subway. In rush hour, it's probably faster than the car."

"I don't want to take the subway."

"And if you took the subway, you'd be off the hook. You wouldn't have to drive her."

"I already said I'd drive her."

"So you change your mind. You call her up and tell her the car's too much trouble, you're taking the subway down."

"I don't want to do that."

"Why not?"

I took a breath. "Look. I don't want to do signups

in Harlem on foot. I don't like it, I don't feel comfortable. If court runs late, by the time I finish my evening signup it's gonna be getting dark. I don't like walking around Harlem alone after dark. I don't want to walk ten blocks to the subway. I wanna park right in front of the client's house, zip in and zip right out.''

Which was true. I also didn't want to renege on my promise to Sherry Fontaine. And it pissed me off to have to defend my right to keep that promise. And it also made me feel defensive and stupid as hell.

It didn't help any when Alice said, ''And what you gonna *do* with your car, now? If you're in court, how you gonna get out and put money in the meter?''

I winced.

''What's the matter?''

I sighed. ''I got a parking ticket.''

''When?''

''This afternoon. I was in court. I couldn't get out at four o'clock to put money in the meter, and—''

''How much?''

''Thirty-five bucks.''

''So,'' Alice said. ''You can't take the car. It's ridiculous. You keep getting tickets and what's the point of doing the work?''

''I'll work it out.''

''How?''

''I don't know, I have to figure it out.''

Alice shook her head. ''This is really stupid. All you have to do is the call the woman and tell her you can't drive her to court.''

''She's got nothing to do with it.''

God, what a miserable situation. I mean, here I was being forced to defend my right to drive to court. The thing was, what I said about driving to Harlem was perfectly true. I didn't like walking the streets in a suit and tie. I'd hate it like hell trying to do signups there on the subway. If Sherry Fontaine didn't exist, I'd still be holding out for the car. But if Sherry Fontaine didn't exist, we wouldn't be having this conversation. I would have said, "I got a parking ticket, I gotta figure out something about the car," Alice would have said, "Why don't you take the subway?" I would have said, "I don't want to take the subway to Harlem, I'll work something out," and that would have been the end of it.

But because Sherry Fontaine *did* exist, here I was, embroiled in an argument, which from Alice's point of view was nothing more than me defending my right to drive the woman to court. Which really wasn't fair.

But which didn't help me from having self-doubts. I mean, if Sherry Fontaine didn't exist, would I *really* not have considered the possibility of taking the subway to Harlem? I mean, I didn't think so, but how could I be sure? I couldn't say to myself, "Consider Sherry Fontaine doesn't exist, now what do you do?" That's like saying, "Don't think of an elephant." The premise is self-defeating. Can't be done. So even though I knew I was in the right, I couldn't prove it. Even to myself.

It was not a good evening. The argument finally ended, resolved in that I had determined to take the car in the morning, and unresolved in that we could not agree on it. It hung in the air like a cloud, putting a damper on everything from dinner to putting Tommie to bed to watching TV to going to bed ourselves. And, surprise, surprise, guess who wasn't gettin' nothing tonight?

We turned out the lights and I lay in the dark, replaying the fight in my mind. I do that a lot because I'm slow on my feet, and I can never best Alice in mortal argument. Even when I know I'm right, Alice can turn my brain to Jell-O. It's only later, when she isn't in front of me, that I can think of what I *should* have said. The perfect answer, the snappy comeback, the devastatingly logical crushing argument.

I replayed the whole thing in my mind and came to the conclusion in this instance I was entirely in the right. As far as I could see, I'd been totally fair, open and honest concerning the whole business of Sherry Fontaine. The only thing I could think of that I'd neglected to mention was the fact that in my opinion Sherry Fontaine was wearing no bra. But that was surely irrelevant to the conversation. Alice certainly had enough material to deal with. No need to bog her down with too many details.

13.

SHERRY FONTAINE was late.

That figured. I just knew she'd be late.

I did my signup in Harlem—which went smooth as silk, even with having to run down in the subway and take pictures of the platform where the client fell—got in my car, drove down to the eighties, pulled up in front of Sherry Fontaine's building at 9:15, the time we'd agreed to meet, and sure enough, Sherry wasn't there.

I was in no mood for waiting. I double-parked the car, hopped out and went in.

Sherry Fontaine's building was one of the smaller ones on West End Avenue, the kind that doesn't have a doorman, just a buzzer system in the foyer. She hadn't told me what apartment, but the bell for 4A said "Fontaine." I pressed it, and seconds later a voice saying, "Be right down," squawked over the intercom.

I went out and sat in my car with the flashers on.

She was out ten minutes later. She came tripping out the door with a big smile and a wave, as if nothing was wrong.

I unlocked the passenger door and she hopped in.

She was obviously just out of the shower. Her hair was wet, and she had not bothered to dry it. On some women, that would be a holy horror, but it just made her look fresh and clean. She was wearing a light blue cotton sleeveless pullover, again with no trace of a bra. In fact, her nipples were poking out quite conspicuously.

Which somehow made me angry. Or maybe I was just angry to begin with.

"You're late," I said.

"Yeah," she said, without a trace of remorse. "Isn't it awful? Rehearsal went till one o'clock. I didn't get home till two. The clock rang this morning, I simply couldn't believe it."

I started the car and pulled out. "I got a problem with the car," I said. "It's a very tight schedule. I can't drive you if you're going to be late."

"Your blinkers are on."

I switched off the blinkers.

"I mean it," I said. "I really can't afford to be late."

She smiled. "Don't be an old grouch. We got plenty of time. You'll see."

It was not a pleasant drive. Traffic was heavy, and the going was slow and I just knew I was going to be late. I also resented being called a grouch. Or perhaps it was her choice of adjective. At any rate, I was not in a good mood, and if Sherry Fontaine had brought up the trip-and-fall scam again, I was gonna tell her where to get off.

But she didn't. Instead she jabbered on and on about the rehearsal, and her part in the play, and the director, with whom she was having some sort of argument. The play was, of course, an experimental piece by a new playwright. To the best I could determine, it had something to do with three lesbians and a baseball player. The dispute with the director was over her interpretation of her role, of course. It seemed to center on her relationship with the baseball player, and the issue of who was seducing whom.

Somehow I found this hard to relate to.

Traffic thinned out, and we pulled into the municipal parking lot at ten to ten.

"See," Sherry said. "What did I tell you? Here you were so worried, and we're early."

She was early. She got out of the car and went in. I had to circle the parking lot. I was lucky and got a parking space five minutes later. I fed ten quarters into the meter, hustled up to 111 Centre Street and got in the elevator. I didn't take it to four, though. I got out at three and hurried to the Juror Assembly Room.

A clean cut young man in slacks and a polo shirt was sitting in the back of the room reading a newspaper. I went up to him and said, "Excuse me."

He looked up and said, "Yes?"

"I'm sorry," I said, "but I'm in a real bind. I wonder if you could do me a favor."

He frowned, but he folded his paper and stood up. "What's the problem?"

"I got put on a jury and I have to be in court." I pointed through the back door of the Juror Assembly Room. "My car's in the municipal lot over there at a two-hour meter. It's gonna run out at noon, I'm gonna be sitting in court, I'm gonna get a thirty-five dollar ticket. I got one yesterday." I whipped an envelope out of my jacket pocket. "I got a tan Toyota. Here's the licence number on this envelope. It's in the second row you come to. There's ten quarters in here. At five to twelve, if you haven't been called, could you run out and put 'em in the meter?"

He smiled, the way people do when they feel slightly put upon, but they're gonna say yes. He took the envelope. "Yeah, sure," he said.

"Thanks a lot," I said. "You're a lifesaver."

"Hey, no problem. It's my third day, I haven't been called, I got nothing to do."

"Great," I said. "If you get called for a case and you can't do it, no hard feelings, thanks for trying."

"Don't worry," he said. "If I get called for a case, I'll pass it on to someone else."

As he said that, a man emerged from the direction of the men's room and came walking up the aisle.

It was my buddy. Damn. They hadn't excused him. They'd called him back for his tenth day.

He saw me, stopped short, glared, turned, and slouched into a chair. It was like a spector, haunting me. Christ, even the back of his head looked malevolent.

I thanked the guy again, beat it out of there, and caught the elevator upstairs.

I got up there at five minutes after ten. Of course, the hall was empty. Sherry Fontaine and the rest of the jurors had already been escorted in. And now the door was locked, and there was nothing for me to do but stand and wait.

Ralph showed up five minutes later. He stuck his head out the door and snarled, "All right, come on."

I walked over. Ralph didn't open the door for me, however. He stood in it, blocking my path.

"You're late," he said. "I told you not to be late. I told you if you were late, you couldn't get in.

"I told you something else, too. I told you if you were going to be late, to call and let me *know* you were going to be late. Then I would know, and I could tell the court. If you *don't* call, I *don't* know, and I *can't* tell the court. I have the judge and the lawyers and the witnesses all sitting around waiting on you. I came out here just now, I didn't know if you'd be here. And if you *hadn't* been here, I wouldn't know what to tell them still. Did you lose the number I gave you to call?''

"No."

"Then why didn't you call it?"

"I didn't have time."

"You had time to be late. Next time take the time to call. But there better not *be* a next time. From now on, *be on time.*"

With that, Ralph threw the door open wide and let me pass. As I followed him meekly down the corridor to the deliberation room, it occurred to me this was entirely typical of the syndrome. I *had* left time to get here. Sherry Fontaine was the one who'd been ten minutes late. But, of course, she'd gotten away with it. *She* hadn't been late. She'd simply *made me* late. It was entirely her fault, and yet I was the one in trouble.

Ralph opened the door of the juror deliberation room, and stood there sternly holding it as I marched in, as if he were the truant officer, and I were the naughty pupil he'd caught.

As I walked in, I wondered if Sherry Fontaine would expect me to sit with her, since we were friends. That seemed a little much. I looked around and everyone seemed to be sitting where they were before. I went and took my place at the head of the table.

As I sat down, Ralph gave me one final glare, and went out, closing the door behind him.

The Professor looked at me, rubbed his index fingers together and said, "Bad, bad boy."

Everyone in the room cracked up. Jurors who had

been silent as the grave when Ralph was in the room, now all began jabbering at once, and I gradually got the story.

I had not noticed it, but College Boy was not in the room. He'd phoned in sick this morning, and had to be replaced. Mrs. Abernathy, as first alternate, had been elevated to the rank of juror. Chuckles, as the other jurors persisted in calling Ralph, had taken this as a personal affront, and was in a particularly foul mood, even for him. My coming late on top of all that was simply the last straw.

It was also wholly unimportant in the workings of the higher order of the universe. For, despite what Ralph had said, if the judge and the lawyers and the witnesses were all in court waiting on me, then Ralph must not have told them I arrived, because he didn't come back for us until after eleven. So we had over an hour in the juror deliberation room to cut up Ralph, and shoot the shit, and just get generally acquainted.

I began sorting other jurors out. I mean, aside from the arbitrary designations I had given them. Here, as usual, my observations had been somewhat less than accurate.

College Boy, no longer with us, was not a college boy at all, but an assistant manager at Burger King. It was Eraserhead who was the college boy. He was, in fact, in law school at Columbia, and was actually happy to be on the jury and get some firsthand courtroom experience. He turned out to be bright, sharp and articulate, and was probably gonna make a damn fine lawyer some day, if his hairstyle didn't hold him back. I realized the last thought was just prejudice on my part, that I'm just a old fogy who can't relate to the kids of today any more than my parents could relate to me as a long-haired hippie, and that it was

Eraserhead who was hip, cool and with it, and I was the one out of step.

I also found out his name was Ron, which was good, because then I could stop thinking of him as Eraserhead. Ron was our foreman too, by the way, by virtue of sitting in seat number one, and it occurred to me that was fortuitous, because when the jury finally got down to their deliberations, he'd be on top of things and be a good leader and move things along.

Only I wouldn't see that. For as the alternate, while I had to sit through the trial, I didn't have to stay for the deliberations. As soon as the jury was sent to deliberate, I'd be excused. Thank god for small favors.

As to the other jurors, I already knew Mrs. Abernathy, and I already knew Sherry Fontaine. That left the Professor, Hoop Earrings, and Business Woman. Hoop Earrings foxed me by wearing small studs today, which left me up in the air as to just what to call her. Fortunately, her name turned out to be Maria, which is one of those names I can remember—Maria, I just met a girl named Maria.

Business Woman's name was one of those I can't remember, so I missed it again, but I did learn that she wasn't a businesswoman at all, but a housewife and the mother of three. It was Hoop Earrings who was the businesswoman. She turned out to be a buyer for a large textile company. So Hoop Earrings, who *was* a businesswoman became Maria, and Business Woman, who *wasn't* a business woman got pushed into limbo and became the Nameless Mother.

That left only the Professor. He turned out to be a clerk at OTB.

At eleven-fifteen, Ralph Chuckles came and got us and we marched into court.

I am pleased to announce that we found our respective seats without incident. Of course, with College Boy dropping out, Mrs. Abernathy was now in the second row, which meant I only had to count up to one, but I still took pride in the accomplishment.

When we were all seated I looked around the courtroom. Judge Davis, the Silver Fox, and Peter, Paul and Mary were all in place, but today we had an added starter. There was a man sitting in the spectators' section in the very back of the courtroom. An old Hispanic, dressed in work clothes. He looked oddly out of place in the courtroom, as if he'd been looking for the Department of Motor Vehicles and come in the wrong door.

But he was in the right place, all right. After Judge Davis called court to order, she turned to the Silver Fox and said, "Mr. Pendergas, call your first witness."

Pendergas rose and said, "Your Honor, I call Hernan Medina."

The old man in the back of the court rose and shuffled up to the witness stand. After he'd been sworn in, the Silver Fox said, "What is your name?"

"Hernan Medina."

"And what is your occupation, Mr. Medina?"

"Custodian."

"And where to do you work?"

Medina gave an address in Brooklyn.

"I see," Pendergas said. "And how long have you worked there?"

Medina shrugged. "Two, three years."

"I see. And can you tell us where you were working on February 15, 1982?"

"Yes."

There was a pause, then Pendergas said, "Please do."

"What?"

"What was the address?"

"Oh." Medina thought a moment, then gave the address of the office building on 26th Street.

"And you were working there in what capacity?"

Medina frowned. "What?"

"What was your job?"

"Oh. Same job. Custodian."

My interest picked up somewhat. Medina appeared as if he would at least make a colorful witness. As custodian he must have discovered the fire. We would hear tales of smelling smoke, rushing up, seeing the flames, calling the fire department, the arrival of fire engines, police, and the whole shmear.

Wrong again. None of that happened. It truly *was* the most boring case in history. There had been no alarms, no fire engines, in fact, no firemen at all. The fire had occurred over the weekend while the building was locked up. Apparently it had started on the third floor at Veliko Tool and Die, spread to the fourth floor where it had damaged some of the equipment of Dumar Electronics, and then *burned itself out*. Medina had indeed smelled smoke in the building, but not while the fire was burning. He had smelled smoke when he'd come into work Monday morning. He'd investigated, opened the offices of Veliko Tool and Die and Dumar Electronics, and discovered that there had indeed been a fire. And he had been on hand to report that to the owners of those respective companies when they had showed up later that morning to open up for business.

Hernan Medina's story was dull as dishwater.

And we got to hear it four times, because when the Silver Fox was done, Peter, Paul and Mary led him through it again. Trust me, it did not improve with repetition.

There were, however, some bones of contention. Veliko Tool and Die had a die-press machine that had been consumed by the fire. Pendergas tried very hard to get Medina to say that in his estimation the fire had originated from that machine. Not in those words, of course, but the general idea. Medina, however, held firm. There'd been a fire, he'd seen the damage, but he didn't know how it had started or where it had started. That wasn't his job.

Pendergas *did* get Medina to say that he'd seen no water on the floor, and as far as he knew, nothing seemed wet. He tried to get Medina to say that in his opinion the sprinkler system had not gone off, but Mary objected on the grounds that that was a conclusion on the part of the witness, which he was not qualified to give, and Judge Davis sustained her on the point.

If you find any of that at all interesting, that's 'cause it only took a minute to tell it. Try listening to it for close to two hours, 'cause that's what we did. At which point it was one o'clock, and Judge Davis mercifully broke for lunch.

As we filed back into the deliberation room, we all looked slightly numb.

Ron, formerly Eraserhead, blew out a breath and said, "Lawyers."

I smiled. "I thought you were in law school."

OTB Man, formerly the Professor, grinned and said, "What's the matter, Ron? Havin' second thoughts?"

Ron shook his head. "Naw. It's just like they teach you in law school, you can argue either side of anything. That's why everyone's always suin'."

I frowned. "Excuse me, but what do you mean?"

Ron jerked his thumb in the direction of the courtroom. "Pretty Boy's suin' everyone because the sprinklers didn't work so his equipment burned, right?''

"Yeah. So?''

Ron smiled. "Think about it. If the sprinklers *had* gone off, his equipment would have got wet, and he'd be suin' everyone for water damage.''

14.

I DIDN'T WANT to have lunch with Sherry Fontaine. I mean, it would have been okay if a bunch of us jurors had gone out together, but I didn't want to have lunch with her alone. In view of the whole controversy about driving the car, I didn't want to have to tell Alice I'd gone out to lunch with the woman. If you can't understand that, all I can say is you're probably single. At any rate, if Sherry had asked me what I was doing for lunch, I was gonna tell her I was busy.

She didn't though. As soon as we were released, she sailed out the door without so much as a backward glance at me.

That pissed me off. Which was strange. I mean, I didn't *want* to have lunch with her. I just would have liked to have been given the option.

At any rate, I really *was* busy. First I had to run out to the parking lot to see if the guy had put my quarters in the meter. He had, and at the right time too. By my calculations, he'd put the money in at five of twelve, meaning the meter'd run out at five of two. Perfect.

I'd already checked my beeper on the way to the parking lot, so I knew the office wanted me. I called in and Wendy/Janet already had a case for tomorrow morning and one for tomorrow night, again both in Harlem. All right. So far things were working out.

I ran across the street and got a cheeseburger and a can of soda to go, went back to the parking lot and ate 'em sitting on the hood of my car. I tried eating them *in* my car, but every two minutes someone would pull up behind me and honk to see if I was going out, so I gave that up.

I finished my lunch, disposed of my garbage in the proper receptacle, and hung out in the parking lot until a quarter to two. That was early, of course, but I wasn't taking any chances of being late. I fed ten quarters into the parking meter, making it good until a quarter to four, and hotfooted it back to 111 Centre Street.

Sherry Fontaine was just crossing the street as I got there. She saw me and waved. I waved back, but half-heartedly. Seeing her was like an omen. I had a flash that somehow, someway, she was going to make me late.

"Going in so soon?" she said. "We still got fifteen minutes."

I wasn't gonna be distracted. "I gotta find someone to put quarters in my parking meter."

"That's how you're workin' it?

"Yeah."

"Okay. I'll go with you."

Again, I felt a portent of doom. Somehow, some way she was gonna fuck me up.

"Fine," I said. "Let's go."

I expected her to stall, somehow, but she didn't. She went right inside and got in the elevator. We went up to three and down to the Juror Assembly Room.

It couldn't have been better. The guy I'd given the quarters to was sitting right there in the same chair reading a book.

I walked up and said, "Hi."

He looked up, said, "Hi," then cast an appreciative glance over Sherry Fontaine.

"Hi," she said.

"Listen," I said. "I want to thank you for putting the quarters in the meter, and if it's not too much trouble, could you do it again?"

There was no way the guy was gonna say no. He couldn't take his eyes off Sherry Fontaine. And he sure wasn't gonna be a grouch with her smiling at him. He was a nice guy, and I'm sure he would have done it anyway. But with Sherry there, it was a lock.

He smiled. "Sure thing," he said. "How's the case going?"

"We're not really supposed to discuss it," I said.

"Don't be silly," Sherry said. "How can you not discuss it?"

"You on the jury too?"

"Sure thing," Sherry said, smiling. She slipped her arm through mine. "Me and Stanley are the super jurors. The best jurors on the best jury on the best case in the whole system. We're lucky to be on it."

The guy was grinning like a zany, and it flashed on me my worst nightmare would be Sherry would stand there flirting with him until she made us late.

No, there was a nightmare worse than that. At that moment, my buddy came walking in from the hall just in time to see me standing there with Sherry on my arm, and her sayin' how great it was for the two of us to get put on this great jury together. Here he was on the afternoon of his tenth day of doing absolutely nothing, and he had to hear that. If looks could kill, his would have.

But aside from that, it went smoothly. The guy accepted the quarters, agreed to put them in at three-thirty, and I managed to spirit Sherry away from him and pilot her upstairs by five of two.

The other jurors were already waiting in the hall. Maria, formerly Hoop Earrings, attempted some innuendo by giggling, ''Where did you two go for lunch?'' and OTB Man winked and whispered, ''You sly dog, you,'' which was slightly embarrassing, but could not dampen my spirits at the relief of not being late for Ralph.

Ralph showed up at two on the dot, seemed not at all pleased to find all of us there, led us back to the deliberation room, and eventually into court.

If the morning session was dull, the afternoon session was torture. In the morning, at least we had a witness. In the afternoon we had nothing. See, since the case was eight years old, some of the witnesses were not available. But they'd all been questioned at prior hearings. So the afternoon session consisted of the Silver Fox reading their depositions into the record.

The depositions consisted of two former employees of Veliko Tool and Die, and two former employees of Dumar Electronics, all of them reporting what they saw when they came to work on the morning of February 15, 1982.

The Silver Fox tried to read with expression, but even so, I have to tell you, I thought I was going to die. When Judge Davis finally adjourned court at ten to five, it was an incredible relief.

I'd gotten through the day. And I hadn't gotten a parking ticket. And on the ride home, Sherry Fontaine didn't ask me to do anything illegal. And Alice only put up a mild argument about me driving the car, since everything had worked out today, leaving her with no ammunition. And Tommie cooperated and was easy to put to bed. And Alice cooperated and was easy to put to bed—the sexist pig strikes again.

As I lay cradling Alice in my arms, the happy thought crossed my mind, on top of everything else, when I got to court tomorrow morning, my buddy wouldn't be there. Just before I dropped off to sleep, I felt a warm glow, and I had to admit things could be worse.

I gotta stop thinking that.

15.

THURSDAY STARTED off great. Sherry Fontaine was on time. In fact, she was early. I had a piece-of-cake signup in Harlem—the kid had fallen on a school playground, Location of Accident pictures to be taken at a later time—whizzed downtown, pulled up in front of Sherry Fontaine's building at five after nine, and she was already standing there. She gave me a big smile and a wave and hopped in.

Once again, her hair was wet, and once again she was wearing a cotton something or other without a bra. But today her nipples didn't bother me. Yesterday they had been blatant, suggestive, intrusive, obnoxious, late nipples, and they pissed me off. Today they were casual, friendly, comfortable, on-time nipples, and I didn't mind them at all. In fact, they were actually rather pleasant.

Sherry was in a good mood, too. More than a good mood. She was higher than a kite. Apparently rehearsal had gone very well. She was all keyed up talking about it. The director was starting to listen to reason (i.e., her), and coming up with some good ideas (i.e., hers), and was beginning to get a handle on the more important aspects of the play (i.e., her part).

The baseball player was pretty much of a stiff, but he was at least good-looking, and was showing signs of having potential if someone (i.e., her) could get it out of him. The author of the play was a numbnuts who didn't like her improvisation (from which I gathered she was rewriting all her lines), but she was sure the director was coming around to her point of view, and probably would have said so more explicitly had he not been inhibited by the presence of the playwright.

It was a totally egotistical and self-serving monologue, and had Sherry Fontaine been late, I'm sure I would have found it annoying. But since she was early, I found it only amusing, and her high spirits didn't bother me at all.

She was also excited because there was no rehearsal Saturday night, and the director had invited the cast to a party, and it was rumored that Al Pacino was going to be there. She went on about the party so much I was beginning to think she was leading up to inviting me. Not to fear. Sherry was off in her own world, and I might not have even been there at all.

We hit the parking lot at twenty to ten. Once again, Sherry got out and went in ahead of me, but I found a parking spot right away, and had plenty of time to search out someone to take care of putting quarters in the meter. Again I was in luck. The guy from yesterday was in the Juror Assembly Room. He seemed disappointed Sherry wasn't with me, but he accepted the quarters without hesitation. He also confirmed the fact that yesterday afternoon my buddy had, indeed, been dismissed. They kept him there all day until four-thirty before doing it, but they had finally let him go, and he'd gone stomping up the aisle, clutching his jury service certificate in his hand as if it were a sword, and muttering under his breath. That was a tremendous relief. I'd had the paranoid fantasy that yesterday afternoon they'd finally called him and put him on a jury, and he'd be there to haunt me forever. But no, just like that, he was gone. Things were really working out.

I got upstairs in plenty of time for Ralph. In fact, when I got there, OTB Man wasn't there yet, and I had a momentary flash of panic that maybe he wasn't coming, and then I'd be *on* this damn jury, instead of just the alternate. But he arrived minutes later, grumbling about a subway delay, and everything was fine. So, considering I was a reluctant juror who shouldn't have been there to begin with, on the worst case in history, it was the best of all possible worlds.

The rest of the day went smoothly too. In the morning we met the owner of Dumar Electronics, a middle-aged man named Dumar, which shouldn't have surprised me, but did. (I mean, like, What a coincidence, they got Gary Shandling to host the "Gary Shandling Show.") At any rate, Dumar was plump, bald and aggrieved. He told a tale of coming to work that morning and finding a scene of devastation. According to him, the fire had been catastrophic in proportions and had all but wiped him out. He described TVs, amplifiers and answering machines as if they were his children.

Peter, Paul and Mary all had a whack at him, which was probably as fruitless as it was boring. They had copies of two previous depositions he'd made in this case, and they went over them painstakingly, looking for contradictions between what he'd said in them and what he'd said today, harping on things like, "In 1984 you testified that when you entered the office, Hernan Medina and your employee Frank Small were with you, but today you only mentioned Hernan Medina, now which is correct?"

None of the answers to any of these questions was particularly enlightening, but many of them led to objections followed by long, tedious arguments. The Silver Fox seemed slightly off his game today. Not that he was losing many points—he was still sharp as ever, it was just that every now and then he'd let his usual genial façade slip and let his irritation show. It was as if eight years of this bullshit was finally wearing him down. But considering that, he was doing fine.

In the afternoon we were treated to the appearance of the adjuster called in by Dumar Electronics to assess the damage. He was a flashy-looking dresser with dark hair, a dark moustache and a confident manner. He identified a document the Silver Fox produced which turned out to be the assessment he had made back in '82. He itemized the damaged equipment, and estimated the total value at two hundred and twenty-five thousand dollars.

I found the guy pretty impressive until Peter, Paul and Mary got a whack at him. The first thing they brought out was how he got paid, and when I heard it, it floored me.

He got a percentage. Ten percent of the recovery. Good lord. This was an impartial estimate? I could envision the guy standing there thinking, ''Okay, here's a two-thousand-dollar stereo. If I say it's worthless, I get two hundred dollars. All right, it's worthless.''

But that didn't seem to bother the judge or the Silver Fox or the adjuster any. The man stated that taking a percentage was a standard practice, and I guess it was. Once again, the thought crossed my mind, boy am I in the wrong line of work.

And that was the day. Dumar and the adjuster were it. It occurred to me at this rate I would indeed fulfill my prophecy of being on this jury forever, but aside from that the day was very smooth. I had no problem getting quarters put in my meter, my buddy wasn't around to bug me, the office gave me two more sign-ups for tomorrow, and before I knew it the day was over and I was driving Sherry Fontaine back uptown to drop her off on my way to Harlem.

The ride uptown was perfectly pleasant too. Sherry Fontaine seemed to have given up trying to get me to do anything illegal. Either that, or she was now so into her play she didn't care. At any rate, she was just bubbling over with good will, and the ride uptown was fine.

I pulled up in front of her building at five-thirty. Actually, I pulled up in front of the building across the street, since I was heading uptown and her building was on the other side of West End. She hopped out of the car at the corner and crossed the street.

I sat in the car and watched her go.

Now, I want you to understand. I wasn't watching to see she got safely in. After all, five-thirty in the afternoon in the summer in New York City is broad daylight. And West End Avenue is a perfectly respect-able street, and a thirty-year-old woman can cross it and go into her apartment building with no trouble. So I was not watching her for that reason. It was just that my car was at the corner, and the light happened to be red. And while I was waiting for it to change, I watched Sherry Fontaine cross the street and enter her building.

Only she didn't. There was a man leaning against the building next to the front door. When he saw Sherry, he straightened up to meet her. He was a youngish man, maybe Sherry's age, with long brown hair dangling down the side of his face, and blue jeans and a gray sweatshirt with a hood hanging down the back. He wasn't tall, but he was kind of thin and gangly, and that coupled with the sweatshirt made him look sort of like a hippie basketball player.

At any rate, Sherry walked up to him and the two started talking. I was across the street with the windows up and the air conditioning on, so naturally I couldn't hear a thing. But from the tilt of their heads and the way their lips were moving, I could tell the conversation wasn't particularly amicable.

The car behind me honked, and I realized the light had changed. I didn't drive off, though. Instead I pulled on the emergency brake and hit my flashers. The car behind me gave one more impatient honk, then pulled out and went around me. I paid no attention. I kept watching the scene across the street.

I know, it was none of my business. Sherry Fontaine had never mentioned a boyfriend, but she probably had one, and this was probably him. And they'd probably had a fight, and probably the reason she'd seemed in such good spirits all day was she was upset and overcompensating.

All of that flashed on me, and I knew I should drive off.

But I stayed.

And there was something in the guy's manner that told me I *should* stay. That this was not just a domestic spat. At least, I'd like to think I thought that, and I *do* think I thought that, but maybe that's only because of what happened next.

He reached out and grabbed her arm. He grabbed her by the wrist and held her firm. And when she reached for his hand he grabbed her other wrist.

I felt sick.

You have to understand. I'm not a physical person by nature. I'm athletic, but I'm not particularly strong.

And I've never been in a fight in my life. I avoid fights like the plague. Fights, hell, I avoid confrontations. I don't even like to argue. That's one of the reasons I feel so silly telling people I'm a private detective. It's as if, how can they consider me a private detective if I've never even punched anyone?

I know, I'm rambling. But that's why I felt sick. All that emotional baggage was flashing on me when the guy grabbed Sherry's arms. Because I knew I had to do something, something I didn't think I had it in me to do. But I had to, so I did.

I jerked the door open, got out of the car. I caught a break in traffic, and went striding across West End Avenue like the calvary to the rescue. I hit the sidewalk not ten feet from where they were standing, stopped, stuck out my finger straight at him and said, ''All right, buddy, hold it right there!''

They both turned and saw me and my heart sank. At least that got it out of my mouth. But still.

The guy was younger than I thought, say twenty-five. He was also more muscular. Thin, yeah, but wiry. Strong. And slightly taller than he'd looked from across the street.

But all that's subjective and incidental. The bottom line was, I suddenly realized this guy could rip me apart.

He didn't.

He ran.

He took one look at me and he let go of her hands and he turned and ran. He darted across the street, dodging traffic, flashed around the corner, and just like that he was gone.

I watched him go. As he did, all I could think of was, what a fucking relief.

I turned to find Sherry Fontaine looking after him.

Son of a bitch. I'd done it. I was like some crazy movie hero, I'd actually saved her. Actually rescued a damsel in distress.

She turned to me, that damsel in distress. She turned to me, and just like in the movies, her eyes were red with tears.

She didn't fall into my arms sobbing, though. Instead, she clenched her fists, stamped her foot, said, "God damn it! Why the fuck did you have to do that?" and stalked into her building, slamming the door behind her.

16.

A LICE WAS not pleased.

"You *fought* for this woman?" she demanded.

"I didn't fight for her."

"You were going to."

"No, I wasn't."

"You got out of your car. You crossed the street."

"I had to do something."

"Oh yeah? What were you going to do?"

"Stop him."

"How?"

"I don't know."

"But you weren't going to fight with him?"

"No."

"What were you going to do, tell him he was a bad boy?"

"I don't know what I was going to do."

"But you weren't going to fight him?"

"If I had, he'd have killed me."

"You took a risk like that for this woman?"

"Person."

"What?"

"This person. She's just a person. If you'd stop

thinking of her as 'this woman,' you'd understand. I'd have done the same thing for any of the jurors."

"But it wasn't any of the jurors. It was her."

"It happened to be her."

"Yes, it did. Of all the jurors, she's the one you happened to drive home. And then she yelled at you."

"She was upset."

"I'm sure she was. So she told you to mind your own business?"

"Not in those words."

"Well, what words did she say?"

"She said, 'God damn it, why the fuck did you have to do that.' "

"Nice talk."

"She was upset."

"You keep saying that."

"Well, she was."

"Sure. Fine." Alice took a breath. "Well, I guess you're not driving her anymore."

I didn't say anything.

"Well, are you?"

"Yes, I am."

"Why?"

"I said I would."

"That was before she yelled at you. You don't have to drive someone who's gonna yell at you."

"She's expecting me to pick her up in the morning."

"So call her and tell her you're not going to."

"I don't want to do that."

"Why not?"

"I just don't. It would be stupid. I'd feel like a little kid. 'You yelled at me, so I'm not gonna drive you anymore.' "

Alice held up her hand. "Wait a minute. That's not the point here."

"What's the point?"

"Do you *want* to drive her?"

"That's not the point."

"Oh, yes it is. The point is, are you doing what you want to do?"

"Yes, I am."

"Oh really? Do you *want* to drive her?"

I took a breath. "Well, no."

"So call her and tell her you're not going to drive her."

"I don't want to do that."

"Why not?"

I took another breath. "I don't want to have to call her and tell her my wife won't let me drive her anymore."

"That's not true."

"Yes it is. If you weren't telling me not to drive her, there'd be no issue."

"Aren't you angry at her for yelling at you? I mean, doesn't that make you mad?"

"Yes, but—"

The phone rang. Alice scooped it up. "Hello?"

One look at Alice's face told me who was on the phone.

Alice covered the mouthpiece and said simply, "It's for you."

Those words spoke volumes.

I picked up the phone and said, "Hello?"

"Stanley, hi. I just called to say I'm really sorry."

With Alice standing there looking at me, the best I could manage was an, "Uh huh."

"I know, I know, it's not enough. Look, I'm at rehearsal now, I can't really talk. I just called to say it was a horrible misunderstanding, and I shouldn't have yelled at you, and I'm really sorry, and I'll see you tomorrow morning nine-fifteen. Okay?"

"Okay."

"Thanks. You're an angel. Sorry again."

And she hung up.

I hung up to find Alice looking at me.

"I take it that was her?" Alice said dryly.

"Yes."

"Hmm," Alice said. "Nice voice."

In my humble estimation, Alice did not sound entirely sincere.

17.

S HERRY WAS late. Wouldn't you know it. Nine-fifteen I was waiting outside her building, and she wasn't there. And after yesterday, I just wasn't in the mood to cope with her being late.

I was sorely tempted just to drive off and leave her. But I'm just not that kind of guy. I'm not that hostile on the one hand, or that gutsy on the other. What I mean is, if I drove off and left her, I wouldn't want to deal with the ugly scene when she finally did arrive for jury duty, late and pissed off at being left. Being finally free of my buddy's hostile presence, I didn't need someone else sitting there hating me day after day.

So I didn't want to leave her, but I didn't want to wait, and there I was, sitting in my car, impotent, frustrated and mad as hell.

I put the flashers on, went into the foyer and rang her bell. No answer. I rang again, longer this time. Nothing. I leaned on the damn bell. Still nothing.

I knew why. She was in the shower. What with her coming down with her hair wet every morning, it didn't take a detective to figure that out. She was in the shower, so she couldn't hear the bell.

But if she was in the shower and not even dressed yet, we were gonna be late. Or rather, *I* was gonna be late. She'd sail in at one minute to ten, while I was still circling in the parking lot or handing out quarters for the meter. She'd be on time and I'd be late, transported back to high school again, sent to detention study hall by Ralph, made to stand in the corner like a bad boy, or kept after court and made to clean the blackboards.

It was the last straw. I was through having fights with my wife over this woman who was pissing me off. You make me late today, Sherry, so help me, this is your last ride.

I rang the bell again. Still nothing.

The foyer door had been propped open, understandable in the heat, but still a serious breach of security. If I'd lived in the building, I wouldn't have allowed it. Or at least, Alice wouldn't have. Not without a super in the lobby.

But it meant I could go up if I wanted to.

I sure didn't want to. If she was in the shower, maybe I could make her hear by pounding on the door. But if so, I didn't really want her coming to the door in a bath towel. The woman was hard enough to deal with with her clothes on. I didn't need any adventures with her naked. With my luck, she'd drop her towel and run giggling into the bedroom to get dressed. And I was having a hard enough time with Alice. I didn't need Sherry Fontaine's naked body on my mind the next time Alice and I discussed her pros and cons.

But I was too pissed off to stand in the lobby, and as I said, I just couldn't bring myself to drive off. So I checked the apartment number again, 4A, got in the self-service elevator, and pushed four.

I got off on the fourth floor and looked around. 4A

turned out to be at the end of the hallway in the front of the building. I walked up to it and pounded on the door, hard.

The door swung open. It had been closed, but not latched. When I knocked, it opened a good four inches.

I grabbed the knob with my left hand to hold the door steady, and pounded some more.

Nothing. No response.

I pushed open the door a few more inches and bellowed, "Sherry."

No answer.

I leaned my head closer to the open door and, sure enough, I could hear the sound of the shower running.

Damn. My worst nightmare. She was in the shower, and I was either gonna stand here like an asshole, or go in and find her naked.

I bellowed, "Sherry," again, once more to no response.

Aw, hell.

I took a deep breath, pushed the door open, and went in.

Jesus Christ!

It was my worst nightmare, all right.

She was stark naked, just like I'd imagined.

She was also dead.

18.

I THREW UP.

I staggered into the bathroom with my head spinning, guided largely by the sound of the running water from the shower, and vomited in the toilet. I ended up on my knees, gripping the edge of the toilet seat, hanging on for dear life.

I threw up when I found my first dead body. And when I found my second. I broke myself of the habit during the Rosenberg and Stone murders, when a bizarre twist of fate had made finding dead bodies just a matter of course. I managed to steel myself to it, blot it out, take it in my stride.

But this was a woman's body.

A naked body.

Sherry Fontaine's body.

That was it.

Sherry Fontaine's body.

For the first time, the body was someone that I *knew*.

I rubbed my head to clear it, steadied myself and got to my feet. I flushed the toilet. Then I turned on the sink, got some water to rinse my mouth. I knew I shouldn't be doing those things—I shouldn't be touching anything, destroying any evidence. I didn't care. I wasn't going to leave a toilet full of vomit, and god knows I had to rinse my mouth.

There was a tube of toothpaste on the sink. Crest. "Look ma, no cavities." I picked it up, took off the cap, squeezed some toothpaste out on my finger and stuck it in my mouth. I added some water, sloshed it around, got rid of the horrible taste.

I straightened up and looked at myself in the mirror. I looked terrible. I splashed some water in my face. It didn't help.

I squeezed my eyes shut. *Come on, pull yourself together.*

I took a few deep breaths, calmed down, steeled myself.

And went back into the other room.

Sherry Fontaine was lying in the middle of the floor. She was lying on her back, with her head twisted to the side. Her legs were apart like a porno magazine, and I could see the slit of her vagina. It was pulled slightly open by the position in which she'd fallen.

And then her breasts. Those braless breasts that I had found so disturbing. A woman's breasts are de-emphasized when she's lying on her back. Compound that with her being dead, and you can't even begin to imagine.

What I'm trying to say is, there was nothing sensual or erotic about Sherry Fontaine's naked body. The sight was nauseating, sick and sad.

There was a wet pool emanating from between her legs. In death, her bladder had released, the final humiliation. I didn't notice and almost stepped in it. Thank god I didn't. It flashed on me, Jesus, just like Lincoln Monroe Jackson. Slipped in urine.

I tried to compose myself. I ran my hand over my face. My god, what do I do, what do I do?

Of course, I knew what I had to do. I had to call the cops.

But not from here. I'd touched enough things in the apartment already. I couldn't touch the phone. I had to go out and call.

But not yet. First I had to look around. Occupational hazard. If you're a detective, you have to look around.

I told myself that. Never mind what you think, never mind what you feel, never mind that it's personal, never mind that you knew her—you're a detective and you have to look around.

The front door was open. Lying just inside it was a towel. Sherry Fontaine's body was about ten feet further into the room from that. And the shower was going. She'd been in the shower, someone had knocked, she'd wrapped a towel around her and she'd opened the door—Jesus Christ, an old Bobby Darin song—the man had grabbed her, she'd dropped the towel, and then—

Oh, Christ. It was obvious what happened, but that didn't help. Nothing helped. And nothing would help. Shit, I gotta get out of here.

Yeah, you're a detective so you gotta look around.

Some detective.

I went out to the street and called the cops.

19.

S ERGEANT THURMAN was not exactly the most sensitive of men.

"Gees, look at that twat. Ten-to-one it's a rape."

A TV detective would have punched him in the face. Except on TV Thurman couldn't have said that. But a movie detective would have punched him in the face. I, of course, just stood there and seethed.

That remark alone was sufficient to insure my not liking Sergeant Thurman. Sufficient, but not necessary. I wouldn't have liked him anyway. Thurman was a barrel-shaped man with a bullneck, a flattened nose, and a crewcut. Probably it was the broken nose that did it, but somehow he looked like a man with zero IQ. The eyes, though hard, seemed vacant, as if what they were taking in had nothing to do with what his mouth was spewing out. As if his brain was processing information on some prehistoric, caveman level. His speech, guttural, and flavored with the "duh" sound, added to the primitive image.

The simple ideas his one-cell brain could process, he clung to like the gospel, and his opinions, such as they were, he barked out in a preemptory fashion, as if his word were law.

Which, of course, it was. For though he looked and acted like an army drill sergeant, he was actually a homicide sergeant with the NYPD.

It was about a half-hour from the time I'd called in. Sherry Fontaine's apartment was a flurry of activity. A Crime Scene Unit was already processing the place for evidence, dusting for fingerprints, and doing the things Crime Scene Units do. A police photographer had already taken a million pictures of Sherry Fontaine's body, including several closeups of her vagina. I couldn't help wondering if those were really for evidence, or just to give the boys back at the precinct a thrill. Now the medical examiner was having a crack at her.

"What's the word, doc?" Thurman barked at him.

The medical examiner, a plump black man with an easygoing manner, looked up from where he knelt by the body and shrugged. "She appears to have been dead for some time. I'll pin it down when I get her to the morgue."

"Was she fucked?"

"No obvious signs of semen. I won't know till I do an internal."

"Don't you doctors know anything?"

"I know she's dead."

"Gee, you college boys are smart. Wanna tell me what killed her?"

"Most likely she was strangled."

Shit. I'd figured that. The Rosenberg and Stone murders had been stranglings. I'd recognized the look. The protruding tongue, the slightly bug-eyed look. The look I'd hoped I'd never see again.

I was residing in the company of a young officer

whose instructions were to keep me off to the side and not let me touch anything. I hadn't moved, so I guess he was doing a hell of a job.

So far, no one had questioned me. That was because the cops had arrived all at once, so there was too much to do. Thurman had ascertained that I was the one who'd called the police, assigned the young cop to ride herd over me, and that had been it.

He turned his attention to me now. He strode over, stuck out his chin at me as if I were a young recruit, and demanded, "You the one called this in?"

"As I told you, yes, I did."

"What's your name?"

"Stanley Hastings."

"You found the body?"

"Yes, I did."

"How'd you happen to find the body?"

"I came to pick her up. She was late and didn't answer the bell. The door was open, so I went up to see what was keeping her."

"The upstairs door was open?"

"The downstairs and the upstairs door. The downstairs door was propped open. When I knocked on the upstairs door, it swung open."

"You saw the body then?"

"No. First I banged on the door and called her name a few times. She didn't answer. Then I heard the shower running. Then I opened the door and found her."

His eyes narrowed. "You heard the shower running?"

"That's right."

"You were gonna walk in and surprise her in the shower?"

"No, I wasn't."

"Then why did you open the door when you heard the shower running?"

"I figured she was in the shower so she couldn't hear me. I went in so I could shout through the bathroom door for her to hurry up."

"Shout through the bathroom door?"

"Yeah."

"Not go in the bathroom and find her?"

"Absolutely not."

"Absolutely?" He chuckled. "Oh, it's absolutely, is it?" His eyes narrowed. "You fuckin' her?"

I controlled myself with an effort. "No, I was not."

"You sure?"

"Yes, I'm sure. She wasn't my girlfriend. I'm a married man."

His eyes widened. "Oh, gee," he said with elaborate sarcasm. "Excuse me. A married man. How stupid of me. Then you couldn't have been fuckin' her, could you?"

I took a breath. "Sergeant, I'm a little upset at finding a friend of mine dead. I know you gotta ask your questions, but your bedside manner stinks. So let me tell you, I did not have any physical relationship with Sherry Fontaine. I was just picking her up because we're jurors and—Jesus Christ!"

"What is it?"

"What time is it?"

The young cop guarding me looked at his watch and said, "Ten to ten." It was an automatic reaction, and one he instantly regretted. Sergeant Thurman glared at him as if he'd just given away military secrets. The young cop seemed to wilt under his gaze.

"Oh, shit," I said. "I gotta make a call."

"What?" the sergeant demanded.

"I gotta make a phone call."

141

He shook his head. "Not now, you don't. You wanna call a lawyer, you got that right. But no one's accusing you of anything. There's no reason to take that attitude."

"I don't wanna call a lawyer. I gotta call the court."

"What?"

"I'm on a jury. I gotta call the court and tell 'em I'm gonna be late."

"Yeah, well that's tough," he said. He jerked his thumb at the detectives processing the apartment. "Phone's off limits."

"So have this guy take me down to a pay phone."

He stuck out his chin. "Where the hell you get off telling me what to do? This isn't fun and games. This is a murder case, and I need you here."

"You're not gonna let me call?"

"You can call when we're good and ready. Right now we got things to do."

I smiled. "Thank you, sergeant. You just let me off the hook."

He frowned. "What are you talking about?"

"With the court, I mean. I was gonna be in a lot of trouble with the court for showing up late. Now I'm not. When Judge Davis demands to know why I was late for court and didn't call in, I'll be able to state that I asked to call her at ten minutes to ten before court convened, but Sergeant Thurman of the NYPD refused to let me. So thanks for taking the responsibility and letting me off the hook."

Thurman looked like he wanted to bite my head off. But he was a cop, and he had to work within the court system. He didn't need the flack. Plus, I hadn't mentioned that it was a civil suit, which might have made a difference. At any rate, the end result was the young cop took me downstairs to the corner to a pay phone.

Ralph answered on the first ring. I could tell he was not in a good mood. Of course, Ralph was never in a good mood, but even for him. I guess in his business, calls this time of the morning were always bad news.

"Yeah?" he growled.

"Ralph, it's Stanley Hastings."

"Hastings, god damn it. Do you know what time it is?"

"Not exactly, but—"

"It's two minutes till ten, that's what time it is. Wherever you're calling from, you're gonna be late."

"Yes, I know, but—"

"God damn it, two minutes to ten, you're not supposed to call at two minutes to ten. I told you that. You're gonna be late, you don't call at two minutes to ten, you call earlier. So I can inform the judge. I shouldn't even be on the phone now, I should be out in the hall bringing the jurors in. Instead, I'm on the phone listening to some jerk who calls in at two minutes to ten.

"So where are you, and how late are you gonna be?"

"I'm uptown, and—"

"Uptown!"

"Yes, and I may not make it at all."

"What?!"

"Listen, Ralph, you don't understand. I—"

"No, *you* don't understand. You can't call in like this and say you may not make it at all. What happens now is, you'll be replaced, that's what. And don't think it gets you out of service. All you do is lose the time you put in. You go back in the pool, and you start over from day one. And don't think they'll take exception and let you go, because *I* will keep on top of it, and *I* will see that they don't. Understand, you've blown it, and you're gonna be replaced.''

''No, I'm not.''

''What?'' Ralph said. ''You talkin' back to me? I just told you you're out. You're off the jury. You're replaced. I'm bootin' you off, and bringin' in the alternate, and—'' It hit him. ''Hey, wait a minute. *You're* the alternate, aren't you?''

''Not anymore.''

20.

THEY BROUGHT me downtown and took my statement. They took my fingerprints too, so they could compare 'em with the ones in the apartment. I told them that wasn't necessary, I'd had my fingerprints taken in a previous case and they'd be on file, but they took 'em just the same.

They also held me for several hours without a charge, which they had no right to do, and if I'd felt like it, I could have called Richard Rosenberg and he'd have come over and kicked some ass. But I didn't want to do that. Not at this stage in the proceeding. Because Richard Rosenberg, for all his ambulance chasing, is actually a frustrated Perry Mason, and the mention of a murder case gives him a hard-on. He'd come to my aid before a couple of times, and when he did, his method was not to win friends and influence people. If I called him in there'd be hell to pay, and eventually I'd be the one paying it.

Which would be fine, if I were actually suspected of anything. Richard would come trotting in, growling and snapping and barking at everyone like a rabid dog until he got me out of there. But as long as I wasn't being charged as a suspect, there was no reason to make waves.

Particularly since I didn't have to get to court. Yeah, I explained to Ralph what I'd meant by the cryptic, "Not anymore." I know that wasn't kosher, and if he hadn't been such an asshole and had let me get a word in edgewise, I wouldn't have done it. But he was such a schmuck I just couldn't resist.

After he understood the situation, Ralph was actually rather chastened. Sherry Fontaine was dead, so I was no longer the alternate, I was the juror filling her spot. And since I was the only alternate, there was no alternate to fill *my* spot, so if I couldn't be there, court was off. It was a series of circumstances even Ralph couldn't argue with.

Ralph finally left me hanging on the phone and went off to confer with Judge Davis. He was gone long enough for the mechanical operator to make me deposit two more quarters to avoid being cut off, and finally came back with the word that court was adjourned until Monday morning at ten o'clock.

So I was off the hook, as far as court was concerned.

Whether I was off the hook for murder was something else.

I hung around downtown, and it was hours before anyone got around to me. Finally Sergeant Thurman showed up, and ordered me into an interrogation room where he and a stenographer took my statement.

I was careful during this part, first because what I said was being taken down, and second, because no one had read me my rights. I knew that technically made me safe, but in dealing with the police I'd learned to be wary. I'd also learned that being wary isn't enough, because I'm not as smart as I think I am. So I was on my guard.

Sergeant Thurman shot a glance at the stenographer and began, ''Your name's Stanley Hastings?''

''That's right.''

''You're a private detective and you work for the law firm of Rosenberg and Stone?''

''No.''

He frowned. ''No? When I questioned you uptown, you said you did.''

''We were talking informally then. You're taking down the answers here.''

''Wait a minute. You saying you were lying before?''

''Not at all.''

''I don't understand.''

''This is a formal interrogation. You're taking down my answers. I have to be very accurate about what I say.''

''Come on. Isn't the truth the truth?''

''Not at all. You ask me informally if I work for Rosenberg and Stone, I'll say sure. You ask me in a formal hearing, I have to say, no, I do not work for Rosenberg and Stone, I am self-employed. But my company does business for Rosenberg and Stone.''

''What's the difference?''

''Big difference.''

''To whom?''

''The IRS for one. The Juror Selection System for another.''

Thurman frowned. ''What's that got to do with anything?''

''I just went through a big hassle with the Juror Selection System over whether or not I'm self-employed. I'm not going to make any formal statement that contradicts that position.''

''Now, see here. That's not what this is all about.''

"I understand. I think I've answered your question and I think I've made my position clear."

Sergeant Thurman took a breath. "All right. You and Sherry Fontaine were on a jury together?"

"That's right."

"When did you first meet her?"

"Tuesday."

"This past Tuesday?"

"That's right."

"How did you meet her?"

"I got selected as an alternate on the jury. Tuesday afternoon I met the other jurors."

"And she was one of them?"

"That's right."

"And you drove her home?"

"Yes."

"Why'd you drive her home?"

"We both live on the upper West Side."

"You drove to court every morning?"

"That's right."

"Why'd you do that? Parking down there is impossible."

"I know."

"Then why'd you do it?"

"I was working my other job, and I needed my car."

"Your job as a detective?"

"That's right. I was doing cases in Harlem. I'd drive up to Harlem, do a case, and drive down in time for court."

"And pick her up on the way?"

"That's right."

"Why didn't you take the subway?"

Jesus Christ. There probably are not two people in the world as unlike each other as Sergeant Thurman and Alice, and yet, here he was, putting me through the same interrogation she had, in practically the same words.

It was hard to take, under the circumstances. I mean, Jesus Christ, Sherry Fontaine was dead. Unbelievable. Incomprehensible. A beautiful, vibrant woman was dead. And for no apparent reason. Unless she'd been raped—which I didn't know, and which Sergeant Thurman sure wasn't letting on—it was an utterly pointless crime. The sort of brutal, mindless crime you grow accustomed to living in New York City, after years of hearing one described every night on the evening news. That's all it was. A name. At most a face, a photograph of a person, depersonalized by the event. The victim. An element in a sad, but inevitable news story.

But Sherry Fontaine was real. A real person. A real woman.

Someone I knew.

I told that to Alice, later that afternoon, when they finally dismissed me, after they'd taken my statement and let me go. I told Alice, and Alice understood. I knew she would. Alice is wonderful that way. She knew I'd been involved in other murders before, found other bodies, knew the horror of it. But she understood why this one was different.

"I *knew* her," I said. "I *knew* her."

"I know," Alice said.

And she held me while I cried.

21.

"**Y**OU GOTTA DO something."

That's the thing with Alice. Predictably, with Sherry Fontaine's death, Alice had come a hundred and eighty degrees. Alive, Sherry Fontaine was "that woman," an obnoxious, scheming coquette. Dead, Sherry Fontaine, whom Alice had never met, was Alice's best friend, a poor, harmed woman who had to be avenged.

I quite understood. I felt that way too. I just didn't see what I could do about it.

"There's nothing I can do," I told her.

Alice stared at me. "Don't you *care?*" she demanded.

"Of course, I care. But there's nothing I can do."

Alice smiled. "You always say that. You always run yourself down. But you're so resourceful. You can do more than you think you can."

I sighed. "Come on."

"You helped Pamela Berringer out, didn't you? And that police sergeant's daughter?"

That police sergeant was Sergeant MacAullif. Helping his daughter out was a favor I wouldn't soon forget.

I don't know about where you live, but in New York City, that simply doesn't happen. The doorbell doesn't ring. Not when you don't expect it. In New York, no one comes to see you without calling first. It just isn't done. An unexpected doorbell is a rare and remarkable event.

Alice and I gave each other a look that said, "Were you expecting someone?" which also automatically conveyed the response, "No."

I frowned and went to the front door.

Another thing no one does in New York is open the front door without looking through the peephole. Even in our building with manned elevators, no one does that. So I slid the metal disk away from the peephole and looked out.

I blinked. It couldn't be.

I slid the cover back over the peephole and opened the door.

Sure enough, the man standing in the doorway was Sergeant MacAullif.

22.

OOD LORD.

This was an occurrence far beyond the scope of just an unexpected ringing doorbell. I knew MacAullif, sure, from various homicide investigations. I'd done a favor for him once, and he'd done a favor for me. And I liked MacAullif, in a sort of strange, adversarial way, and I had a feeling he felt the same. But it was at best a business relationship. A relationship of convenience. Or necessity, if you will. I mean, we'd never go to the ballgame together. Or have an outdoor barbecue. I'd never been to his house, and he'd never been to mine. And I couldn't imagine that ever happening, somehow.

And yet, here he was.

There was a pause while I stood there gaping at him.

"Well," he said. "You gonna invite me in, or should I just stand here like a schmuck?"

I exhaled. I hadn't realized I'd stopped breathing, but I must have, because a lot of air came out. "Sorry," I said. "Yeah. Come in."

I stepped aside and MacAullif came into the foyer. He turned and saw Alice standing there.

I'm poor at social situations, and particularly with

introductions. When I suddenly realize two people I know don't know each other, the ball is in my court. When that happens, I have a tendency to immediately panic and blank out on either name, even though both of them are people I know well.

That didn't happen in this case. I knew the name Alice and I knew the name MacAullif. I even knew his first name, William, although I'd never used it. But even so, I felt totally awkward and embarrassed and on the verge of total panic. I mean, Jesus Christ, introductions. What the fuck was it? In proper etiquette you introduce the person you want to honor to the other person, who I guess is the person you don't want to honor. Or was it the other way around? Anyway, in this case, who did you honor—your wife or your arresting officer?

"Oh," I said. "Excuse me. Alice, this is Sergeant MacAullif. Sergeant MacAullif, this is my wife."

Alice has no problem with social graces. She smiled charmingly, held out her hand and said, "Sergeant MacAullif. How nice to meet you."

MacAullif took her hand and mumbled, "Pleased to meet you." He seemed as awkward and embarrassed as I was. He took a breath, said, "Excuse me, ma'am, but I really need to talk to your husband."

Alice said, "Sure. Why don't you two go in the living room."

MacAullif hesitated, looked at me. "I think we should talk outside."

"There's a coffee shop up the block."

"That would be fine."

A few more awkward pleased-to-meet-yous and MacAullif and I were out the door. We waited in silence for the elevator, rode it in silence to the lobby.

Jerry, our young elevator man, gave us a funny look.

MacAullif is big and beefy, and even in plainclothes he looks like a cop. Jerry had to be wondering what was going on.

We walked up Broadway to Au Petit Beurre, a coffee shop on the corner of 105th. We chose a table off in the corner and ordered coffee. MacAullif said nothing until it came. He dumped in cream and sugar, stirred and took a sip. He nodded. "Not bad coffee."

"Yeah. I like it. So what's up?"

MacAullif sighed. "You know what's up. The Sherry Fontaine case."

"What's that got to do with you?"

"Nothing."

"Then why are you here?"

MacAullif took another sip. "The case crossed my desk this afternoon. Nothing to do with me, but a case comes in, it gets passed around. A homicide, I mean. 'Cause in a homicide they're always looking for any connection, any similarity to anything that's gone before. So even if it's not your case, the word gets around."

"So?"

"So your name popped up as a witness. More than a witness. Guy who found the body. Guy who phoned it in. Guy who knew the dead woman."

"Witness or suspect?"

MacAullif shrugged. "Same thing. With no known perpetrator, witness or suspect means the same thing."

"But I'm not officially listed as a suspect?"

MacAullif grimaced. "Jesus Christ. You're such a fucking amateur. All your ideas come out of story-books—suspect with a capital 'S'. You're either a 'suspect' or you're not." MacAullif shook his head. "It doesn't work that way. If you're involved and there's no perpetrator, you're in trouble. Your only chance of getting out of trouble is if a perpetrator appears."

"Shit, MacAullif. You came up here to tell me I'm in trouble?"

MacAullif exhaled. "Not entirely."

"Well, what then?"

MacAullif took another sip of coffee. He held the cup in both hands, seemed to be studying it. "The cop in charge of the investigation is Sergeant Thurman, is that right?"

"Yeah. So?"

"He interrogated you at the scene, took you downtown, took your statement, right?"

"Yeah. So?"

"So what do you think of him?"

I took a breath. "He's crude, obnoxious, overbearing, looks like he couldn't find his couch in the living room. Setting that aside, I suppose he's good at what he does and knows his job."

MacAullif exhaled and shook his head. "Jesus Christ," he said. "I don't know what it is with you. You're fucking amazing."

"What do you mean?"

"Unbelievable. Uncanny. If I had the time, what I ought to do is take you to the track, ask you what you thought, and then bet the other way."

"What are you saying?"

"I'm saying your judgment of character's so bad I could make book on it. Jesus Christ, I never seen anything like it. I ask you what you think of Sergeant Thurman, in spite of everything you've seen of him you say underneath he's probably a good cop."

"Wait a minute, MacAullif. Are you telling me he isn't?"

"No," MacAullif said. "I'm a cop, and I don't bad-mouth other cops.'' He took a sip of coffee, added, ''As a rule.''

He took another sip, set the coffee down, studied it for a moment, then looked me right in the eye.

''Just between you and me,'' he said, ''Sergeant Thurman is the pits.''

23.

I STARED at MacAullif. "What?"

"You heard me."

"You're sayin' Thurman is a bad cop?"

MacAullif winced. "Again with the capital letters? Bad Cop, like on TV? Everything black and white? No, he's not a Bad Cop, not like you're thinkin'. Not like bein' on the take, or shooting some unarmed kid and then laying a gun on him. No, he's just a bad cop in that he isn't good."

"You're saying he's honest?"

"With a capital 'H'?" MacAullif shook his head. "It's hard getting through your TV mentality, so let me spell it out for you. Thurman's the type of cop, he thinks he's on the side of the angels. Us against them. The good guys and the bad guys—there, something you can relate to. Thurman's the type of cop, he thinks someone's guilty, he's not above cuttin' a few corners to put him away. That don't make him a bad cop in his eyes, see? He's still on the side of the angels. See what I mean?"

"Yeah, I see. Seems to me you said something like that yourself a while back."

MacAullif frowned and held up his hand. "Let's not

go off on a tangent. I said something like a lot of recent court decisions are bullshit, and there's assholes walking the street 'cause their rights were violated, and I don't give a shit if they were, they're scum and I want 'em put away.''

"What's the difference?"

"The difference is I wouldn't manufacture evidence, frame a guy and give false testimony in court.''

"You sayin' Thurman would?''

"No, I'm not sayin' that, but you can draw your own conclusions. All I'm sayin' is, if Thurman thinks a guy's guilty, then that guy'd better look out.''

"Why are you telling me this?''

MacAullif sighed, ran his hand over his head. "Yeah, why? Well, because I know and you don't. And I hate like hell to tell you. But if I didn't tell you, and you took a fall in this case, then I'd feel responsible.''

"But that's ridiculous. I'm not involved.''

"Yeah, but Thurman doesn't know that. And Thurman doesn't have a perpetrator. And if Thurman can't *find* a perpetrator, then all he's got is you. And that could just elevate you to bein' the suspect with a capital 'S' you were talkin' about.''

"Yeah, but someone killed her. So Thurman ought to be able to come up with something.''

MacAullif frowned. "Yeah, well that's the other thing. You really ought to trust your first impressions more. You say Thurman doesn't seem very bright, but underneath it all he must be pretty sharp. Wrong. Thurman *isn't* very bright. He seems stupid 'cause he *is* stupid. Now, I know that's too simple a concept for you to handle, but it happens to be the case.''

I rubbed my head. "Why are you telling me this? You wanna warn me, okay, I'm warned. Now I know

Thurman may be out to get me. Fine, but what the hell can I do about it?''

MacAullif looked at me. ''Are you really that dense? Thurman will pick you if he can't figure out who did it. And he's not bright enough to figure out who did it. So you gotta protect yourself.''

MacAullif took a sip of coffee, shrugged. ''Only way to do that is to figure out who did it.''

24.

I T WAS ENOUGH to give me a complex. I mean, first
I drive to Harlem, and Alice and Sergeant Thurman both tell me I should be taking the subway.
Then I decide I can't get involved in this case, and
Alice and Sergeant MacAullif both tell me I have to
solve it. It was as if, no matter what decision I make,
no matter how logical and sound it might seem to be,
everyone immediately tells me I'm wrong.

I exhaled. "Jesus Christ."

MacAullif nodded. "Yeah, I know. It's a hell of a
position to be in. But you're in it, so accept it, and
let's take it from there."

MacAullif reached in his jacket pocket and pulled
out a folded manila envelope. He unfolded it and
pulled out a stack of papers. "This is the case so far."
He put the papers on the table, held up his finger.
"Now let me make one thing clear. This is not my
case. This is Sergeant Thurman's case. If you come
up with anything, you tell me about it, fine, but you
gotta take it to him. I can't step on his toes here, you
understand?"

"Yeah."

"I just wanna make that clear. 'Cause I shouldn't

be doin' this at all. But that's neither here nor there. Anyway, here's the dope."

MacAullif picked up a paper. "Preliminary autopsy report. It's not official at all—shouldn't even be called a report. Wouldn't be evidence in court, but perfectly fine for our purposes.

"First off, time of death—eight to ten hours before the body was examined. That puts it roughly between midnight and two A.M." MacAullif looked at me. "Where were you between midnight and two A.M.?"

"In bed asleep."

"Can you prove it?"

"How the hell could I prove that?"

"What about your wife?"

"She fell asleep before I did."

"So," MacAullif said. "No alibi."

"My wife can swear I was undressed in bed watching the eleven o'clock news."

"Sure," MacAullif said. "And then she fell asleep and you got up, got dressed, went out and killed a woman."

"No, I couldn't have," I said.

"Why not?"

"Because we have elevator men. And the elevator man can swear I didn't go out."

"The guy's seen you going in and out all day, how's he gonna remember one particular trip?"

"He would. Because the shift changes at eleven o'clock at night. The night man comes on then. Alice can swear I was in bed at eleven, and the night man can swear he didn't see me at all."

MacAullif frowned. "Your building have stairs?"

"Of course it does."

"Then you could have taken the stairs."

"I could have taken 'em down, but I couldn't have taken 'em back up."

"Why not?"

"The stairwell door's locked. You can open it going down, from the inside, to get from the stairwell to the lobby. But from the lobby side the door to the stairwell's locked, and none of the tenants has a key."

"You could prop it open."

"What?"

"Stick a matchbook in it so it didn't latch. Come down the stairs, wait till the lobby's clear, till the night man's up in the elevator. Fix the door open with a matchbook cover. Go out, kill the woman, come back, wait till the lobby's clear again and go up the stairs."

"Jesus Christ."

MacAullif shrugged. "Hey, it's your alibi. If it ain't airtight, it's no alibi. If it was really airtight, maybe we could stop doing this, but my recommendation is we keep going."

I sighed. "Good lord."

"I know," MacAullif said. "Let's move on. Cause of death: strangulation. Someone choked her."

"I knew that."

"Well, now it's confirmed. It's too bad, 'cause it probably took a man to do it. You're big enough and strong enough."

"That's debatable."

"No, it isn't. Physically, you could have done it. You wanna argue you're too chickenshit, that's an argument, but it don't let you out.

"All right. Was she raped? Probably not. No semen in the vagina, mouth, anus, or on the pubic hair."

"Good," I said. The image was horrible enough without having to think of her being raped as well.

"No, it isn't," MacAullif said. "If there was se-men, you could prove it wasn't you by blood types and this DNA shit. It wouldn't let you off the hook en-tirely, 'cause the guy who fucked her didn't have to be the guy who killed her. She could have been out gettin' laid, and then came home and got killed."

"Do you have to talk about her like that?"

MacAullif's eyes narrowed. "Unless, of course, you were fuckin' her anyway, in which case the semen type *would* match."

"I'm gonna pretend I didn't hear that. For your information, I just met this woman, I drove her to court a few times and that's all. I'd never been in her apartment before, or anywhere else with her. But I did know her, and this whole thing has me very upset and on edge. Now I expect this sort of shit from Sergeant Thurman, but it's a little much hearing it from you."

MacAullif shrugged. "Hey, no offense, I'm just trying to get the facts. I seen the woman's pictures. A saint would be tempted. I keep forgetting you're a storybook hero, slightly more principled than a saint."

MacAullif flagged the waitress. "Hey, can I get some more of this coffee?"

She came over and filled his cup. He dumped in cream and sugar, stirred it up, took a sip.

"Still good the second time around.

"Okay, let's get back to it. The point is, according to the medical report, she probably wasn't raped."

"Why probably? I thought there was no semen."

"Yeah, but the guy could have used a condom."

"A rapist?"

"Hey, even a rapist don't want AIDS."

"That's farfetched."

"Maybe, maybe not. Anyway, odds are, she wasn't raped, and there's no way to prove she was.

"Let's move on." MacAullif pulled out another sheet of paper. "Report of her movements yesterday up to the approximate time of her death. This is less than helpful, since most of the information comes from you. But for what it's worth, this is it: She spends the day in court. You give her a ride home, drop her off in front of her building around five-thirty. She has an altercation with a young man in a hooded sweatshirt. You intervene and the guy runs, not realizing you're a cream puff. She cusses you out and goes home, presumably to change for rehearsal. You go up to Harlem to interview a client named Margaret Frazier who fractured her ankle in a trip-and-fall. Then you go photograph the crack in the sidewalk that tripped her. You point to the signed retainer and roll of film as corroboration. The woman in question confirms a man came to see her, but didn't know your name, can't describe you accurately, and claims the man who called on her was a lawyer."

I held up my hand. "That's Rosenberg's advertising. His TV ads say, 'We'll come and see you in your own home.' It's slightly deceptive. The clients expect a lawyer. I never say I'm a lawyer, but I walk in in my suit and tie and they just assume I am."

"Wonderful," MacAullif said. "The point is, the woman didn't identify you."

"She'd know me if she saw me."

"Yeah, if it came to that. But big deal. It's early in the evening, has nothing to do with the murder anyway."

"So what's the point?"

"The point is, she didn't identify you. And anything

about your story that fails to check out, just gets Thurman interested in you.''

"It *will* check out."

"Yeah. Later, if he bothers to do it. Right now it's a detail that doesn't check out."

I sighed. "Jesus Christ."

"So, you do all that, you're home seven-thirty, quarter to eight. This can be confirmed by your wife.

"A short time later, say eight-fifteen, you get a phone call. Sherry Fontaine, presumably at rehearsal, 'cause that's where she claims she was, apologizing for getting angry and saying she'll see you tomorrow. The phone call is also confirmed by your wife. Not what was said, but the fact that you got the call. And the fact that the caller was a woman, whom you claim was Sherry Fontaine."

"What do you mean, 'claim?' "

"I'm talking about what can be proved. Your wife doesn't *know* it was Sherry Fontaine on the phone. She didn't know her, couldn't recognize her voice. She only has your word for it."

"This is getting ridiculous."

"It's ridiculous to you because you know it was her. It's not ridiculous to Sergeant Thurman."

"Shit."

"Yeah. Anyway, with regard to the rehearsal, confirmation is still sketchy. After all, this just happened this morning. Actors Equity confirms that Sherry Fontaine was indeed doing a showcase. Something called *Love Strikes Out*. They also supplied the name of the director, Walter Shelby. Shelby, contacted, expresses usual surprise and horror. States Sherry Fontaine was indeed at rehearsal last night from eight to twelve. He has no idea who she left with, or how she intended to get home. Other actors are yet to be contacted.''

MacAullif took a sip of coffee. ''Anyway, the rehearsal hall's a loft in SoHo. That puts Sherry Fontaine in SoHo at midnight. She might have taken a subway, a taxi, or private car. If she took a subway, there's nothing to trace, but if she took a taxi, the cops'll be looking for the driver. She took a private car, same thing. The point is, if she's in SoHo at midnight, no matter how she got home, she couldn't have got uptown before twelve-thirty, quarter to one.

''That leaves two theories: She brought someone home with her and he killed her, or she came home and someone came later and killed her. Everything points to theory two. Body naked, shower running, bath towel by the door. She came home hot and tired from rehearsal, took off her clothes, hopped in the shower. Doorbell rang, she grabbed a towel, went to the door, man pushed his way in and strangled her. Simple and straightforward. So simple and straightforward, if it were in one of your goddamned books you'd think there had to be some other explanation. But basically, I think we can assume that's what happened.''

''Okay. Is that it?''

''One more thing. It's incidental, but it's in the report. Apparently she was using drugs. Cops found drug paraphernalia in her apartment. Not drugs, just paraphernalia. Gram scale, grinder, straws. Apparently she used coke.''

''Is that a motive for murder?''

''Not likely. A lot of these actresses, they do drugs. The cops found it, so it's in the report.''

''All right, what are you going to do with all this?''

MacAullif grinned. ''Me? I'm not going to do anything with it. I'm gonna give it to you." He passed the report across the table. "And then I'm gonna forget I gave it to you, and so will you. Should you be caught or captured, I will disavow any knowledge and all that shit."

I took a breath. "MacAullif. Thank you for your concern, and all that. But, Jesus, what am I supposed to do with this? I mean, most of the stuff in here is about me."

"This is true."

"So what the hell am I supposed to do?"

"You want me to hold your hand? You're a detective, start detecting. And just 'cause I'm not working on the case, don't feel you're all alone. The cops find out something, I'll pass it along.

"Meanwhile, you want a point of departure, you got the director, the names of the actors in there, the address of the loft where they're rehearsing. A hot tip—according to the director they got an understudy and they'll be rehearsing tonight. Show must go on, and all that shit."

"So?"

"So, you wanna talk to the actors, here's a good chance to get 'em all together."

"You said all the evidence points to the fact she went home alone and the guy came later."

"That's right."

"So talking to these people probably won't tell me a thing."

MacAullif grinned. "Probably not."

"What are you smiling at?"

"Ninety percent is like that. You talk to people, you don't learn a thing."

"Fuck you. You ever investigate a case where you were one of the suspects?"

"Certainly not," MacAullif said. "I'm just like Sergeant Thurman. I'm on the side of the angels." MacAullif pointed to the folder. "I have to admit, it's a pretty unpromising mess. I'm glad it's not my case."

MacAullif raised his coffee as if he were making a toast. "Happy hunting."

25.

THE REHEARSAL HALL was in a fourth-floor loft on Grand Street. The elevator wasn't a self-service elevator. It wasn't a manned elevator either. It was an unmanned manned elevator, making it a non-self-service elevator you used yourself. In other words, someone had to be in it to run it. If it was on the fourth floor, you couldn't push a button and call it down to one.

I didn't know all that till later, so I stood out on the street, pressing the button and wondering why the fucking thing didn't show up. I was standing in the street because the elevator actually ran up the outside of the building, making it more like a construction elevator than anything else. Anyway, I kept pushing the button, and I could hear a faint buzz up above, but that was it.

After what seemed like forever, but was probably not more than a few minutes, a voice said, "Hang on, for Christ's sake." Then I heard a clank, and the sound of the elevator rumbling down.

The gentleman running it turned out to be a plump young man, with long but thinning yellow hair, a rather artsy-fartsy-looking sweater and slacks, and a formidable-looking watch that probably cost more than my car.

He pulled the cage door to the elevator open and said, "What floor?"

"Fourth."

The rather put-upon look on his chubby face turned to one of pure exasperation. "No, no," he said. *"We're* on the fourth floor. We're rehearsing."

"I know," I said. I flashed my ID at him briefly, stuck it back in my jacket pocket and said, "It's about Sherry Fontaine."

Please understand, I did *not* impersonate a police officer. I flashed my ID as a private detective, which I have every right to do. And I said it was about Sherry Fontaine, which it was. And I happened to be wearing my suit, which I usually am. And if the guy wanted to *assume* I was a police officer, that was his business. I wasn't impersonating one any more than I'm impersonating a lawyer when I call on Richard's clients.

At any rate, the guy's expression changed. I wouldn't say he was pleased, but he was less overtly hostile.

He stepped aside, let me in, and ran the elevator up to the fourth floor.

On the way up, he cautioned me. "Now I understand you gotta ask your questions. But I don't want you interrupting rehearsal. They're in the middle of a scene, so let 'em finish. We got problems enough without this."

"And who might you be?" I asked him.

He stuck out his chin. "I," he said, "am Marshall Crane."

It was a pronouncement, as if I should have heard of him. As if, if I were anyone in the theatre world, I *would* have heard of him. Of course, I wasn't, and I hadn't.

So I wouldn't have to comment, I nodded, whipped out my notebook and wrote it down. It was a small spiral pocket notebook I use to write down my cases. When I wrote his name in it, it occurred to me it didn't look official, that it would tip him off to the fact that I wasn't a cop. Then I recalled Peter Falk scrawling notes on all kinds of things in the old "Columbo" series, and again in the new "Columbo" series. So I figured, what the hell.

Marshall Crane, whoever he was, didn't seem to notice. He was too busy running the elevator anyway. He reached the floor, opened the door in the side of the building, and we stepped off into a small entrance hall.

He turned to me and put a finger to his lips. "Now, do me a favor, don't interrupt. Go in quiet, sit in the back, let 'em finish the scene. When it's over, you can talk to 'em."

Without asking me if it was okay, he pulled the door open and ushered me in.

It was a small makeshift theatre with maybe a hundred to a hundred and fifty seats. The loft was high-ceilinged, and the seats had been tiered on risers. The floor of the back row was about up to my chin. It was theatre-in-the-round, or at least three-quarters round, with a thrust stage coming out the long sidewall of the loft, and the audience chairs tiered around it on three sides.

We'd come in from the back of all this, so directly ahead of us was the black curtained back of the riser platform. The house lights were out, making visibility close to zero. I followed Marshall Crane around the back of the risers, down a short side aisle, up a step onto the lower platform, and up a series of platform steps to the back row. Crane slid into the second chair, leaving the chair on the aisle for me. I slid into it next to him.

We were sitting top row center in the very back of the audience. The only other occupied chair was dead center, about halfway down. It was occupied by a skinny man with wire-rimmed glasses, a short red beard, and short clipped red hair with a bald spot in the back. A misaimed work light was shining directly off the bald spot, making it look like a bullseye.

The rest of the work lights were shining on the stage where the actors were performing on a set consisting entirely of folding chairs and a card table.

There were four actors, one man and three women. The man was young, with curly dark hair and a kind of athletic, pretty-boy look. The kind of look I consider the male counterpoint to the dumb blonde stereotype—the goofily handsome young stud. Kind of like the pitcher in *Bull Durham*. Which wasn't that far off, since he was a baseball player in this play. It occurred to me to wonder if the play had been written after the movie.

As to the three actresses, one was a blonde, one was a brunette, and one was a redhead. That made life easy.

The brunette was the one that interested me. Of all the actors on the stage, she was the only one holding a script. That meant she must be the understudy, Sherry Fontaine's replacement.

I felt a cold chill as I thought that. She was the understudy, replacing Sherry Fontaine in the play. Just as I was the alternate, replacing Sherry Fontaine on the jury.

Life goes on.

The understudy was tall, taller than the other two

girls. In fact, when she stood up and crossed to the baseball player, she was his height.

That gave rise to another unsettling thought. Having once been an actor, how often I had heard the words, "I'd kill for that part." In New York City, with competition so fierce, there were lots of actors who felt that way. Even for an unpaid piece-of-shit showcase, there were hundreds of people dying to do it. Christ. Dying to do it. Kill for the part. The theme of death and desperation pervading the theatre.

Well, it seemed absurd, but with Sherry Fontaine's understudy being that tall, would she have been strong enough to do it?

In one of those movie moments that sometimes happen in real life, the understudy said, "I'm strong enough to do it, Carl."

Carl laughed at her, a goofily handsome laugh.

That was enough to snap me out of it. Jesus Christ, get your head out of the clouds before you start coming up with psychic solutions.

I took out my notebook, turned to Marshall Crane. I whispered, "Why don't you save some time and tell me who's who?"

"Okay," he whispered back. "The guy is Claude Breen. The redhead's Audrey Lake. The blonde's Jill Jenson. The understudy with the book is Miranda Vale." He pointed to the bald bullseye below us. "The director, of course, is Walter Shelby."

"Fine," I said. "You mind telling me how you're all rehearsing here, with Sherry Fontaine just having been killed?"

He drew back as if I'd just committed some breach of social etiquette. "The show must go on," he said. "We're upset, of course. But the schedule was damn tight without this. Now we gotta work in an understudy. We're only rehearsing nights, and we open in three weeks. Now, if that seems cold and heartless, I'm sorry, but I happen to have five thousand bucks in this show."

My eyes widened. "Five thousand bucks? In a showcase?"

He looked at me. "Where have you been? That's rock bottom. Showcases don't usually get off the ground for ten."

Jesus. No wonder I'd never made it as an actor. But at least, Marshall Crane's interest in the show was defined. I mean, five thousand bucks. Jesus.

I watched the understudy walking across the stage. It was hard watching her. She wasn't bad, but I couldn't help thinking the only reason she was there was because Sherry was dead.

Then I looked at the script in her hand. A small bound volume. I remembered Sherry reading the script that first day in the jury deliberation room, when I'd thought she was looking at her crotch. Her crotch. Jesus. Naked. Open. Dead.

I shook my head. Never mind that. Think straight.

Something else about the script bothered me. I realized what it was.

I turned and poked Marshall Crane.

"Yes?" he hissed.

"That script she's holding?"

"Yeah."

"I thought these showcases were new, experimental plays, never been done before."

"That's right."

"But that's a bound script. I thought they only published bound scripts of plays after they'd been produced."

176

"That's true," he said. "I had them bound myself."

"Oh?"

"Yeah. Sort of expensive, but I thought it would lend an air of class to the production."

"I see," I said. I didn't see. From what I'd observed so far, *nothing* could lend an air of class to this production. The action on stage, such as it was, was simple, banal, and boring. The three women, whom I knew to be playing lesbians from what Sherry had told me, were totally interchangeable, with no distinct personalities whatsoever. The situation, such as it was, seemed to be that the baseball player had gotten involved with one of these three ladies, in fact, the Sherry Fontaine part the understudy was now playing, and the three women were now deciding what to do with him. The dilemma seemed to be whether or not to tell his wife. This was handled by such on-the-head dialogue as, "Should we tell his wife?" The rest of the dialogue was, at best, sophomoric, and sprinkled with *single* entendres.

As I sat there, I was treated to lines such as this:

BLONDE: "I say, let's tell her."
BASEBALL PLAYER: "No, no."
REDHEAD: "Look at him squirm."
BLONDE: "Is that right, macho man? You squirmin' now?"
UNDERSTUDY: "Leave him alone."
REDHEAD: "You stickin' up for him now?"
BLONDE: "Stickin' up. There's a phrase. You been stickin' up, baby?"
REDHEAD: "Walk softly and carry a big stick."
(BLONDE and REDHEAD laugh. UNDERSTUDY looks put out. BASEBALL PLAYER squirms in

adorable, goofily handsome way.)

BASEBALL PLAYER: "What do you know from big sticks?"

UNDERSTUDY: "Carl."

BASEBALL PLAYER: "No. I'm not going to sit here and take this." (Carl is standing when he says this—the director, on top of everything, scribbles a note.)

BASEBALL PLAYER: "Not from them, I'm not. The only big stick they know comes in plastic."

BLONDE: "Oh, listen to him."

BASEBALL PLAYER: "Yeah, their idea of a cheap date is, batteries not included."

(Squeals of protest.)

BASEBALL PLAYER: (on a roll, goofy laugh) "Yeah, like, how do you make dill bread?—dill dough."

It was too much. I poked Marshall Crane again.

"Yes?" he hissed.

"Pardon me," I said. "But *why* do you have five thousand bucks in this show?"

His chin came up. His eyes narrowed, and he said in a clipped voice, with as much cold dignity as he could muster, "I wrote it."

I have the knack of saying just the right thing.

26.

THEY GAVE ME the stage. Of course, they all thought I was a cop, and I was doing nothing to disillusion them. But as an ex-actor, it was nice to be once again on the stage.

They were all sitting in the front row. The four actors, the director, and the producer/playwright whose dialogue I had demeaned. They were all sitting in the first row, and I had center stage.

Of course, as a failed actor, I have often had the actor's nightmare, the dream where you're on stage in a strange play which you've never rehearsed and for which you don't know the lines. This was that nightmare come to life. I was on stage without a script, and what the hell did I do now?

"All right," I said, "I'm sorry to interrupt your rehearsal, but, of course, you're all aware of the tragedy, and I need to ask you some questions about Sherry Fontaine."

"But I told you everything I know on the phone," Claude, the baseball player, protested. "And I'm coming in tomorrow to make a statement."

So. Thurman had reached him, and god knows how many of the others. Time to tread cautiously.

"I know," I said. "But I want to talk to all of you together. See if any of you noticed anything last night that might be helpful. Maybe you can jog each other's memory."

"But Jill and I weren't here last night," the redhead put in. "It was just Claude and Sherry."

That's what comes of going in blind. Should I, as a presumed police officer, have already known that?

"Right," I said. "But you may have noticed something in her manner at a previous rehearsal. Anyway, let's get the record straight. Just who was here last night from when to when?"

The director cleared his throat. From the front, I couldn't see the bald bullseye, which was a relief, since I didn't have to carefully not stare at it. "As I said on the phone, we were here from eight till midnight. We were working Claude and Sherry's scene. They were here, and Miranda was here understudying. And of course Marshall and I. Audrey and Jill were not."

"And it went till twelve o'clock?"

"That's right."

"Twelve on the nose is pretty specific. Did you really break exactly then?"

"Around then. We'd just finished a run-through of the scene, and I'd given notes. It was about five to twelve. We wrapped things up and left. All that entailed, really, was turning off the lights. I'd say we were out of here by twelve."

"You all went down together?"

"Of course."

"Why 'of course'?"

"You leave the elevator down there, there's no way to get it back up."

"Right," I said. "So you all left together?"

"That's right."

"And how did Sherry get home?"

The baseball player cleared his throat. "Like I said on the phone, we shared a cab."

"Oh?"

"We both live on the upper West Side."

"Where do you live?"

"115th. Up by Columbia."

"So the cab dropped Sherry off first?"

"That's right."

"What time?"

"I don't know. Must have been around twelve-thirty."

"Can't you give it to me better than that?"

"No."

"You phone for the cab?"

"What?"

"You call up and order a cab?"

"Oh. No."

"Where'd you get a cab around here that time of night?"

"We walked down to Canal and got a cab going by."

"Gypsy or medallion?"

"Huh? It was a regular cab, you know."

"With a meter?"

"Yeah."

"How much was on the meter?"

"I don't remember."

"You split it, or pay for it yourself?"

"Split it."

"So what did you split?"

"Sherry gave me five bucks and I paid the cab. I don't remember what. I think it was about twelve bucks."

"And you're not sure what time you dropped her off?"

"Twelve-thirty's best I can do."

I nodded. "We'll find the cabby. They keep a trip sheet. Addresses they go to. The guy may have put the time."

I was watching him when I said that. I couldn't swear to it, but that seemed to make him uncomfortable.

"Listen," I said. "When you dropped her off . . ."

"Yeah?"

"You notice anyone hanging around?"

"In her building?"

"Yeah."

"No."

"She didn't stop, talk to anyone on the street?"

"No."

"What did she do?"

"She went right in."

"You saw her go in?"

"Yeah."

"Before the cab drove off?"

"Yeah."

"The cab was headed uptown. She had to cross the street to go in, right?"

"Right."

"You waited while she did that?"

"Yeah."

"Did you do that on purpose?"

"What do you mean?"

"Did you tell the cabby to wait till she went in?"

"Ah . . . no."

"Then why did he?"

"I'm not sure. I don't remember."

"But you did see her go in the door?"

"Yes."

"And then the cab drove off?"

"Yes."

"What made the cab wait there?"

"I don't know."

"Think."

He did. I could see the wheels turning. He looked like a man drowning. I couldn't tell if it was because he had something to hide, or just because for him thinking was foreign ground.

Then his eyes widened as he got it. "The light must have been red."

"Oh?"

"Yeah. The light at the corner. It must have been red. When it turned green, the cab drove off."

"Yeah," I said. "That would explain it. At any rate, you saw her go into the building and she didn't talk to anyone."

"That's right."

"What did she talk about?"

"I beg your pardon?"

"On the ride uptown. What did you and Sherry talk about?"

"Oh."

"You did talk to her, didn't you?"

"Yes."

"Well, what did you talk about?"

He seemed uncomfortable again, and I thought I'd hit something, until he said, "About the play."

"What about the play?"

"Well, Sherry had these ideas . . ." His voice trailed off.

"About your scenes?"

"Yeah."

"She was giving you direction, telling you how to play your part?"

"Well, yes. And . . ."

"And what?"

"Well, she was talking about changes."

"Changes? You mean in your lines?"

It was as if he couldn't bring himself to say it. He nodded, dismally.

I couldn't blame him. The look Marshall Crane was giving him could have cut glass.

It was disappointing. I was hoping his discomfort was over his relationship with the woman, over something she'd said. But no, it was just the stupid play.

"All right, aside from the play," I said. "Did she talk about anything else?"

"No. Just that."

"Well, what about her mood?"

"What?"

"How did she seem? Was she the same as ever? Was she different than the night before? Did you notice anything that you can tell me that might help?"

He thought. "I would say she was pretty much the same, only more so."

"What do you mean?"

"Well, Sherry was always very opinionated. Very bubbly and up. Well, she was last night, too, only more so. Like when she'd have ideas, sometimes I could discuss 'em with her. Last night she was having none of it. They were her ideas, they were right, and she didn't want to hear anything else."

I frowned. "Did she seem angry or frustrated?"

"What do you mean?"

"I mean, like, these are my ideas, they're right, why doesn't anybody listen to me?"

He shook his head. "No, no. Just the opposite. She was very pleased about everything. Very gung ho. Like, these are my ideas, they're right, let's do 'em."

"Was she the same way at rehearsal?"

"Yeah."

"How about the rest of you—those of you that were there—how did Sherry seem?"

The understudy spoke up. "I think Claude's right."

"Oh?"

"About how Sherry was. Yesterday she was in a good mood. More than a good mood. She seemed . . . I don't know . . . exultant, sort of. Over the top." She frowned. "Look, it's hard to talk about someone who's dead. And I'm playing her part—that makes it worse. But . . . well, I have to say it. She acted like she was queen and we were nothing. Like she was a professional and we were amateurs. Like she knew everything and we didn't know shit."

I turned to the director. "Is that right?"

He stroked his beard. "That's a little strong. But—"

"Strong, hell!" Marshall Crane put in. It was as if a dam had burst, as if he'd been holding it in and could contain himself no longer. "She was wrecking the play. You know it, and I know it. It was like she was doing the "Sherry Fontaine Show," and nothing else mattered. She wouldn't take direction, she wouldn't say the lines." He jerked his thumb at Claude. "She got him so screwed up, it's like we're starting over." He snorted. "Professional, huh? I've never seen anything so unprofessional. I mean, I've heard of things like this happening in the movies, but in the theatre? Damn it, the actors respect the lines. You do the play."

I looked them over. I'm not sure all the actors would have felt so strongly about respecting those particular lines, but at any rate, there were no dissenting votes.

"All right," I said. "But essentially, that attitude is the same one she'd had throughout the production? It's just last night was more extreme?"

The director nodded. "I think that sums it up."

"Aside from the play—did she mention anything else?"

The director shook his head. "Not that I heard."

The understudy said, "She mentioned the jury she was on. Said it was a big pain in the ass, was keeping her from auditions and from learning her lines."

"Yeah," I said. "But nothing else? About her personal life, I mean?"

"She mentioned the party," Claude put in.

"Party?"

"Yeah. There's a party tomorrow night we're all invited to. She was excited about that."

"Oh yeah, and what party is that?"

"It's a private party for theatre people. Upper East Side. No big deal, but it was to her. Thought she might meet someone famous. Always looking to get ahead."

"What's the address of this party?"

"I don't know offhand."

"Who does?"

Marshall Crane did. He gave me the address and I wrote it down.

He seemed rather pained. "Are you *going* to this party?"

"I may have to check it out. If I do, I will be low-profile, low-key, and I'll try not to spoil your fun.

"All right. Can anybody think of anything else?"

Nobody could.

"What about boyfriends? She ever mention anyone?"

They all looked at each other, as if for help, as if no one had the answer.

The understudy frowned. "The way she talked, I don't think she had anybody. At least not now."

"But she had her eye out," the redhead said. It was

a catty remark. I gathered the redhead was not all that broken up over Sherry's demise.

"She was going with someone a while back," the blonde put in. "But they split up."

"You know who?"

"Dexter something-or-other."

"You don't know his last name?"

"No."

"How long ago was this?"

"A while back. Six months. A year."

"This Dexter—is he an actor?"

"Yeah."

"You recall anything he was in, I could get his name from?"

"No. But we know some of the same people. He'll probably be at the party."

The looks the others flashed her were somewhat short of kind. They didn't want me at the party. And now, everyone in the room, me included, knew I was gonna be there.

"All right," I said. "I don't want to keep you, but I do want to take down your home phone numbers in case I think of anything I forgot to ask."

I wrote down the phone numbers, folded my notebook, and stuck it in my jacket pocket. "Fine," I said. "I don't know that I'll have to call you, but I may. In case I do, I'm a detective, Hastings."

I have to admit, I swallowed the "a" so it sounded like I said, "I'm Detective Hastings," as in cop.

"All right," I said. "Thanks for your time. How do I get out of here?"

Claude was on his feet. "I'll run him down," he said.

The director got up. "All right, everybody. Take five, and we'll run it again."

Claude seemed eager to get away. He led me out to the elevator, opened the cage door.

I stepped into the elevator and turned around. As it started down, I saw the redhead come out into the foyer. It seemed to me she gave us a look before heading for the women's room.

Claude and I clanked down into the night. I wondered if Claude had had any reason for wanting to take me down.

He did. He turned to me, and his face spoke volumes.

"Sir?" he said.

It's not often people call me sir, but I was glad he did. If he'd called me officer, I'd have felt bad about not correcting him.

"Yes," I said casually. If he wanted to tell me something, I didn't want to frighten him.

He took a breath. "Ah, what you said—about them finding the taxicab."

"Yes?"

"Do you think they'll find it?"

"I'm sure they will."

He bit his lip. "I have a problem."

"What's that?"

"What I told the officer on the phone."

"Oh?"

He ducked his head in what I was sure was his patented goofily handsome way. It probably worked well with the women, but I wasn't impressed. I waited.

"And with what I just told you," he said.

"What's your problem?"

"The bit about the taxicab."

"What about it?"

"I left something out."

I felt if I were a cop, my face would harden about

now. I attempted a steely gaze. Thank god no one I know was looking, or they'd have been on the floor.

But it seemed to work on him. He started fidgeting, ducking his head again.

I was wondering how to prompt him when the elevator hit the ground. That jolted both of us. He let go of the control, but he didn't open the gate.

"What'd you leave out?" I said.

One more head duck. "The part about Sherry getting out of the cab. That was true. The thing is, I didn't take the cab up to my place. I got out of the cab with her."

"Oh yeah?"

"Yeah."

"You paid off the cab there?"

"That's right."

"You got out with Sherry Fontaine?"

"Yes."

"Why'd you do that?"

He ducked his head again. "Sherry Fontaine was a very attractive woman. I was going to go up to her apartment."

"I see," I said.

"But I didn't," he added quickly.

"You didn't?"

"No."

"Why not?"

"She didn't want me to."

"Oh?"

"Yeah. I know, I know. I'm explaining it badly. See, I misread the situation. I thought she wanted me to, but she didn't. See, we'd been working together, and she'd been kind of coming on to me. At least I thought she had. And she was in such high spirits last night. And then we went home alone, and I just naturally thought . . . Well, I was wrong. Anyway, we got to her place and I got out and paid off the cab. I started walking across the street with her, and she said, "Where do you think you're going?" I said, "I'm walking you home." She said, "I'm a big girl, I can walk myself." I started to say something and she said, "Good night." Real final, like that.

"Then she laughed at me. A teasing kind of way. I'll never forget it. It was the last time I ever saw her and she gave me that laugh. Then she turned around and walked in."

"What did you do?"

"Walked over to Broadway and caught the bus."

"Then there's no record of you ever getting home. You live alone?"

"Yeah."

"Why didn't you mention this before?"

He ducked his head again. It flashed on me if I were a more aggressive person, I'd have punched him in the chin.

"I didn't think it mattered. And I didn't think anyone would know. Then you mentioned talkin' to the cabby. Then I knew I was sunk."

"That's not the question. The question is, *why* didn't you mention it?"

"Oh," he said. He ducked his head again. I felt my hand forming a fist.

"Well," he said. "You see, Audrey"—He jerked his thumb upstairs—"the redhead? Well, she and I have been seeing each other. But she wasn't at rehearsal last night and I rode home with Sherry. She was miffed enough about that. I didn't want to have to admit I'd gotten out of the cab."

"I see," I said. "Tell me. You and Sherry—aside from last night—was there anything going on?"

"No. Not at all."

"You ever been up to her apartment?"

"Never."

"Then your fingerprints wouldn't be there."

He frowned.

"Would they?"

"No, I don't think so."

"Well, which is it, yes or no?"

"No."

"You don't sound convinced."

He waved it away. "No, no, I was never there. It's just . . ." He looked at me with sheepdog eyes. "Well, does it have to come out? Does Audrey have to know?"

"That's between you and her," I said.

"How about tomorrow, when I make my statement?"

"I would advise you to tell the truth."

"You mean what I just told you?"

"If it was the truth, yeah."

"What will they do to me?"

"What do you mean?"

"For not telling them this on the phone."

Frankly, what I hoped they'd do would be elevate him to Suspect Number One, knocking yours truly down to the second position.

"Nothing," I said. "You weren't under oath. You didn't sign anything. They may be pissed off, and they may give you a hard time, but they can't *do* anything."

He didn't seem convinced. "Uh huh."

I wasn't in the mood to try to cheer him up. "Look," I said, "you better get this elevator back upstairs before your friends wonder what you're confessing to."

That snapped him out of it. I could see thoughts of the redhead flash in his eyes.

"Yeah, right," he said.

He slid the cage door open. I stepped out, and the elevator started back up.

I watched it go.

Well, that was interesting. The case wasn't twenty-four hours old, and one of the people who'd known Sherry had already lied to the police.

Of course, it could have been just as he'd said. He could have tried to make a move on Sherry, and then not wanted the redhead to know about it. And from the look she'd given us when we'd gone down in the elevator, I could understand that. Yeah, he could have done that, all right.

He also could have walked about a bit, gotten pissed off at being rejected, gone back, gone upstairs, rung her bell and strangled her.

27.

I DRESSED DOWN for the party so I'd blend in, so I wouldn't look like a cop. I wore jeans and a short-sleeve blue sports shirt, and left the suit and tie at home. I didn't know it till I got there, but I also should have taken off ten to fifteen years.

It was a modern high-rise in the East 70s. The guy who came to the door looked young enough to be my son, assuming I'd knocked up my high school sweet-heart. He didn't step aside and let me in. Instead, he looked at me as if I were from another planet.

"Yes?" he said.

Fortunately, I knew the magic word. "I'm Stanley Hastings," I said. "I'm a friend of Marshall Crane and Walter Shelby."

His face went through a transformation. Suddenly he was all smiles. "Pleased to meet you," he said. "Do come in." He grabbed my hand, pumped it up and down. "I'm Steve Muldoon. Walter and Marshall are already here, if you can find them."

Stepping into the apartment, I knew what he meant. It was a huge layout, and it was mobbed. The lighting was dim and atmospheric, but still bright enough for me to tell that I was virtually the oldest one there.

Which explained Steve Muldoon's sudden cordiality. Bein' so ancient, and knowin' Walter and Marshall and all, had to make me a producer, director or money man. Not the worst thing to be taken for at a party of young aspiring actors.

Fortunately, the doorbell rang again before my young host, who was obviously preparing to do so, could run through his list of stage credits. I escaped and threaded my way through the throng.

The apartment seemed to consist of a large living room, connected to a large dining room connected to the kitchen. That was in one direction. In the other was a hallway, leading off presumably to the bedrooms. In yet another was a door leading off into what appeared to be a game room. It was hard to tell, looking through the crush of people, but it seemed to me I saw the corner of a pool table.

I figured somewhere in all this there had to be a table with drinks, and after a little research I spotted it on one side of the dining room. I figured I would look more natural with a glass in my hand, so I threaded my way over there and poured myself a diet Coke.

I turned around to find the redhead standing there in front of me. Up close, I could see her face was covered with a light sprinkling of freckles. On her they were kind of cute.

She also had green eyes. Somehow, that didn't surprise me.

"Hello," she said. "Mr. . . . Hastings, is it?"

"Stanley," I said. "And you're . . . ?"

"Audrey."

"Right. Audrey," I said. "Are the others here?"

"Claude and Miranda are. And Walter and Marshall. Jill's not here yet, but she's expected. You seen anyone yet?''

''Just you.''

''Uh huh,'' she said.

''Well, nice party,'' I said.

''Yeah, isn't it? What did you talk about?''

''What?''

''Last night. When Claude took you down in the elevator. What did you talk about?''

''I don't know. I guess we talked about the case.''

''Claude was gone a long time. Walter sent me out to look for him.''

''Oh?''

''Yeah. And he still hadn't come up yet. So I figured you must have been talking about something.''

''I suppose we were, but I doubt if it was important.''

''Uh huh,'' she said. ''Claude went downtown and made a statement today. To the cops.''

''Yeah. He said he was going to.''

''Were you there?''

''No, I wasn't.''

''Uh huh.''

''Why? Did Claude say I was there?''

''No, he didn't.''

''Then what's the problem?''

''The police didn't ask me for my statement.''

''Sure. 'Cause you weren't there that night.''

''So,'' she said. ''You won't tell me what you and Claude talked about?''

''Absolutely not.''

That jarred her. She'd expected a subtle evasion or deflection. The flat denial caught her by surprise.

''Well, why not?''

I smiled. ''Because you're all witnesses in one way

or another. And since we don't know who did this, strange as it seems, that makes you all suspects in one way or another. So what we wanna do is get your stories individually and compare them, to see if there are any discrepancies. We're certainly not gonna tell one of you what another one of you said.''

She looked at me. ''Are you kidding? About us being suspects?''

''Only half. Somebody killed her, and we have to find out who. Until we get a lead, we have to consider all possibilities. Now, I know that sounds absurd to you, but try to see it from my point of view.''

She exhaled. ''Jesus Christ.''

''Hey, don't let me spoil your party. I'm actually here chasing down other leads. So, what about this Dexter fellow? Is he here yet?''

''I don't know him. Jill does. You'll have to wait till she gets here.''

''I see,'' I said. ''If you spot her, let me know.''

She gave me a look, then turned and threaded her way though the crowd.

I watched her go.

So, there was a very jealous woman. Shrewd, hard, calculating, and possessive. And she had every reason to think Sherry Fontaine was making a play for her man.

I turned around and bumped into Walter Shelby. He had the understudy in tow.

''Enjoying the party?'' he said.

I smiled. ''It's not exactly my style, but I'm getting along.''

''You seen Al Pacino yet?''

''Is he here?''

''He's *rumored* to be here. Miranda here's all excited. So far, no one's seen him.''

I felt a rapport talking to Walter Shelby. He seemed more my age somehow, but maybe that was just the bald spot. I'm sure he was at least ten years my junior.

And the understudy, Miranda, at least ten years his. He had his arm around her, and I wondered if they were an item. More than that, I wondered if they had been an item *before* last night. Back when Sherry Fontaine was still alive.

Walter was looking me over, and his eyes were sort of twinkling. "Do you have a cover?" he said. "So that we don't blow it?"

"I'm Stanley Hastings," I said. "I'm a friend of yours and Marshall Crane."

"Where do we know you from?"

"I'm vaguely connected to the movies, but I like to keep a low profile, so you're not supposed to talk about it."

"Hey, I like that," he said. "And what movie are you vaguely connected with that I'm not supposed to talk about?"

I shrugged. "You might let it drop that I've worked with Arnold Schwarzenegger."

He smiled, shook his head. "You know, you got a sense of humor for a cop."

"I'm not a cop," I told him. "I'm a person vaguely connected with the movies."

"Right, right," he said with a big wink. "The soul of discretion. We'll put it around."

He moved off with the understudy in tow.

I must say I resented him. Sherry Fontaine's death meant nothing to him. As far as he was concerned, it was just fun and games. An acting opportunity. Just good theatre.

Unless that's what he wanted me to think. Unless his act was simply that, an act.

I turned around to find Claude bearing down on me.

"I saw Audrey talking to you."

"That's right."

"What did she want?"

"Wanted to know what we were talking about when you took me down in the elevator."

"What did you tell her?"

"That we were discussing the case in general, but I couldn't go into specifics, because until the murderer is caught everyone's a suspect, and I have to get their stories individually."

He frowned.

"What's the matter?"

"I'm trying to remember if that jibes with what I told her."

"Why wouldn't it?"

"I don't know."

"What I said was so general, it should jibe with anything."

He frowned. Thinking obviously wasn't one of his strong points. "I guess so. What do you mean, we're all suspects?"

"I wouldn't take it personally. Until we figure out who did it, everyone's a suspect. So, you make your statement today?"

"Yeah."

"They give you any trouble?"

"They sure did. The cop who questioned me—the bull-necked one—"

"Sergeant Thurman?" I loved saying it—as if I knew the whole damn police force.

"Yeah, that's him. He was pissed as hell. Wanted to know why I didn't mention getting out of the cab before."

"What'd you tell him?"

"That I didn't think it mattered, and I didn't want my girlfriend to know I'd done it."

Great. Two conflicting reasons. Couldn't the guy just have picked one?

"That satisfy him?"

"No, it didn't. He was most abusive."

"Yeah. I'll bet. He ask you why you were telling him now?"

"Yeah."

"Whaddya say?"

"I didn't know if it was important or not, but thinking it over I didn't want to do anything that might screw up his investigation."

"Not a bad answer. You mention talking to me?"

"No. Should I have?"

"Not at all," I told him. "Much better to let him think you made that decision on your own."

"That's what I thought."

"You thought right."

Well, that was a relief. It hadn't even occurred to me to tell him not to mention me to the cops. Well, actually, it had occurred to me, but not until I was on my way home from the rehearsal, when it was too late to do me any good. I had his phone number, and I could have called him up to suggest he didn't mention me, but I thought that might be a little much, even for him, getting a special phone call just to tell him that. Even an intellect as slow as his might get suspicious. I figured it better just to let him blunder through. Apparently, for once I figured right.

Jill arrived about then, and I extricated myself from Claude's clutches and fought my way across the room to tackle her.

The host, Steve Muldoon, was still greeting her when I arrived.

"Jill," I said. "I was afraid you weren't going to make it."

She turned, saw me. "Oh, hello, Mr. Hastings."

"Stanley," I said.

Steve Muldoon had undergone a major transformation. "Stanley Hastings," he said. "You know, I have to apologize. I should have caught the name." He lowered his voice. "Is it true you did a movie with Schwarzenegger?"

"Yeah, it's true," I said. "But don't spread it around."

He winked conspiratorially, then moved off, I'm sure to do exactly that.

"What's that all about?" Jill asked.

"Your director thought I should have a cover story. Evidently he's been spreading it around."

"Oh."

"Yeah. He seems to be getting a kick out of the whole thing."

"Yeah. He would."

I looked at her inquiringly.

"I dated him once," she said. "It was a long time ago, and I don't want to talk about it. But yeah. That fits. Sherry's dead, and he's having fun."

"You mean he didn't care about her?"

"No, I mean he's totally self-centered. I think he had the hots for her. I don't think he scored. I don't think he's *glad* she's dead, but he just doesn't give a shit, you know what I mean?"

"Yeah. So what about the boyfriend? Is he here?"

"I just got here myself. Let me look around."

She moved off and vanished into the crowd. I elbowed my way back into the center of the room. Marshall Crane passed by me. He didn't stop and talk, just nodded an acknowledgment and kept on going. I wondered if that was evasive and should make me more suspicious, or perfectly natural and should make me less.

A rather attractive young girl maneuvered my way and started up a conversation. She was obviously coming on to me, which might have done things for my ego, if I hadn't known damn well either my host or the director had tipped her off to who I supposedly was.

I escaped her clutches and bumped into Marshall Crane again. This time he stopped to talk.

"Walter tells me you're some movie bigwig. I think that's stupid."

"Probably right."

"Then why are you doing it?"

"Walter thought I needed a cover of some sort."

Marshall shook his head. "Stupid," he said, and moved off again.

I couldn't really disagree.

I spotted Jill pushing her way through the room. I started working toward her, met her halfway.

"Found him," she said.

"Where?"

"In the kitchen."

"Come point him out."

"Okay. But you couldn't miss him."

She was right. The kitchen was an L-shaped affair. The man I was looking for was sitting on a chair in the far corner of the L. He was a young man, about twenty-five to thirty, with straight dark hair, a little on the long side, and a thin face a reviewer was certain to refer to as sensitive. Under other circumstances, he was probably a pretty good-looking guy, in a frail, fragile sort of way. But at the moment he looked like shit. His hair was uncombed, his eyes were watery and bloodshot, and his face was slack and pale. He was holding a glass of some dark liquid, probably scotch or bourbon, and it certainly wasn't his first.

And he was alone. In the midst of this incredibly crowded party, he was sitting there all alone.

I walked over to him. If he noticed my presence, he didn't acknowledge it. He took a sip from the glass, stared blankly straight ahead.

"Dexter?" I said.

He didn't look up then, and for a moment I thought he hadn't heard me. Then he said, "I shouldn't have come."

I was trying to think of what to say next when he went on, "Jack and Vicki came by and got me. Said I had to get out. Said I had to come." He shook his head slightly. "Shouldn't have listened."

"You live alone?"

"Yeah."

"How'd you hear about it?"

"TV. Last night. Evening news. Actress murdered on upper West Side. Watching. Is it anyone I know . . . ? And it's her."

A tear ran down his cheek.

For a few moments, neither of us moved. Then he looked up sideways, saw me.

His eyes at first were dull and vacant. Then they registered puzzlement. "Who are you?"

"Stanley Hastings. I'm investigating the murder."

And now a flick of interest. "Yes. The murder. Talked to the cops. Wouldn't tell me nothing."

"You talked to the cops?"

"Yes."

"When?"

"Today."

"They come to you?"

"No."

"You go to see them?"

"No."

"How you talk to them?"

"Phone."

"You called 'em on the phone?"

"Yeah."

"Told 'em you knew Sherry?"

"Yeah."

"They ask you to come in?"

"No. Didn't want to talk to me. Wouldn't tell me nothing."

Jesus Christ. MacAullif was right. With Sergeant Thurman in charge of the investigation, the cops didn't have a prayer of cracking the case. Here was Sherry Fontaine's ex-boyfriend, the one person the cops should have got on to. But they hadn't. And then he calls up and drops himself in their lap, and they *still* don't talk to him.

"The police didn't say anything?"

"No."

"You tell 'em you used to be her boyfriend?"

"Yeah."

"And they still wouldn't talk to you?"

"No."

"What did they ask you?"

"Asked me when we broke up. Told 'em six months. Asked when I seen her last. I said not in a couple of months. They lose interest. They don't want to talk to me."

"I'm here and I want to talk to you."

"You a cop?"

"I'm a detective investigating the murder. But I don't want to upset people coming in looking like a cop."

"Yeah. Party. Shouldn't have come."

He shook his head and took another drink.

"Can I ask you some questions?"

"Sure."

"You broke up with Sherry six months ago?"

"Yeah."

"You have a girlfriend now?"

"No."

"No one since Sherry?"

"No."

"You live alone?"

"Yeah. Jack and Vicki came to get me. Said I shouldn't be alone." He shook his head. "Wrong. I shouldn't have come."

"Where you live?"

He gave me an address on West 8th Street. I wrote it down.

"What's your last name, Dexter?"

"Manyon."

He spelled it for me and I wrote it down.

"Two nights ago, Dexter, where were you?"

He looked at me. His eyes were wide. "You think *I* killed her? Is that what you think?"

"No, Dexter, but I gotta ask everybody. Everybody who knew her. So where were you?"

"Home."

"What'd you do?"

"Watched TV and went to sleep."

"You live alone?"

"Yeah. Alone."

So. No alibi. Not even a stab at one. Either he didn't need one, or he didn't care.

"All right. Look, Dexter. I need your help."

"Huh?"

"Yeah. You tell me. Who do you think did it?"

His eyes were wide and sad. "Don't know. Who would do such a thing? Horrible."

I felt awful. Yeah, Dexter. You and me both. But I had to keep on.

"What about her other friends?"

"Friends?"

"Yeah. After you. After you two broke up. She have another boyfriend?"

"I don't know."

"Well, what do you think?"

He shook his head. "Don't know. Maybe she was seeing someone. But not special. Not . . ." He groped for the word. ". . . permanent. She was so . . . Oh, Jesus Christ."

He dissolved into sobs.

I figured I'd done as much good as I could. Also as much harm. At least I had his name and address. I could tackle him again when he was sober. Assuming he'd *be* sober any time in the near future. He obviously cared a lot and was taking it real hard.

I wanted to find out if Sherry had any other friends here at the party, but Dexter was in no condition to point them out to me. I figured I'd hunt up Jill, see if she'd bumped into anyone. Then I was gonna call it a day. Talking to Dexter Manyon had really gotten to me and I just couldn't play out Walter Shelby's little charade any more. It was time to pack it up and head for home.

I fought my way back into the living room and looked around for Jill. I spotted Marshall Crane in the corner, having a philosophical conversation with a rather effeminate young man in a purple satin shirt. That gave me a clue as to his sexual preferences, but shed no light on my murder investigation.

On the other side of the room Claude and Audrey

were having a rather earnest-looking discussion. Neither one looked happy, and I had a feeling the topic of conversation might be me.

Over near the drink table, Walter Shelby and the understudy were holding court. They had a small audience of actors around them, and Walter was pontificating on some subject or other. I hoped it wasn't my film career.

I looked around for my host to say good-bye. I didn't give a shit about the social conventions, but I figured it would be better to make my excuses to him, than to make an unexplained departure that might prompt speculation. I spotted him at the door, which was convenient. I could say good-bye and go, without having to fight my way through a room of people, and running the risk of being stopped by someone and having to start apologizing for my exit all over again.

I made my way across the room, keeping my host in sight, so he wouldn't slip past me in the crush and defeat my purpose. Not to fear. He'd gone to the door to let someone in. I'd almost reached him when he turned around, ushering in the new arrival.

I immediately drew back and averted my head.

Jesus Christ.

He looked a lot different from when I'd seen him before. His long hair was pulled away from his face and tied in a ponytail. And he was wearing a light blue turtleneck, instead of a hooded sweatshirt.

But there was no question about it. The young man my host had just ushered into the party was definitely the same man who'd been waiting outside Sherry Fontaine's apartment and grabbed her by the wrists.

28.

I DIDN'T WANT him to see me. The first time he'd seen me, he'd run. I didn't want him to run again. I faded back into the crowd and watched to see what he'd do.

After a brief greeting, he extricated himself from his host and began worming his way into the room. A lot of people seemed to know him. There was a lot of smiling, nodding, high-fives, back-slapping and what have you. That was good. It was gonna be no trouble at all pinning down his name.

As he made his way across the floor it was clear he was not heading for the dining room where the refreshments were. Instead he was heading in the other direction, to the hallway that I figured led to the bedrooms. I followed from a discreet distance, and was close enough to see him and another guy work their way through the edge of the crowd and disappear down the hall. As if by common agreement, no one followed them.

Except me. I did, and found myself in a short hallway with a door straight in front of me. I figured that was where they went. Then the door opened, and a young woman emerged from what proved to be a bathroom. I smiled, walked past her, and discovered another short hallway leading off this one to the left. There was a closed door at the end that had to be it. I gave them about thirty seconds to get settled, then turned the knob, opened the door and went in.

They were standing next to the bed with their backs to me, my guy and another young guy with curly red hair. They wheeled around with guilty looks. I'm not great at interpreting looks, but trust me, these were guilty ones. At first they were just general guilty looks, at being surprised by anyone. Then the guy recognized me. I could see the expression change in his eyes, from guilt to panic. I could tell his first instinct was to run.

There was a leather bag on the bed next to them. The guy glanced at it quickly, then back at me. I figured that told me all I needed to know.

I closed the door and held up my hand. "All right, let's hold it right there. Whatever you're thinking, don't do it. It will do you no good. Just shut up and listen." I held up my finger. "You guys are lucky." I pointed my finger at the redhead. "You are *really* lucky. You know why? 'Cause I don't want to talk to you, that's why." I switched my finger to the other guy. "Now you I want to talk to, but you're lucky too. You're thinking about running, don't try it. There's a whole roomful of people out there, they all know you, and how far are you gonna get?"

I switched back to the redhead. "Now you, you're lucky 'cause I'm letting you walk. So happy birthday. 'Cause I don't want to talk to you, I wanna talk to him. So here's the deal. You walk out of here right now, you're free to go." I held up my hand. "Only one thing. I wanna talk to him alone. So you don't go. You wait by the door. When I come out, if no one's come in here, you've done a good job, I don't wanna talk to you, you can go. But if someone comes in, disturbs me while I'm talking to him, then you done a bad job, and when I come out I wanna talk to you a lot. You got that?"

The redhead gulped. "Yes, sir."

I jerked my thumb. "Fine. Get out of here."

He went, closing the door behind him.

I turned to the other guy. He still looked big and strong, like he could take me apart. But that wasn't the issue now.

"Okay," I said. "Now let's talk about how you're lucky. You're lucky in that you got a choice. You can either talk to me here, or you can talk to the boys downtown. If you talk to me here you're *real* lucky, 'cause I don't give a shit what's in that bag on the bed. And when we get done talking, you walk."

He was staring at me incredulously. "What?"

"You heard me. That's why you're lucky. You see, things are different. It's murder now."

"Oh."

"So talk."

"Whaddya want to know?"

"Tell me what you know about the murder."

"What murder?"

I shook my head. "That's a bad start. Okay, let's go downtown."

He put up his hands. "No, no wait. You mean Sherry Fontaine?"

"That's right. Sherry Fontaine. What do you know about it?"

"Nothing."

"But you know her?"

"Yeah."

"And you know me, don't you?"

He didn't answer.

209

"You saw me outside her building the other day. When you saw me you ran. You'd like to run now, you just know it would do no good. So tell me, why'd you run?"

"Why do you think?"

"I'm not here to play guessing games. You want this deal, you come halfway. I'll give you some help. Sherry Fontaine was a cokehead. Wasn't she?"

"Yeah."

"And you're her connection, aren't you?"

He took a breath, pursed his lips. "I wanna see a lawyer."

I looked at him, shook my head, laughed mirthlessly. "You dumb shit. No, you don't. You're peddling drugs at this party. You got a bag of dope on the bed. And here we are talking informally. Now you wanna press your rights? Sure, you can call a lawyer, we can go downtown, the cops can take your bag of dope away from you and charge you with possession with intent to sell, and then everything will be nice and legal.

"Or you can talk to me here and now, and when we're done you can pick up that bag on the bed, since I don't know what's in it, and you can walk out of here.

"So, that's that. Now, you want this deal or not?"

He thought about it a minute. "All right."

"Fine," I said. "Then start cooperating. First off, let's see some ID."

"I thought this wasn't a bust."

"It isn't. But I wanna know who I'm talking to."

I held out my hand. He scowled at me, then reached in his hip pocket and pulled out a wallet. He flipped it open and passed it over.

I whipped out my notebook and wrote down the

name Luke Brent from his driver's license. I copied the address too.

"What's your phone number?" I said.

He told me, and I wrote it down.

I flipped the wallet back to him. "Okay. That's a good start. Tell me about Sherry Fontaine."

"That's it. She's a cokehead."

"And?"

"And she buys from me."

"How much?"

"Small. Half-gram, gram tops. Not a heavy user. Just recreational."

"How often?"

He shrugged. "Week. Two weeks. Sometimes longer. Depends how she's doin'."

"What about the other day?"

"What about it?"

"The scene in front of her apartment—what was that all about?"

"She got behind."

"What do you mean?"

"Every now and then she'd do the dirty."

"The dirty?"

"Yeah. She'd call me up, order some coke, and when I'd come by she wouldn't have the money."

"And you'd give it to her?"

He made a face. "Sometimes. You understand, I wouldn't do that normally. But there was something about Sherry. She had a way of getting you to do things."

I sighed. "Yeah. You sleeping with her?"

"No. Not that I wouldn't want to. That was part of it, you know? Frankly, I didn't think I'd ever make it with her. But she was so attractive. There was something sexual about her that . . . well, she was just hard to say no to, you know?''

I did. ''Yeah.''

''And then that day. She called me. She wanted another half a gram. She already owed me for one. I told her I wouldn't come unless she had the money. She said no sweat, the money'd be there.''

''When'd she call you?''

''The night before.''

''What time?''

''It was two in the morning, actually. She said she just got back from rehearsal.''

''She called you at two in the morning?''

''That's not unusual. People call me then.''

''And?''

''I told you. She asked for half a gram. She told me she'd be home between five-thirty and six, could I come by before she went to rehearsal. I told her only if she had the cash. She said, no sweat, she'd have it. When I got there, she didn't.''

''That surprise you?''

''Yeah, it did. She was apt to wheedle, but not out-and-out lie, you know what I mean?''

''Yeah.''

''When she told me, I got mad. I grabbed her wrists. I told her, 'You can't do that.' Then you come walking up. Scared the shit out of me. I've got stuff on me. I can't afford a bust. I ran.''

He looked at me. ''Now, is that straight or what? Can I go?''

I shook my head. ''Not yet. What happened after that?''

''Nothing.''

''What do you mean, nothing? Did you call her? Did you come see her again?''

He shook his head. "Shit, no. Frankly, I'd had it. First I get stiffed, then I almost get busted. As far as I was concerned, the ball was in her court. If she wanted to call me up, work something out, she could. Otherwise, she still owes me for half a gram. But I ain't gonna chaise her all over the world to get it. If I never see her again, I eat it, and good riddance. I don't need that kind of shit."

"You come back later that night?"

"I told you, no."

"You weren't waiting for her when she came back from rehearsal, to ask her what the hell she meant siccing the cops on your case?"

"Christ, no."

"Where were you that night from twelve till two?"

"Oh, shit."

"What?"

"I was home alone. No one knows it. No one can prove it. You want an alibi, I ain't got one.

"But I didn't kill her. Jesus Christ, I swear to god I didn't kill her."

I snorted. "Join the crowd."

He looked up at me. "Huh?"

"Sorry, but that's what they all say." I shrugged. "The problem is, someone did."

29.

MACAULLIF WAS in his office. That surprised me. I guess it shouldn't have. Criminals don't take Sunday off, so I guess cops can't either.

I tried him at home first, and his wife told me he was at the precinct. I felt strange talking to his wife. I'd never met her, and I was sure I never would. Just as I was sure he'd never meet mine. At any rate she said try the police station, I did, and there he was.

He wasn't particularly glad to see me, which wasn't fair, seeing as how he was the one who suggested I do this in the first place. At any rate, he grumbled a bit, and then put aside the file he'd been going over, sighed, and said, "Okay, what you got?"

"I found the guy."

"What guy?"

"The guy I told you about. The guy who stopped Sherry outside her apartment."

I told him about my encounter with Luke Brent. I can't say he seemed that impressed. "So?"

"So, what do you think? Should I give it to Thurman?"

"Give him what?"

"The guy. Luke Brent."

MacAullif picked up a cigar and turned it over in his hands. He didn't smoke 'em, he just played with 'em every now and then when he wasn't particularly happy. Which seemed to be every time I was there.

"I don't think you've thought this out," he said.

"What do you mean?"

"If you give this to Sergeant Thurman, what you gonna give him?"

"The guy accosted her in front of her apartment. The day she got killed."

"The afternoon of the day she got killed. Some six hours before. That's hardly conclusive."

"The guy's a dope dealer. She owed him money, and she didn't pay."

"Half a gram." MacAullif leveled the cigar at me. "You want to go to Thurman and say she got killed over half a gram? You'll be lucky he doesn't think you're making it up."

"Hey, I saw what I saw. Maybe it's only half a gram, but the guy was pissed off. He grabbed her by the wrists."

"That's a far cry from strangling her."

"Yeah, but I showed up and he took off. If I hadn't, who knows what he might have done."

"So he takes off, comes back six hours later and strangles her over half a gram." He shook his head. "Very persistent. The guy should be working for loan sharks. Even they aren't that tough."

"The guy thought I was a cop. He could have thought Sherry set him up. Maybe he killed her 'cause of that."

"Come on," MacAullif said. "Why would Sherry set him up?"

"You're a cop, and you have to ask me that? She gets busted for drugs. The cops say they'll let her go if she'll roll over and give 'em her source. I'm sure shit like that happens all the time.''

"Not over half a fucking gram.''

"Well, I've only got his word for that. Maybe it was more.''

"Finally!'' MacAullif said, striking himself on the head. "I only had to say half a gram a couple of hundred times before you got the point. Now you're talkin' like a cop. That's right. You've only got his word for that. You corner the guy, he's got to tell you something, so he does, but it don't have to be true.

"And not just the half a gram. *None* of what he told you has to be true.''

"I know that.''

"So whaddya got? The unsubstantiated word of a dope dealer. Great. You wanna take that to Thurman?''

"The guy's lying, all the better. Let Thurman sweat it out of him.''

MacAullif grimaced. "You've seen Thurman. You think Thurman's gonna get the truth? No, let me tell you what you got. You got a guy who substantiates your story—that's why you like it. So the guy says, yeah, he was there with the broad, you showed up and he ran away. That leaves you there with the broad. Thank god she went to rehearsal, so that doesn't make you the last person to see her alive. But you happen to be the *first* person to see her dead. And this guy's story right now doesn't help you one bit.''

"Hey, give me a break. The guy's a dope dealer and she was into him. Whether it's half a gram or not and whether he told the truth or not, there's still that. He admitted that much.''

MacAullif shook his head pityingly. "Yeah. To you. Because you had the goods on him and he was carrying dope. Whaddya want to bet by now he's clean as a whistle, you could drop by his place you wouldn't find a thing, and if the cops pick him up he'll sing a whole different tune? Hell, it's your word against his, he can deny he ever said it.''

''I don't think so. If push came to shove, there's enough people we could shake down and prove he was selling dope.''

MacAullif shrugged. ''Maybe, maybe not.''

''Plus he had the hots for her. That's another thing. He had the hots for her, he never got anywhere, but he wanted to.''

''So,'' MacAullif said. ''He goes there because he has the hots for her. He rings the doorbell, he finds her naked, and instead of fucking her he strangles her.''

''He tried to rape her and she resisted.''

MacAullif sighed and ran his hand over his head. ''It's a theory. At best, it's a theory. You don't go to Thurman with a theory. You got the information, that's fine. If the cops start hasslin' you, you got the ammunition to shoot. But don't take something half-baked and go running to them. 'Cause coming from you, it's gonna make 'em skeptical. Anything you take 'em, it's well thought out on the one hand, and something you can prove on the other.''

MacAullif drummed his cigar on the desk. ''Sorry to be so hard on you, but I'm not gonna let you slit your throat. What you got is good, but you gotta check it out further. Now, what else have you got?''

''I also found the ex-boyfriend.''

''Oh?''

I told him about Dexter Manyon. His interest picked up somewhat.

''Now, that sounds promising,'' MacAullif said.

"For my money, he's a better bet than your dope peddler. Most violent crimes are committed by intimate partners—husbands and wives, boyfriends and girlfriends. They have more reason, see? More emotional involvement. You usually kill someone you know well. Now, this guy's really carrying a torch for her. She's through with him and running around with this wild lifestyle, drugs and casual flings and what have you. Well, that could get to him. That could drive him to something like this. You always kill the one you love, right?

"Well, that works much better for me. The obsessed lover. Waits outside her building all night for her to come back. Watches her go in. Stands on the sidewalk, vacillating. Should he or shouldn't he? Finally, he can't bear it anymore. Goes in, knocks on her door. She comes to the door in a bath towel. He's outraged. The slut. Coming to the door like that. He pushes the door in, rips the towel off her. Sees her naked and snaps. If he can't have her, no one can. Strangles her."

MacAullif found himself strangling his cigar. He frowned and put it down. "Yeah, for me that works much better. But it's still just a theory, nothing you take to the cops. You got anything else?"

I sighed. "Well, I sat through rehearsal."

"And?"

"I got a lot of possibles. Most of 'em pretty thin, but they're there."

He sighed. "Okay. Let's have it."

"The actor in the piece. The guy she was working with. Claude Breen."

"What about him?"

"He had the hots for her. He rode home with her in a taxi from rehearsal. On the phone he told the police he dropped her off and took the taxi on home. That was a lie. He paid the cab off at her place and tried to go upstairs with her. According to him, she wasn't having any and left him on the sidewalk."

"The cops know this?"

"Yeah. The guy's none too swift. When I pointed out they'd get a hold of the taxi driver to confirm his story, he got cold feet and confessed. So when he gave his signed statement, he changed his story."

"Well, that's something. You think he's a possible?"

"Frankly, I think he's too stupid to do it. But I've been wrong before."

"No shit. Who else?"

"Claude has a girlfriend. Actress in the show. Redhead named Audrey Lake. She wasn't there that night, they were just working Claude and Sherry's scene. But she's a very jealous and suspicious woman, and had every reason to hate Sherry Fontaine."

"To the point of killing her?"

"Hey, I'm just giving you what I got. Then there's the writer/producer. Marshall Crane. Seems to be gay, so a sexual motive is out. But the guy's got five thousand bucks invested in the show."

"Five *grand?*"

"That's what I said. Apparently in the theatre it's a trifle. Anyway, he's putting up the money largely to see his own work produced. In other words, the show's a vanity piece. It's a big deal to him. He had his scripts bound professionally at his own expense. That shows you how dear they are to him. And Sherry Fontaine was throwing her weight around and making a big stink about changing all the lines."

MacAullif frowned. "You sayin' that's a motive for murder?"

"Hey, I'm a writer. I've never had anything substantial published, but even the simple shit I do, if someone rewrites me, I wanna kill. So I understand artistic passion. And believe me, it could be just as intense as sexual passion.''

MacAullif shook his head. ''I don't know.''

''Then there's the director. Walter Shelby. From everything I heard, Sherry was giving him a real hard time. Complaining about everything, undermining his authority, and trying to direct the show. Which put him in a hell of a position. Marshall Crane was footin' the bills, wrote the script, and wanted it intact. Sherry Fontaine was doing her best to tear it down. That put Walter Shelby right in the middle. He didn't want to piss off his backer and playwright on the one hand, or his lead actress on the other. And he couldn't please both. From what I heard, Sherry was getting more and more assertive and aggressive, pushy and demanding. Her death had to be a blessed relief to him.

''Add to that the fact he seems to have the hots for the understudy Sherry's death elevated into her role. She's a sweet young thing, seems completely infatuated with him, and should be putty in his hands, a joy to work with, and a breath of fresh air after Sherry Fontaine.

''Then, of course, there's her. The understudy. Miranda Vale. Sherry's death lands her in a starring role. True, it's just a lousy showcase production, but still. The problem with it is, the play is such a piece of shit a moron ought to be able to see that being in it's gonna do absolutely zero for their career.''

I exhaled and rubbed my head.

''Is that it?'' MacAullif said.

''There's one other actress. Jill Jenson. She had no personal involvement with Sherry Fontaine, wasn't there the night of the murder, had nothing to gain or lose from Sherry's death, and has been nothing but cooperative and helpful in terms of the investigation, and seems out of it altogether.''

MacAullif grinned. ''With your storybook mentality, that probably makes her your chief suspect.''

''Fuck you. In my humble opinion, she's probably safely out of it.''

''You check her alibi?''

''No.''

''So,'' MacAullif said. ''What about the rest of them?''

''Luke Brent and Dexter Manyon have no alibis. You've heard Claude's story, and he's got no alibi either.''

''The director and writer and the understudy and actresses?''

''I don't know.''

''You didn't ask 'em where they were that night between the hours of twelve and two?''

''No, I didn't.''

''Well,'' MacAullif said. ''Looks like you got some work to do. Is that everything you got?''

''Yeah.''

''That's good. This may surprise you, but I actually have work to do too. But hey, don't get depressed. You made a good start. So what's next? What you gonna do tomorrow?''

I sighed.

''What's the matter?''

I shook my head. ''Tomorrow, I'm gonna be in court.''

30.

YEAH, Monday morning I was back on jury duty. Sherry Fontaine's death had held up court for one day but that was it. The case had been dragging on for eight years, it had finally got to trial, and come hell or high water that trial had to finish. As with Marshall Crane's masterpiece, the show must go on.

I don't know how to describe the atmosphere in the jury deliberation room without resorting to gross understatement. Suffice it to say it had changed. Naturally, the enormity of what had happened colored everything. The death of one of the members of the jury would have been extraordinary enough. The murder of one of them was almost incomprehensible.

The initial mood was one of restraint. Quiet, subdued, respectable. Even Ralph wasn't his usual self. He wasn't exactly cordial, but he wasn't abusive either. He was for all intents and purposes a human being, as affected by what had happened as the rest of us. And like the rest of us, he was properly awed.

But that, as I say, was the initial mood. Or perhaps I should say, the surface mood, the outward appearance. Because underneath that there was something else. Because, as with me, it isn't often someone you know is murdered. And, unlike me, these people weren't involved. And none of them knew Sherry Fontaine even as well as I did. And not being involved, and not knowing Sherry that well, but still knowing her, made her murder something else.

It made it exciting as hell.

Which didn't take long to come out. After a few respectful comments, during which all assembled agreed that it was indeed a terrible thing, Ron said, "So you found the body?"

"That's right."

"How'd that happen? You'd been driving her down here, right?"

"That's right."

"And you just went to pick her up and found her there?"

I sighed. "Yeah."

"I heard she was naked," Maria said. Her face looked properly subdued, but her eyes were gleaming.

"Yes, she was," I said.

"Then it was a sex crime?" OTB Man asked.

I shook my head. "Police don't think so." I wasn't going to start discussing semen, much as I was sure they'd have loved it. "There was no evidence of sexual attack," I said.

"And you just walked in and found her?" Nameless Mother said. She was wearing a less severe outfit today, and looked slightly less like a businesswoman.

"Yeah," I said. "She didn't answer the bell and her door was open. I walked in and there she was."

She shook her head. "You poor man."

"She was naked when you found her?" OTB Man said.

I bit my lip. What did he think—I found her dressed and took her clothes off? I took a breath. "Yeah."

"Did she . . ." Maria said. "I mean . . . did she . . . look . . . different?"

"She'd been strangled. It's not a pretty sight."

The others looked at each other. Shook their heads.

"So what did you do?" OTB Man said. "When you found the body?"

What I'd done was throw up. But I didn't think that was really relevant to the present discussion, much as the others might have thought it a juicy tidbit. "I called the cops," I said.

"From her phone?" Ron asked. It occurred to me once again he was going to make a good lawyer.

"No, I didn't touch her phone. I used the one outside."

"Were you there when the cops came?" Maria asked.

"Of course."

"I mean up there in her apartment."

"Yes."

"Did they do fingerprints and stuff like that?"

"Yes, they did."

"You saw them?"

"Yes."

"And pictures of the body?"

I blinked. The image flashed on me of the photographer taking closeups of Sherry Fontaine's crotch. "Yes," I said.

Maria shivered. "Oh, that must have been awful." But her eyes were still bright.

"So, do the police have a suspect?" Nameless Mother said.

"No," Mrs. Abernathy said. She shook her head. "That's what it said on the news. No suspects."

When she said that, it occurred to me the story had indeed been on the evening news. She'd seen it. I'd seen it. Dexter Manyon had seen it. And I was sure the other jurors in the room had all seen it too. It also occurred to me most of the things they'd just asked me, the fact she was strangled, the fact she was naked, the fact she hadn't been assaulted, had all been in that news report. So the questions weren't really questions, just morbid curiosity.

It also occurred to me it wasn't just them, that anyone couldn't help being fascinated at being so close to something so bizarre. But still the tone of the conversation was ghoulish at best, and when Ralph finally led us into the courtroom, it was actually a relief.

But not much. It was excruciating for me to sit there. Considering everything that had happened, and everything that was going on in my head, it was almost impossible for me to concentrate on what was going on in that courtroom. And yet, I had to. Sherry Fontaine's death had kicked me onto the first team. And there I was, sitting in the back row, the new Number Three, sitting in between Number Four, the Nameless Mother I'd thought was a businesswoman, and Number Two, originally College Boy, replaced by the first alternate, Mrs. Abernathy. And as a member of the first team, I now had to judge and deliberate and render a verdict on what was going on here.

Which wasn't going to be easy. For the first few days, I must confess, I wasn't really paying that much attention. Because I wasn't on the jury, I was just the alternate, and it didn't matter anyway. Now, I know that's no excuse and makes me a bad citizen and all that, but it happened to be the case. I had my own problems. My own worries to deal with. And I shouldn't have been there in the first place. I resented it, and resented the system, and was digging in my heels as a matter of course.

Plus, what I'd observed so far, I'd seen from a dramatic point of view. As if it were a stage play. As if the lawyers were actors, performing a bit of courtroom drama. Peter, Paul and Mary, the Silver Fox, Ms. Judge, and their cast of supporting witnesses. Just another badly written, boring, tedious play, inexplicably making it into New York after eight years of floundering in the provinces.

And now, now that I'd been elevated to juror, now that I knew I had to pay attention, I didn't know how I was going to do it. I mean, Jesus Christ, how could I concentrate on this case when my mind was filled with the other case, the murder case? I mean, come on, give me a break. I'm only human. How could I concentrate on a mundane case of property damage when I was involved in a murder case where I just might be a Suspect with a capital "S"?

I had so much to think about, that was it. I'd spent Sunday after I'd seen MacAullif doing what I should have done before, what MacAullif had advised me to do, checking the alibis of the various parties.

Marshall Crane had been the easiest. First, because he was home and answered when I called, and second, because he was so straightforward. He'd gone home alone by cab, he lived alone, no one could vouch for his whereabouts, but frankly he couldn't care less. The idea that he'd killed Sherry Fontaine was absurd, if anyone wanted to prove it they were welcome to try, it didn't faze him in the least, no hard feelings and call any time.

Walter Shelby wasn't so easy. He didn't take offense at the idea of being asked for an alibi, but he didn't seem eager to supply one either. He hemmed and hawed around a bit, and finally said, "Let me think for a minute." If I'd had a watch, I'd have timed him, and I bet a minute would have been a conservative estimate. At any rate, he finally came back on the phone and said he'd thought it over, and decided to tell me as long as I'd be discreet. In point of fact, he'd actually gone home with the understudy, Miranda Vale, and he'd been wrestling with his conscience as to whether it would be chivalrous to say so.

I phoned Miranda Vale to confirm this, with an unexpectedly comical result. I got Walter Shelby again. It turned out she had call-forwarding, and she was at his house. And all that time on the phone when I'd thought he'd been consulting his conscience, he'd actually been consulting her.

When I finally got her on the phone, she had no such scruples. She freely and happily admitted they'd been together that night. Which more or less let them out. Unless they'd been in it together and were lying. Unless that pause on the phone hadn't been Walter asking her if it were all right to tell me, but instead had been him saying, "He's on to me, what should I do?"

Next up was Audrey Lake. She was, as usual, belligerent and suspicious. No, she didn't have an alibi, did she really need one, and why *really* wouldn't I tell her what Claude and I had discussed in the elevator?

Last but least was Jill Jenson. She was, as usual, polite, agreeable and cooperative. She hadn't had rehearsal that night, so she'd gone to the movies with a girlfriend. She'd gotten home about eleven-thirty, she lived alone, and no one could vouch for her. She was sorry she couldn't do better than that, and would I like her to come down and make a statement?

I would not. But in spite of MacAullif kidding me about that very thing, I couldn't help feeling that she was somehow too good to be true, and therefore suspicious.

At any rate, I had all that kicking around in my head when I should have been concentrating on the trial. Fortunately, the morning session was easy to follow. The Silver Fox called a gentleman who turned out to be a private detective who'd taken pictures at the time of the fire. He'd made several enlargements of these, which he identified and which the Silver Fox introduced into evidence. This was good. Looking at pictures was a damn sight easier than listening to testimony. All I could tell from the pictures was there had been a fire and that it seemed to have done some damage, but I suppose that's all they were supposed to show. At least it got me through the morning.

When we broke for lunch I went out and called Rosenberg and Stone. I'd canceled my Friday cases, of course, when the whole thing happened, but I'd told Wendy/Janet I'd probably be back on the job on Monday. But that was when I thought I wasn't involved and wasn't investigating. Before my wife and MacAullif went to work on me. Now that I was mixed up in this mess as well as serving jury duty, there was no time left for signups. I'd left my car home today and taken the subway, just as everyone had advised me to. As far as Rosenberg and Stone was concerned, I wasn't working.

Wendy/Janet wasn't pleased to hear it. In fact, she had a case she'd been planning to give me that afternoon, and was already pissed at me because I wasn't answering the beeper. The reason I wasn't answering it was because I wasn't working today and I'd left it at home. I tried to explain that, but Wendy/Janet was having none of it. As far as she was concerned, I was working. If anyone was going to tell her any different, it was gonna have to come from Richard.

So I had to talk to Richard. Who wasn't particularly sympathetic. As far as Richard was concerned, I either was a suspect or I wasn't. If I was a suspect, then I needed a lawyer and he was it. If I wasn't a suspect, then I wasn't involved and I could damn well do his signups.

Actually, Richard's attitude was nothing more than a sulk. He figured I *was* involved, and wasn't letting him in on it.

"Richard," I said, "I promise you, if the cops start hassling me, you're the first one I'll call. Right now they're leaving me alone and there's nothing you can do. I can't ask you to fight someone who isn't fighting back."

Richard still wasn't convinced, and couldn't see any reason why I wasn't working. I had to remind him that he hadn't wanted me working while I was on jury duty in the first place. I finally left it that I would come back to work as soon as I finished jury duty or the murder case cleared up, whichever came first.

By the time I finished all that, I just had time to run out and grab a quick cheeseburger before rushing back to court.

The afternoon session was worse. We still had the detective and his photographs, but now Peter, Paul and Mary got a crack at him. And as the questioning droned on, I came to the sickening realization that not only did I have to determine negligence in this case, but I also had to apportion it to the various defendants. For instance, the VCR in the picture—was that forty percent Mary's, thirty-five percent Peter's, and twenty-five percent Paul's? Or maybe sixty percent Mary's, forty percent Peter's, and Paul had nothing to do with it? And was the plaintiff himself negligent, as Peter, Paul and Mary were all trying to suggest? If so, what portion of the damage should be allotted to him?

I had no idea.

Some juror.

31.

I TACKLED Luke Brent. I figured he was my most promising lead. Of course, that was just by process of elimination, since my other leads were all so unpromising. But MacAullif had made a good point—there was no reason to assume the guy had told me the truth. Not that the truth would necessarily help me any, but if the guy had any story at all, I needed to hear it.

Plus he was the only one I had any leverage on. If that still held true. If, as MacAullif had predicted, he hadn't already ditched all his dope and would promptly tell me to go to hell.

The address was a walkup on Avenue C. That stirred memories. I'd called on a dope dealer in that neighborhood way back when, the first time I'd been involved in a murder case. I'd called on him but he hadn't been home, and had later turned out to be dead. I sure hoped history wasn't repeating itself. In murder mysteries, whenever the detective went to interview a crucial witness who could have cracked the case, that witness would always turn out to be murdered. I didn't know how crucial a witness Luke Brent was, and I can't say I liked him very much, but I sure hoped the son of a bitch was alive.

He was, but it certainly wasn't the fault of the security in his building. There was none. The front door was open and I walked right in. I went up to the third floor, found the apartment and banged on the door. After a minute or so, it opened an inch on a safety chain, and I could see his eye peering out at me.

"Stanley Hastings," I said.

"Whaddya want?"

"I want to come in."

"Got a warrant?"

"No, I don't."

"You can't search my place without a warrant."

"I don't want to search your place."

"Oh? Then whaddya want?"

"I want to talk."

"I got nothing to talk about."

"That's dumb. Here I am, without a warrant, wanting to talk. If you do, you got nothing to lose. If you don't, I gotta call the precinct, get a warrant, get some cops over here and start hassling you."

"You won't find nothing."

"I know that. You're clean. You'd be a damn fool if you weren't. But how long you wanna stay that way?"

"What?"

"Think it over. You don't talk to me, I gotta keep hassling you. Which means you gotta stay clean. Big pain in the ass. Sooner or later you're gonna figure out, 'Shit, I don't talk to this guy, he's never gonna leave me alone.' Which happens to be the case. If you're smart, you'll talk to me, and then you can get on with your life."

There was a pause. "Whaddya want to talk about?"

"We have to do this in the hall? I got no warrant, you're in no danger. How about being a human being?"

Another pause, then the door closed. I could hear the chain being slipped off. Then he opened it again. "Come in."

I walked in and found myself in a small, modestly furnished apartment. It wasn't luxurious, but it was neat, comfortable. Not a junkie's crash pad. As I'd expected, Luke Brent wasn't some hard-line pusher. Most likely the guy had rich parents somewhere he was rebelling against.

There were playbills from a summer theatre tacked to the wall. I jerked my thumb at them. "You an actor?"

"Isn't everyone?"

I chuckled. "That's a fact."

I flopped into a chair. He sat down on the couch, eyed me warily. "So whaddya want to talk about?"

"Your story."

"What about it?"

I shook my head. "I don't like it."

"What's that supposed to mean?"

"Sherry Fontaine was into you for half a gram. Wow. Big deal."

"So?"

"I saw you outside her apartment. You grabbed her by the wrists. You were very upset."

"Yeah? So?"

"Over half a gram of coke?" I shook my head again. "Doesn't wash. Doesn't add up. You gotta remember. I saw you. You were really pissed off. Half a gram of coke just doesn't make it."

His eyes were defiant. "That's what it was."

"No, it wasn't." I held up my hand before he could

protest again. "Now hang on. We got a problem here, we gotta resolve it. I don't know what your problem is, or why you're feeding me this bullshit. But I got a feeling it's because you're a pusher and I'm a cop.

"So I'm gonna let you in on a little secret. Only you have to promise me you won't tell anyone. Any of your actor friends, I mean."

His eyes narrowed. "What are you talking about?"

"You promise me?"

"Promise you? I don't know what you're talking about. What's goin' on?"

"I'll take that as a yes. So here's the secret. Just between you and me."

I paused, made him ask. "What?"

"I'm not a cop."

"Huh?"

I pulled out my ID, flipped it open, passed it over. "I'm not a cop. I'm a private detective. But that's incidental. My only interest in this case is 'cause I knew Sherry Fontaine."

He looked at my ID, blinked a couple of times, and looked back up at me. "You're kidding."

"Hey, use your head. Why you think I was outside Sherry Fontaine's apartment that afternoon? You think I'm a narc, working undercover, setting up a big half-a-gram bust? If you'd paid attention, you'd have noticed I'd just dropped her off on the corner. I was there 'cause I happened to give her a ride home."

"You sure look like a cop."

"Thanks a lot. I wear a suit 'cause I'm a private detective. You're young, you're an actor, your friends are all actors. To you, anyone in a suit's a cop. The point is, I'm not."

He shook his head. "This is crazy."

"Yeah, ain't it?"

"Then why are you doin' this?"

I sighed. "Yeah, that's the question. Well, in the first place, I knew Sherry. Someone killed her, and I want to know who.

"In the second place, I came to pick her up the next day and happened to find the body. The cop in charge of the investigation's a moron, and if he can't find out who did it, he just might pick me.

"But that's neither here nor there. The thing is, I'm not a cop, so what you tell me, it won't get you into any trouble. Unless, of course, you killed her."

"I didn't kill her."

"Then you got nothing to lose. 'Cause your drug dealing, frankly, I don't give a shit. It's a murderer I want. So you might as well talk to me."

"What if I don't?"

I shrugged. "Then I got friends on the force, I could pass the information along. Maybe they'll do a better job on you than I can."

"I don't like threats."

"Me either. That's why I'm not making any. That's why I'm sitting here telling you I'm not a cop. I'm a friend of Sherry's, just like you, and, damn it, I want the guy who did it."

A pause. Then he sighed. "All right."

"All right, what?"

"I'll tell you, but I don't think it's gonna do you any good."

"Maybe, but I still want it."

"Okay. Here it is. Everything I told you's true except for one thing."

"What's that?"

"It wasn't half a gram."

"What wasn't?"

"What she wanted. It was half a gram she owed me for, that was true. I mean, what I was bringing her."

"Which was?"

"You sure you're not a cop?"

"Hey, we've come this far."

"Yeah. So, it wasn't half a gram. It was a quarter of an ounce. Seven grams."

"That's the truth?"

"Yeah."

"Tell me about it."

"It's just like I said. She called me up. Only she don't want half a gram, she wants seven. I told her she owed me for the last half, she said no sweat, she'd have the money. And not just for that—she'd have all the money. No problem."

He paused. Shrugged his shoulders. "Well, that was something new. She'd always done half a gram, gram tops. Suddenly she wants a quarter-ounce. I asked her about it. She just laughed it off. She had a way of doing that. Never answering your questions if she didn't want to. Same as if you were comin' on to her. She wouldn't say no, she'd just laugh it off. I can't get anything out of her, like who's this for, where's the money gonna come from. All I get is, she wants it, the money's there, and I should bring it."

He looked at me. "And that's what happened, so help me god."

"Why couldn't you tell me this to begin with?"

"I thought you were a cop."

"So?"

"So, I was scared. When you're dealin', there's different degrees. Class B felony, class A misdemeanor, god knows what else. I sure don't. I never been in trouble with the law before. You're the first cop I met. Or thought I met. Anyway, I know there's different penalties. I don't know what, but there's gotta be a big difference between half a gram and a quarter ounce. See what I mean?''

I frowned. ''Yeah, that tells me why you lied. But . . .''

''But what?''

''It still doesn't explain.''

''Explain what?''

''What happened. I don't care if it was a half-gram or a quarter-ounce. I saw what happened. You were really pissed. It still don't add up, even if you were bringing her more. 'Cause the bottom line is, she only owed you for half a gram. If she didn't have the money, you didn't have to give her the stuff, so what was the difference how much you brought?''

He shook his head. ''Yeah. I know. It wasn't the money.''

''Well, what was it?''

''It's hard to explain. I don't think you'd understand.''

''Try me.''

''Well, it was just the way she was. Like I said, never taking you seriously, always kidding you out of it. Well, she was real pretty. And I never got anywhere with her. And I doubt if I ever would. But she *knew* she was pretty, you know what I mean? And she used it. Like wheedling me for half a gram.

''Only this time it was a quarter-ounce. She told me she'd have the money, and she didn't.''

He stopped, took a breath. ''This is what you won't understand. It wasn't the money. It was the idea of the thing. I come there, I got the quarter-ounce on me, and she tells me she doesn't have the money. Screw the money. It was the whole idea of the thing.

''She *expected* me to give it to her. She'd just have to smile and giggle and say something cute and I'd give it to her. She could get away with shit like that because she was pretty. 'Cause she knew it and knew how to use it. That was the thing. Not the money. The idea that I was a sucker, and she was a cute young girl and I'd just give her anything she wanted.''

He ran his hand over his head again. ''Yeah, I over-reacted. I was pissed at her, and I was pissed at myself for the way I felt about her. It wasn't the money, and it wasn't the coke or any damn thing like that. I grabbed her wrists just 'cause I was pissed at her for bein' who she was.''

He looked up at me. ''I suppose you couldn't un-derstand that.''

I sighed. ''Yeah,'' I said. I nodded. ''Yeah. As a matter of fact, I could.''

32.

MACAULLIF wasn't impressed. "So?"

"So, you were right. He changed his story."

MacAullif shrugged. "So what?"

"So what? You told me he was lyin'. I went and checked it out, it turned out he was lyin'."

"So what does that get you?"

I stared at him. "Are you kidding? Now I know what the real story is."

MacAullif shrugged. "Maybe."

"What do you mean, maybe?"

"The guy was lyin' before, how do you know he's not lyin' again?"

I shook my head. "Aw, shit."

We were in MacAullif's office. After a dreary morning of the Silver Fox reading yet another bunch of depositions into the record, Judge Davis had mercifully broken for lunch early at twelve-thirty. I'd taken advantage of the extra half-hour to zip over to MacAullif's office to fill him in on what I'd found out the night before.

He was, once again, less than encouraging. And if there was any doubt as to whether or not I was doing well, MacAullif dispelled it by unwrapping a cigar to play with.

"The trouble with you," MacAullif said, "is no matter how hard you try, you can't seem to think like a cop. You think the guy's lyin', you go confront him, he changes his story, you think, whoopie, you got it made. It never occurs to you just 'cause he changed his story what he's telling you now doesn't have to be the truth."

"Maybe, but I think it is."

"Oh yeah? On what basis?"

I took a breath. "On a hunch. What's the matter with that? Don't you cops ever go on a hunch?"

"Oh, absolutely," MacAullif said. "If you didn't go on hunches, you'd never get anywhere." MacAullif held up the cigar like a teacher holding up a blackboard pointer. "The thing is, you have to remember a hunch is a hunch, and not start treating it as fact."

"All right," I said. "Granted. But I talked to him, and in my humble opinion, the guy's telling the truth. So if he is, what have we got?"

MacAullif shook his head. "Not much. She was buyin' coke, now she's buyin' more."

"Yeah, but that's interesting. 'Cause she didn't have any money. She either came into some money, or she was buying it for someone else."

"Right," MacAullif said. "And who would that be?"

"I have no idea."

"Of course you don't," MacAullif said. " 'Cause you're goin' at this thing ass backwards. You come in here yesterday, you run down your list of possibles, and you got two main suspects, this dope dealer and the boyfriend. Who do I tell you is the best bet? The boyfriend. Do you check him out? No. You put in your

240

time with the dope dealer. Now, you got some information that may or may not be true. If it's true, it's interesting. But that's all. Meanwhile, the boyfriend's runnin' around free, the only time you talked to him he was corked to the gills, you couldn't really get his story, and you still haven't followed up on him.''

"I couldn't follow up on him. I happen to be serving jury duty on the dullest case in history and I haven't got much time.''

"You had time for the dope dealer.''

"Give me a break, willya? I'm not particularly enjoying this. I'm doing the best I can.''

MacAullif looked at me. "What's the matter, I hurt your feelings? So you got the dope dealer to change his story, whaddya want, a pat on the back? I'm not a cheerleader, I'm trying to help you here.''

MacAullif waved the cigar. "Now, it's free advice, and you don't have to take it. I just throw it out for all it's worth.''

"I appreciate it,'' I said. I had a feeling the fact I said it through clenched teeth was not apt to impress MacAullif with my sincerity. I took a breath. "While you're dolin' out free advice, you got any more? Aside from the boyfriend, I mean.'' I held up my hand. "I promise, I'll check him out, but frankly I think he's a dead end. Aside from him, what the hell can I do?''

MacAullif leaned back in his chair, rolled the cigar around in his fingers. He chuckled. "Remember those books you had me read once? You know, the Agatha Christies, with the detective with the weird name?''

"Hercule Poirot.''

"Right. Him. You know, in one of them the young hero's running around gettin' information, and he comes to him, just like you, askin' what he should do next. You remember what the detective says?''

Jesus Christ. MacAullif was throwing Agatha Christie back at me. "No. What?"

MacAullif pointed with his cigar. "It was in that book with all the clocks in it. In fact, that was the name of it. *The Clocks*. The guy asks him what to do and he says, 'Talk to the neighbors.' That's what he said. Talk to the neighbors, 'cause in a murder case someone always knows something."

I stared at MacAullif. "The neighbors?"

"Yeah, the neighbors. Sherry Fontaine's neighbors. Did you talk to them?"

"No."

"Well, why not? You wanna know about the girl—what her habits were, who her friends were—the mystery man who was giving her money for cocaine." MacAullif shrugged. "What better source of information than the neighbors?"

I ran my hand over my head. "Maybe, but . . ."

"But what?"

"Well, won't Thurman have already done that?"

"Sure, but Thurman's a moron and he won't know what to ask." MacAullif shrugged. "Hey, it's free advice, and no one likes free advice. But you asked for it, so there it is."

"And that's it?"

"Hey, whaddya want for nothin'? This ain't my case, I'm not investigating it, I don't have all the facts. You want suggestions, I'll make suggestions. But this is really up to you."

"I don't see how talking to the neighbors is gonna help."

"Maybe not. Couldn't hurt."

I felt my spirits sinking fast. "MacAullif."

"What?"

"All right, I'll do all this, you know, but . . . I

242

don't know. I just have a horrible feeling this case is never gonna be solved.''

MacAullif nodded. "Entirely possible. A large percentage of these things aren't.''

"So what if it isn't?''

MacAullif shrugged. "Either it lapses, Thurman drops it and it goes in the Unsolved Crimes file, or Thurman picks on you.''

"What if he picks on me?''

"Then you get that Rosenberg character to come down and bite him in the leg till he lets go.''

MacAullif set his cigar down, leaned back in his chair and ran his hand over his head. "Look,'' he said. "You're getting all worked up over this. Which is stupid, 'cause you've really only just begun. You ask me what to do and I don't know 'cause I got no information. And you don't know, 'cause you got no information. Of course it looks hopeless. So you go out, you dig around, you see what you can find. That gives you an idea which way to go. Maybe it's hopeless, but maybe it ain't. Right now it's too soon to tell.''

"So what do I do?''

"I told you. Talk to the boyfriend, talk to the neighbors. You come up empty, we think of something else. You get something, we don't gotta think so hard. That's good. Thinking's a bitch. No one wants to think too hard.''

He looked at me, cocked his head. "A guy like you should avoid it at all costs.''

33.

I WAS PISSED as hell when I got off court that night.
I was pissed because the afternoon session had
been as boring as the morning one, with the Silver
Fox calling a succession of former employees to testify
that they'd been there the day after the fire and seen a
number of burned and damaged goods. Having already seen the photos, I found this redundant and un-
illuminating. But it sure was time-consuming, what
with Peter, Paul and Mary getting a crack at them too.
By five o'clock I thought my head was going to come
off, and if Judge Davis hadn't adjourned court I was
about to start screaming for mercy. So I was pissed
about that.

I was also pissed at MacAullif. Jesus Christ, what
right did he have to be so cocky and so smug? All
right, he was a cop and he knew his job, and I was an
amateur and I didn't.

But still. Considering how little he had to offer, considering what small contributions he had to make, what
right did he have to be so high and mighty? After all,
it was my ass on the line. I was the one gonna get
strung out for this thing. And there he was, sitting
back, smugly dispensing advice, as if he were the all-

knowing detective and I were the hapless boob. I mean, hell, he'd even compared himself to Hercule Poirot, hadn't he? Given me the same advice.

And what great advice. Talk to the boyfriend. Talk to the neighbors. Having met Dexter Manyon, I knew damn well talking to him wasn't going to do any good. But I was going to do it. And what irritated me, was I knew damn well the only reason I was gonna do it was so the next time I saw MacAullif, he couldn't ride me for *not* doing it. That and the satisfaction of being able to tell him it had been a waste of time. But that would be a hollow satisfaction, since MacAullif had admitted it would probably be a waste of time in the first place.

So as far as I was concerned, talking to Dexter Manyon was bad news all around, and I was in a foul mood as I dropped a quarter in the pay phone and punched in the number.

He wasn't home. Shit. I didn't know whether to be pissed or glad. But there I was, five o'clock at night without my car at 111 Centre Street, and Dexter Manyon wasn't at home and what the hell did I do now? Give up on him and talk to the neighbors?

Somehow that seemed an even less rewarding exercise. I didn't really expect anyone to tell me anything. They wouldn't know Sherry well. They wouldn't have their doors open, observe who went in and out. It would be yet another futile endeavor suggested by MacAullif.

I was getting really pissed.

I figured no matter what I did, I was gonna have to head uptown, so I walked across Franklyn Street to catch the Broadway IRT. After two days of riding the subway after abandoning my car, I had worked out the fact that Chambers Street was actually one stop below where I needed to go. Franklyn is actually the cross street with 111 Centre Street, and there was a Franklyn Street stop on the Broadway line. So I walked crosstown to the station.

When I got there I tried Dexter Manyon again. He still wasn't home. Damn. I bought a token, waited for the train. It came, and I got on and headed uptown.

And immediately had a choice to make. Did I give up on Dexter Manyon and try the neighbors? Or hang out near his place to see if he came home? He lived on West Eighth Street, so if it was gonna be the latter, I'd get off at Sheridan Square. So which was it gonna be? Faced with two unpleasant alternatives, I had trouble trying to decide.

Sheridan Square stop came up. Fuck it. I got off.

There was a pay phone in the station. I dropped a quarter, made the call. No answer. Great. So what did I do now?

I was still on the platform, so if I wanted, I could wait and take the next train. Or I could go out, walk over to his apartment building and hang out there. A wholly unappetizing proposition. But should I do it?

I stood there trying to make up my mind, and what finally decided me was coming to the realization that the only reason I was thinking of hanging outside Dexter Manyon's apartment was that I found the idea of talking to Sherry Fontaine's neighbors an even less attractive proposition. It was unattractive not because there was anything to fear, or even that I might learn something that I didn't want to know. It was unattractive only because doing it was going to make me feel like a fool.

When I realized this, I felt like a fool, and knew I had to do it. So I stood there on the platform, dropping quarters in the pay phone and punching in Dexter

Manyon's number, and by the time the next uptown train arrived he still hadn't answered, so I got on.

I got off at 86th and Broadway and walked over to West End. I walked up West End Avenue, feeling like a fool, but knowing I had to do it. I was a good little boy, who knew the medicine was going to taste awful, but was still gonna get it down. So I walked up West End Avenue, engulfed in a feeling of gloom.

Since I had come from Broadway and hadn't crossed West End, I was walking up the east side of the street, walking uptown with the traffic, the same way I'd come when I'd dropped Sherry Fontaine off on the way home from court. So her building was across from me, on the west side of the street.

Which is why I almost missed it. That and the fact I was so preoccupied with my thoughts and wasn't really paying attention.

I was on the corner a block away, just getting ready to cross the street when I saw him.

I blinked.

I couldn't believe it.

Good lord. The one person in this whole affair that I had never even suspected. Who wasn't even on my list of suspects. Not even on my list of *improbable* suspects. A person I'd never even thought of.

But it was him, all right.

As I averted my head and turned away so he wouldn't see me, I knew damn well the man I'd just seen on the other side of the street walking away from Sherry Fontaine's apartment building was none other than my nemesis, my conscience, the one person I had hoped with all my heart I would never see again.

My old buddy from jury duty.

34.

"**I** THINK YOU'VE lost your marbles."

"You don't understand."

MacAullif shook his head. "I *do* understand. It's absolutely clear. You've cracked up. The thing's too much for you. You can't take being a suspect and getting nowhere in the case, and now you've gone off the deep end."

"I saw what I saw."

"You saw what? An old man walking down the street."

"Away from her building."

"Big deal. Maybe he lives in the neighborhood."

"He lives on 33rd Street. I followed him home."

"So? He's got friends in the neighborhood."

"Then it's just a coincidence?"

"Yeah."

"I thought you didn't believe in coincidence."

"There's coincidence and there's coincidence. Some exist. What I meant was, when you start getting similarities in murder cases it usually ain't a coincidence."

"This is a similarity in a murder case."

"This is a guy you knew one place showing up in another place."

"I don't see the difference."

"You don't see anything. You've lost your marbles."

"MacAullif—"

"No. Hang on. You've gone off the deep end. You gotta relax, take a deep breath, get yourself together. You're at the point now where you're all upset by this, you can't think straight and you're suspecting everyone indiscriminately."

"It's not indiscriminately. Damn it, it makes sense."

"Yeah, sure," MacAullif said. He ran his hand over his head, then said with heavy irony, "Let me make sure I understand your new theory of the case. You are now convinced some old man bumped off Sherry Fontaine because he was pissed off at you for getting him kicked off a jury in a civil case?"

"It's not just that."

"Oh?"

"Well, it *is* just that. But it adds up."

"How does it add up?"

"For one thing, you didn't see it happen. But I understand the personality involved. Here's this guy, this old man. He's retired, he's got nothing going in his life. He's a sour, opinionated old cuss. And he confides in me. His secret plan. He's gonna beat the system. He's not gonna serve his two weeks. He's gonna get on a simple civil case, serve two days and get out of there.

"But he's unlucky. He doesn't get called. He sits there, and he doesn't get called. But finally he does. And when he does, it's the perfect case. A simple trip-

and-fall, gonna be one day, two days tops. He's got it made.

"Then I open my mouth and get him booted out of there."

"For which he kills an actress he never met?"

"He spent a week hating me. Every day. You should have seen the venom. If looks could kill, his would have.

"And then, the final humiliation. His last day there. After serving his full two weeks and never being called. The day he's gonna leave. He walks into the room and what does he see? Me, with a gorgeous blonde hanging on my arm, who's telling everyone in her chirrupy voice how great it is the two of us are on this jury together."

"So he kills her?"

"Absolutely."

"Why her? You're the one he's mad at. Why not you?"

"Two reasons. Or theories. I don't know. Two some-things. One, he's fairly big and probably strong, but he's an old man. And he couldn't handle me. Or at least, thought he couldn't."

"Great," MacAullif said. "And the other?"

"The other, you wanna punish someone, you want to make 'em suffer. You don't kill them and put 'em out of their misery. You kill the one they love."

"You loved Sherry Fontaine?"

"I'm talking from his perception."

"You're talking out of your asshole." MacAullif shook his head. "You want a motive for murder, I mean, Jesus Christ, that's as bizarre as you can get."

"Some motives are bizarre."

"That don't make 'em likely."

"What's so unlikely?"

"Jesus Christ. To kill her 'cause he's mad at you? The guy would have to be nuts."

"Oh? Are most murderers sane?"

"Not necessarily. But they're usually rational. Even a demented motive should make sense."

"This might make perfect sense to him. After all, the man may well *be* nuts."

"He's not the only one. Jesus Christ."

"All right, look," I said. "I traced the guy home and got his name. Nathan Hargraine."

"So?" MacAullif said. "So what?"

"That's why I'm here. To see if you could run a trace on him."

MacAullif snorted. I went on as if he hadn't. "To see if he's got a record or anything. A history of mental illness. Maybe he'd been committed somewhere."

MacAullif sighed. "You come here and interrupt my lunch hour for the second day running just for that?"

"Hey, it could be important."

"So's my lunch."

I looked at him. "You won't do this for me?"

MacAullif pursed his lips. "Let's see here. You talk to the neighbors?"

"No."

"You talk to the boyfriend?"

"No."

"Why not?"

"I was on my way when I ran into this guy. Then I got caught up following him."

MacAullif nodded. "I'll say." He shook his head. "Jesus Christ. I don't know what it is with you. I tell you talk to the neighbors. I tell you talk to the boyfriend. You don't do either. Instead you come in here with some little old man who was just unlucky enough to happen to be in the neighborhood.''

''We've been through all that.''

''We sure have.''

''So, you gonna help me or not?''

MacAullif rubbed his head. ''It's not my case. And hard as this may be for you to understand, I got my own work to do. I'm not sayin' I won't help you, but there's a limit to what I can do. I can't drop everything and start working on your case every time you come running in here with some wild idea. So I gotta slam your brakes on. You want help, well, figure I'll do one thing for you. One unauthorized, extralegal bit of investigation that I really shouldn't be doin'. So figure you got a credit from me, okay? But only one. So you shouldn't waste it. Not on this. At least, not now. You get a little further, you learn a little more, then maybe you come up with something you really want. Talk to the boyfriend. Talk to the neighbors. Exhaust your possibilities. You hit a dead end, you got nothing else, you really want me to do it, I'll do it. Stupid though it is. But do me a favor. Try something else first.''

It was infuriating. MacAullif was wrong, I knew that. He hadn't been there, he hadn't seen, he didn't know. Yeah, MacAullif was wrong.

He was also inflexible. Nothing I said was going to sway him. Like a tree that's standing by the water, he shall not be moved.

I sighed. ''Okay,'' I said.

35.

THE SILVER FOX rested his case!

That was the good news. The bad news was that it was now Wednesday afternoon. We'd begun the trial Tuesday afternoon the previous week, which meant we'd put in six full days in the courtroom already. And now Peter, Paul and Mary got their shot. If the plaintiff's case took six days to put on, did it follow that the defendant's case would take six days too? Or, since there were three defendants, did that mean it would take *eighteen* days to put on? The mind boggled.

Still, the Silver Fox resting his case was a milestone, and the atmosphere was one of excitement in the jury deliberation room during the ten-minute recess Judge Davis granted us before allowing the defense to start putting on their case. Considering how down everyone had been, what with the murder on the one hand, and the dreariness of the trial on the other, the jurors were practically bubbling over now.

Maria, the Nameless Mother and OTB Man immediately started talking about the case. About the Silver Fox (whom they still called Pretty Boy), and how well he'd done and what they thought he'd proved, and what

Peter, Paul and Mary could do now, and the whole bit.

Ron soon put a stop to that. As foreman or law student or whatever, he took charge. He reminded them all that they were not to discuss the case until they had heard all the evidence and Judge Davis had given them their instructions to deliberate. This wasn't popular, but was at least obeyed. The conversation became general. Talk about the case died out.

So did the feeling of elation. It evaporated like the snow. By the time ten minutes was up and Ralph arrived to lead us back into court, the grim realization had set in that the case was *not* over, was not likely to be over soon, and we were still stuck with it.

And what happened next was not encouraging. Peter (or Paul), the attorney from Veliko Tool and Die, called an employee from that company to testify about the fire all over again. Which was just like the testimony we'd heard before. Except that, whereas the witnesses called by the Silver Fox all attempted to say how great the damage had been, Peter/Paul's witness did his best to minimize it.

This did not fool me in the least. The witness, an elderly mechanic, still worked for Veliko Tool and Die, and obviously knew which side of the bread his butter was on. He wasn't going to say anything that was going to hurt his boss. As the guy droned on with his testimony, the only thing that really cheered me was the realization that while there were three defendants, there was only one plaintiff, so this time around only one person would have to cross-examine.

Wrong again. We were dealing with comparative negligence here. All the defendants had a stake in how responsible Veliko Tool and Die had been for the fire, and so Mary and Paul (or Peter, if Veliko Tool and

Die's lawyer was Paul) both got a crack at him too. This was dreary, depressing, and, needless to say, time-consuming, and the most ominous portent of all was that this one stupid witness took up the whole afternoon.

So at five o'clock, here I was, once again, bummed out and faced with the unappetizing choice of the neighbors or Dexter Manyon.

Once again, Dexter Manyon wasn't home, making it an easy choice. So, what the hell. MacAullif wasn't going to help me if I didn't get it done, so I walked across Franklyn and caught the subway uptown to interview the neighbors.

This time I saw no one outside Sherry's building. Thank god. If my buddy, Nathan Hargraine, had been going by again, I'd have flipped out. But this time there was no one there.

And this time her foyer door was locked. Shit. That was an unwelcome development. I know a TV detective could slip a lock with a credit card, but I couldn't even begin to try. The only way I know to get in a locked door is with a key.

I didn't have a key. Which was real bad news. I was gonna have to ring the intercom and try to get someone to buzz me in. Which wasn't gonna be easy, 'cause when they said, "Who is it?," I wasn't gonna know what to say. I knew "Stanley Hastings" wouldn't do the job. But I didn't want to say I was a cop. So what *did* I say?

I had no idea, but I didn't want to stand in the foyer all night like a schmuck. Sherry Fontaine's bell was 4A. I rang 4B.

Sometimes you get lucky. No voice said, "Who is it?" Instead, after a few moments there came the buzz of the occupant of 4B releasing the lock on the front door.

I pushed through it gratefully. Hot damn. Now that I was inside, I could ring all the fourth-floor doorbells in turn. I doubted if it would get me anywhere, but that wasn't the point. It would satisfy MacAullif. Then I could get what I really wanted.

I got in the elevator, rode up to four, and rang the doorbell of 4B.

The occupant of 4B obviously hadn't stayed by the door to wait for me after buzzing me up, because I wound up standing there for a bit. While I did, I glanced across the hall at the door of Sherry Fontaine's apartment.

It was open.

Not much, which was why I hadn't noticed when I walked down the hall. But it was unlocked and standing open a crack, and the light inside was on.

And through the crack in the door I could hear the sound of someone moving around in the apartment.

36.

I WAS SCARED to death.

Good lord, what did I do now?

I knew what I *should* do. I should get out of there and call the cops.

But what if there wasn't time? What if I did that, and the guy in there got away? What if—

There was a click behind me and I jumped a mile. I wheeled around to find it was the sound of the door to 4B opening. Good lord. I'd forgotten I'd even rung the bell. I'd forgotten what I was there for. But I'd rung it, and someone had answered it, and the door was opening and what the hell did I do now?

The door swung open. Standing there was a little old lady, who might well have been ninety. Good lord. How had she lived so long? Buzzing me in without asking who it was. And then swinging her apartment door open wide. The tough young Luke Brent had used a safety chain. And here she was, so frail a breath of wind might knock her down, flinging her door open to anyone, without even looking through the peephole first.

Jesus Christ, what an added complication. I didn't know who she was, but I didn't want her to die. And

I had the thought that if she stayed out in the hall, that was a strong possibility. I had to get rid of her fast. And here she was, smiling at me sweetly, oblivious to the fact that anything was wrong.

"Yes?" she said, in a tiny, bird-like voice.

I gulped. "Zeke Finklestein?" I said.

She frowned. "What?"

Great. She was deaf. "Zeke Finklestein?" I said in a much louder voice.

She winced. "I *hear* you," she said. *"Who* do you want?"

"Does Zeke Finklestein live here?"

"No, he doesn't."

"I'm sorry," I said. "I must have the wrong address."

I turned, walked quickly back to the elevator and pushed the down button. Unfortunately, the damn thing was right there. The elevator door opened.

I glanced back down the hallway. She was still looking after me. Damn.

I stepped into the elevator. In New York City a lot of the elevators are as slow as hell. Unfortunately, this wasn't one of them. The minute I stepped in, the door started to close. As it did, I heard her apartment door slam.

I lunged for the buttons, pressed four. The elevator door stopped midway, then slid open again. I held it open, poked my head out.

Yes, the door to 4B was closed. It was diagonally across the hall from me, so I could tell that. 4A was on the same side of the hall as the elevator, however, so from this side I couldn't see it at all. I presumed it was still open a crack.

So what did I do now?

Call the police. That had been my first thought. That

was probably what I should do. And if I'd talked my way into the old lady's apartment, I could be calling the police from there right now. But I hadn't thought of it in time. And I didn't really want to do it, anyway. I didn't want to alarm her, and I didn't want to have to explain. And I didn't want to be in her apartment with the door closed, when maybe whoever was in Sherry Fontaine's apartment might be leaving. No, I'd done the right thing there.

But what about calling them now? I had the elevator, I could ride it down and call 'em from the pay phone on the corner.

Well, same thing. What if the guy in her apartment left? No problem. The pay phone was right on the corner, I'd see him when he went out.

Assuming I knew him. Assuming the murderer was someone I knew. Which I had no right to assume. But what if he wasn't? If a stranger came out the front door, I wouldn't know if he was the guy in Sherry's apartment or not. He could be just some tenant in the building, how the hell should I know? And if someone did come out the front door, should I follow him or not? If I *didn't* follow him and he was the murderer, he'd escape. And if I *did* follow him and he was just some tenant in the building, then the murderer would also escape.

Shit. Calling the police was out.

Not unless I'd seen him. Not unless I knew who he was.

Damn.

I eased my way out of the elevator, released the door. It closed behind me, and I could hear the elevator start down. Great. I'm trapped here now.

I stood in the hallway a moment, listening for sounds. I heard none, either from apartment 4B or 4A.

All right, ace detective. You're on.

I stepped down the hall to Sherry Fontaine's door. Sure enough, it was still open a crack. I put my ear to it. Listened. Heard nothing. Christ, could he possibly have gone?

No, he couldn't have. I'd been right there in the hall. He was in there, all right.

I took a breath, put my hand on the door. Pushed it open an inch.

Through the wider crack I still saw nothing. Just a portion of the living room. No sign of an occupant.

I pushed the door a little farther.

The hinges creaked, slightly.

I stopped, held my breath.

Still no sound.

I pushed a little more. It was open about a foot now, wide enough for me to stick my head in.

I didn't want to do it. It was quiet in the apartment. Too quiet. Like someone was lying in wait. I'd stick my head in the door and get sapped. Come to hours later wondering what the hell hit me.

Assuming I *did* come to. Assuming after I was sapped, I wasn't strangled as well.

Oh, shit. Did Sam Spade ever hesitate like this? Come on, asshole. Do it.

I stuck my head in, peered behind the door.

Nothing.

I looked around the room.

Nothing.

Empty.

I pushed the door open a little further, eased myself into the room.

The first time I'd pushed my way through Sherry Fontaine's open door I'd found a dead body. Hers. Lying there, naked on the floor.

Christ. There was a chalk outline on the floor where the body had lain, just like in the movies. Life imitates art. Aside from that, the room was just as it had been then.

So where was he?

Well, either the bathroom, bedroom or the kitchen. You know he's still here. You gotta see his face.

My palms were sweaty and my breath was coming short. This guy had killed someone. Strangled them. I told myself he'd killed a woman, a woman smaller and frailer than I was. He'd strangled her, so he probably wasn't armed. It would be him against me. And I was bigger, stronger than Sherry Fontaine. I'd have a chance. Wouldn't I? I'm not a fighter, but I'm athletic. I can dodge, I can run.

What a hero. Think about running. I hadn't seen the guy, and was already thinking about turning tail. Come on, schmuck. Do it.

I crept across the room. Quickly eliminated possibilities. There was no door on the kitchen, it was a small hole-in-the-wall affair, and he obviously wasn't there.

I crept to the hallway to the bedroom and bathroom. As I reached it, I saw the bathroom door was open and he wasn't there either.

That left the bedroom door around the bend. Shit. What a narrow hallway. What a hell of a place to get cornered in.

I crept down the hallway, reached the corner, peered around. Yeah, there was the bedroom door. And directly in front of me, the bed. But I could only see half the room. And the guy wasn't in my line of sight.

But he was there. I could hear a sound, like a drawer opening or closing.

I took a breath. Oh, Jesus.

I slipped around the corner, crept down the hall. I reached the door to the bedroom, flattened myself against the wall. Leaned out, peeked in.

There he was. A man going through her dresser drawers.

I could hardly contain myself. Good lord, this was it. What was he after? What clue was it that the police had overlooked that the murderer knew he had to destroy?

I had no idea.

And I still hadn't seen his face. His back was to me and his head was down, and I just couldn't see him at all.

I leaned farther into the room, trying to catch a glimpse.

The man suddenly slammed the drawer, straightened up and turned around.

And saw me.

He saw me at the same moment I saw him.

It happened so fast, I didn't have a second to think, a second to react, a second to do anything. One moment I was looking at the back of the guy's head. The next moment, there I was in Sherry Fontaine's bedroom, standing face-to-face with a killer.

Her ex-boyfriend, Dexter Manyon.

37.

I HAVE a slight ego problem. My problem is, practically everything that happens to me is a blow to my ego.

MacAullif said talk to the boyfriend. I'd scoffed at the idea. MacAullif said you always kill the one you love. MacAullif said in violent crimes the most likely suspect was always the husband or the boyfriend. But I hadn't even been willing to consider the possibility. Instead, I'd gone chasing off after some harmless old man.

But none of that was my main concern at the moment. From the time Dexter Manyon turned around, my main concern was getting out of that room alive.

I'd only seen Dexter Manyon once, that time at the party. When I'd seen him, he'd been drunk and he'd been sitting down. Now he was sober and standing up. And, presumably, a murderer.

Which made my perception of him entirely different. His face was slender and sensitive, yes, as I had first observed. But without the effect of drink and tears, it was also lean and hard. And his body was by no means frail. He was, in fact, broad-shouldered and muscular. He was inch for inch as tall as I was. And perhaps an inch more. In short, yet another guy who could take me apart.

He made no move toward me, though. Instead, he frowned and said, "Who are you?"

That was something. Unless he was acting, he didn't remember me at all. Of course, he'd been pretty drunk.

I wondered if I should jog his memory. I wondered if that would be wise. At the moment, I wasn't sure if *anything* would be wise. Except, perhaps, running like hell.

I chose a neutral course. "I'm Stanley Hastings," I said.

My name meant no more to him than my face had. "Oh yeah?" he said. "What are you doing here?"

"I was about to ask you the same thing."

He frowned. "Pardon me, but who *are* you?"

I decided to go for it. "I guess you don't remember me," I said. "I saw you at the party."

"The party?'

"You probably don't remember. You'd had quite a bit to drink."

He frowned again. "Oh yeah. The party. I seem to remember someone spoke to me at the party. Was that you?"

"Yeah."

"Then who are you?"

I decided to leave it neutral, so I could go either way. "I'm a detective," I said. Which could mean police or private.

He took it as police. At least I think he did. His eyes narrowed. "I see," he said.

He wasn't wearing a jacket, just a polo shirt and slacks, so he wasn't carrying a gun. And he was across the room from me and I was by the door, so if he made a move on me I could run. And he hadn't made a move on me yet. So I figured it couldn't hurt to push him some, get him on the defensive.

"How'd you get in here?" I said.

"Huh?"

"The apartment. How'd you get in?"

"Oh," he said. "I have a key, of course. I used to live here, you know."

"I didn't know that," I said. "I knew she was your girlfriend, but I didn't know you lived together."

"Well, we did. Not like I moved in permanent, I still had my own place. But I stayed here. I had a key." He frowned. "But you didn't answer my question. What are you doing here?"

"I told you. I'm a detective. I'm investigating the murder."

"You a cop?"

Damn. The guy was sharper than I thought. And it was the type of question, if I answered it wrong I might wind up dead. And I only had a split second to make the decision.

I opted for the truth. I didn't want to lie to him, somehow. And saying I wasn't a cop had worked well with Luke Brent. Maybe it would work with him.

Or maybe it was just that confronted with the direct question, I was too chickenshit to pick a lie I'd have to carry through.

"No, I'm not," I said. "I'm a private detective."

He looked puzzled. "Then why are you here?"

"Because I knew Sherry," I said. "Not well, I just met her. But we were on a jury together. And I'd been driving her to court."

He thought that over. I saw comprehension in his eyes. "Then you're the one who found the body."

"That's right. How did you know?"

"From what the cops said. They wouldn't tell me

much, but that much I found out." He frowned again. "But what are you doing here?"

"Investigating the murder. Not officially or for anyone. Just personally, 'cause I knew her."

"You got a key?"

"No."

"Then how'd you get in?"

"You left the door open."

"Yeah, maybe I did. But if you don't have a key, how were you gonna get in?"

"I wasn't. I just came to question the neighbors. Then I saw the open door."

He thought that over. I couldn't tell if he was buying it or not. I suddenly realized, since I'd told him I wasn't a cop, I was as much a suspect to him as he was to me.

Unless he knew better because he'd done it.

"All right," I said. "Your turn. What are you doing here?"

"Oh," he said. "I just came by to get some things."

"Oh?"

"Yeah," he said. "I spoke to Sherry's parents. Her father's flying in tomorrow to pack up her stuff. What they want to send home. The rest will go to Good Will, I guess. So I wanted to get my stuff out first."

"What stuff?"

He took a deep breath. Sighed. "Nothing much. Keepsakes, really. Sentimental value. I had a bracelet with my name engraved. Athletic award from high school. Baseball team. I gave it to her and she never gave it back." He jerked his thumb at the dresser. "That's what I was looking for when you came in.

"And some pictures. Of me and her together. I didn't have any, but she did. I just wanted one."

He turned, picked up a snapshot from the top of the bureau, held it up.

I couldn't see it from where I was in the doorway. And I didn't really want to walk into the room.

But there was no help for it. He was sharp. If I ignored the picture and stood there poised for flight, he'd figure out that's what I was doing.

I strolled casually into the room. Or as casually as I could. I felt I was walking on eggshells.

I took the photo from him and looked at it. It was a Polaroid. He had his arm around Sherry's shoulders and she was snuggled against his chest. Her face was turned to the camera with a big smile. Happy, contented.

He wasn't looking at the camera. He was looking down at her. That look spoke volumes. That look spoke love.

It was enough to break your heart.

And it was something else.

To me, it was proof positive of a love strong enough, obsessive enough to kill for.

I handed the photo back. He looked at it, sighed. I could see tears welling up in his eyes. He put the photo down, looked back at me.

"If I don't find the bracelet it's too bad, but I think what I really wanted was this."

"I see," I said. I wasn't sure what I saw, but I needed to keep the conversation going. "You say her father's coming in tomorrow?"

"That's right."

"The funeral's tomorrow, then?"

"No," he said. "The funeral isn't here. They're shipping the body back home to Atlanta."

"What?"

"The funeral's in Atlanta," he said. "This Sunday. I still can't decide if I should go."

"Cincinnati," I said.

He looked at me. "What?"

"She's from Cincinnati."

He shook his head. "No. She's from Atlanta."

"Are you sure?"

"Of course I am. Come on. You say you knew her. Didn't you notice the southern drawl?"

"I thought it was an affectation. Because she was an actress."

He smiled sadly, shook his head. "Just the other way around. She tried to hide the drawl. Thought it would limit her in casting. But when she'd get excited about something, she'd get careless, let her guard down, and the accent would come through."

"When was she in Cincinnati?"

He frowned. "Cincinnati?"

"Yeah, was she in college there?"

He shook his head. "She never went to college. After high school she came straight to New York to make it as an actress. Why?"

"She mentioned a friend of hers from Cincinnati. Girl named Velma."

"Velma?"

"Yeah."

He nodded. "I've heard the name. I'm sure she mentioned a Velma now and then. I think it was someone she knew from acting school."

"Acting school?"

"Yeah. I don't remember which one. It wasn't the Neighborhood Playhouse. But which one was it?"

"You mean an acting school here in New York?"

"Of course."

It smacked me in the face. My stomach felt hollow. I ran my hand over my head. "Oh, good lord."

"What's the matter?"

I had to take a breath. "I'm sorry," I said. "I just realized I've been incredibly stupid."

He picked up the picture and his eyes misted over again. He chuckled softly, sadly. "Join the club," he said.

I could feel sorry for him then, knowing he wasn't a suspect anymore.

38.

I N THE MOVIE *The Verdict* there's a great scene
where Paul Newman's been up all night in his office thinking about the case and getting nowhere,
and now it's morning, and there comes the plop of
letters being slid through the slot in the office door.
He walks over, picks them up and riffles through them,
and one of them is the phone bill. He holds it and
looks at it, and you know he's thinking something but
you don't know what. Then you cut to the house of the
woman who's been holding out on him, and he's
breaking into her mailbox and stealing her phone bill,
since what he realized was everyone's phone bill arrives the same day, and there among all the long-
distance charges is the phone number of the witness
she'd been trying to hide.

I'm not the type of guy to go breaking into people's
mailboxes. But I didn't have to. 'Cause I had Mac-
Aullif.

Not that he was overjoyed to see me.

"Oh, shit," he said when I walked into his office
on the lunch hour. "Not again."

I held up my hand. "Last time. I promise."

He blinked. "What?"

"Sorry to bother you, but you said you'd do one thing for me. Well, I want it now."

"That figures," MacAullif said. "Don't tell me. Let me guess. You struck out with the boyfriend and the neighbors, and you want the dope on the old man."

"Not at all," I said. "The old man's out of it."

"What?"

"Oh yeah. That was a stupid idea to begin with, don't you think?"

MacAullif eyed me suspiciously. "I certainly do. I'm a little surprised to hear *you* say so. So whaddya want?"

"I want Sherry Fontaine's phone bill."

He frowned. "What?"

"Her phone bill. I don't need the whole thing. I'm really just concerned with last week."

"Last week? That bill won't even be made up yet."

"I know that."

"So you can't get it."

"I know that too. It'll take a police officer making a specific request."

MacAullif looked at me in exasperation. "You can't just ask for someone's phone bill. There's such a thing as invasion of privacy."

"Yeah, but there are legal ways to obtain it, and if you're a cop and you want it, you can get it."

"And if it doesn't pertain to something you're investigating, it's not entirely kosher."

"Right," I said. "One unauthorized, extralegal bit of police procedure. That's what you promised me, and that's what I want."

MacAullif took a breath. "All right," he said. "Why do you want it?"

I shook my head. "I'm not going to tell you."

His jaw actually dropped open. "What?"

"If I tell you, you'll tell me I'm being stupid and try to talk me out of it. I'm not up to that. I'll tell you after it checks out."

"What if it doesn't check out? Then you'll be back here after me for something else."

"It'll check out."

"Then tell me now."

"No way."

MacAullif scowled. He looked ready to jump over his desk and bite my head off.

I held my ground. "You gonna do it or not?"

MacAullif took a breath. He leveled a finger at me. "After which, you'll tell me what this is all about, whether you're right or not?"

"Absolutely."

"And if this turns out to be just another one of your stupid theories, you'll sit here and tell me your stupid theory, and then you'll say you're sorry you bothered me, and you'll walk out of here and you won't bother me again?"

"You got it."

MacAullif rubbed his hands together. "You got a deal."

"Fine," I said, and walked out.

After that, the afternoon court session was unbearable. It was sheer torture to sit there, knowing what I knew now. I couldn't focus in on any of it. I could barely hear a word. All I could think about was the murder case, MacAullif and the phone bill.

When Judge Davis finally let us go, I raced back to MacAullif's office to see if he'd gotten it.

He had. He picked up a piece of paper from his desk, looked at it. "Getting this was no picnic, believe me. It's not an official phone bill, but a printout

272

of what's gonna be on it.'' He looked at it again and passed it over.

I grabbed it and checked the calls. The area code 513 leaped off the page. I let out a sigh.

MacAullif was watching me carefully. ''That what you wanted?''

''Yes, it is.''

''Confirm your theory?''

''Yes, it does.''

''So, what is it?''

I shook my head. ''I gotta check it out first.''

MacAullif scowled. ''Son of a bitch.''

''I'm sorry to be a hardass,'' I said. ''But you're the one who took the hard line with this, givin' me my one shot. Well, I'm takin' it, but I'm not tellin' you what it is and taking a lot of crap from you before I got the facts to back it up. I promise I'll call you tonight and tell you the whole thing.''

''I won't *be* here tonight.''

''I'll call you at home.''

''I don't *want* you to call me at home.''

''There's no help for it. After I crack this thing, we're gonna have to move fast. You know Sergeant Thurman's home number?''

''Not offhand.''

''Better get it. After I call you, you're gonna have to call him.''

''I don't wanna call him.''

''You're gonna have to. 'Cause he's not gonna listen to me.''

''He's not gonna listen to me either.''

''He will if you're handing him a bust.''

''Damn it,'' MacAullif said. ''I knew it. I said I'd do one thing for you. I did it, now you're askin' me to do something else.''

I put up my hands. "Sorry," I said. "I take it back. I'm not asking you to do shit. I'm *suggesting* you have Sergeant Thurman's phone number handy just in case you feel like giving him a call. Because I have a feeling, after I talk to you, you just might want to do that. But that's entirely up to you. You're a big boy, and you don't have to do anything you don't want to do."

I got out of there before he threw a chair at me.

39.

ALICE WAS WAITING by the door when I got home. The avenging angel.

"Did you get it?"

"Yes."

"Was it there?"

"Yes, it was."

"Did you call yet?"

"Not yet. I gotta do it now."

Tommie came bouncing out of his room, wanting me to play Teenage Mutant Ninja Turtles on his Nintendo system. Alice intercepted him and herded him into the living room, leaving me to make the call.

I went into the kitchen, took out the paper Mac-Aullif had given me and punched the number into the phone.

Three rings. Four rings. Shit, she's not home. Five rings.

Then a click, and a woman's voice said, "Hello?"

"Hello? Velma?" I said.

"Yes. Who is this?"

"My name's Stanley Hastings. I'm a friend of Sherry Fontaine."

"Oh?" she said. "A friend of Sherry's? I don't think

she ever mentioned you. But I haven't seen her in a while.''

"Yes,'' I said. "Then I guess you haven't heard.''

"Heard what?''

"I'm sorry to have to tell you this, but Sherry Fontaine is dead.''

There was a silence on the line. Then a small gasp. "What?''

"I'm very sorry.''

"Dead?'' she said. "Oh, no. It can't be. I just spoke to her last week.''

"I know,'' I said. "That's why I'm calling.''

"What? I'm sorry. This is too awful. I don't understand.''

"I know. This is very hard. Just listen a minute.'' I took a breath. "Sherry's death was no accident. She was murdered last Thursday night.''

"Oh, my god!''

"I know,'' I said. "Velma, listen. I know this is very painful, but it's important. I'm investigating the murder, and I need your help. See, I know Sherry called you last Tuesday night, and I know why. And I know you're not gonna want to talk about it. But you have to. Because someone killed Sherry, and he cannot get away with it. I will not let him get away with it. And you can't let him get away with it either.

"I know this is all sudden, and it's a terrible shock, so I'm asking you. Take your time. Think about it. And then talk to me. I'm asking you. For Sherry. Talk to me. Please.''

She did.

40.

RALPH WAS BACK to his old grouchy self. "You can't do it," he snapped. He seemed pleased at making the pronouncement.

"I'm sorry," I said. "I have to talk to the judge."

"You can't talk to the judge. Not while the trial's in progress. Didn't you hear her instructions at the beginning of the trial? Weren't you listening?"

"Yes, I was."

"Then you know the answer. Can't do it. You can't talk to any of the parties in this case until after deliberation is over."

"This can't wait."

"It will have to. Those are the rules."

"Then how do the rules deal with this? A matter has come up which requires my attention. I am not listening to any more testimony in this case until I talk to the judge."

"That's not your decision to make."

"Whose is it?"

"Hers."

"Then I need to talk to her, don't I?"

"You're not *allowed* to talk to her."

"This is a Catch-22 situation, isn't it, Ralph?"

He said nothing, just glared at me.

"I mean I can't do anything till I talk to the judge, you won't let me talk to the judge, but the judge is the only one—"

"I'm familiar with Joseph Heller," Ralph snapped.

"Fine," I said. "Then you understand the situation. I want to talk to the judge. So what the hell can I do?"

"You cannot talk to the judge. If you must communicate with her—which I *strongly* advise against—then you do it in writing, which is what you'll be doing during deliberation. Any questions you have of the court, you put in writing, and I will deliver them. I'll deliver one now if you really insist."

"Fine," I said.

I turned to the other jurors, who had been watching the scene intently. "Anybody got a paper and pencil?"

OTB Man had a legal pad on which he had been taking notes during the trial. He tore out a sheet of paper and slid it across the table along with a pen.

I wrote on it, "I need to talk to you outside the presence of the other jurors before any more testimony is heard." I folded the paper in half and gave it to Ralph.

He immediately unfolded it and read it. "This won't work," he said.

"That's the judge's decision, not yours," I told him.

He gave me a scowl and stomped out the door.

The minute the door was closed, all the other jurors were on me like flies on honey, wanting to know what was going on. I fended off all their questions, saying I could only speak to the judge. Ron, who was apt to know, agreed with Ralph—there was no way she was going to talk to me.

Ralph was back five minutes later.

"All right, let's go," he snapped.

They got to their feet, began to line up.

"What about my note?" I said.

"Judge Davis will address you on the matter of your note."

"My note said I wanted to speak to her alone."

"I know what your note said."

Ralph pulled the door open, led us out. He pushed the courtroom door open and ushered us in. We filed in and took our seats.

And there they all were, just as they'd been for the last week. The judge, the Silver Fox and Peter, Paul and Mary. All ready to proceed with this boring, eight-year-old civil case about which I couldn't have cared less.

Judge Davis turned to the jury. "Before we proceed, a matter has come up which I must address. A member of the jury has expressed a desire to communicate with me. As I stated at the beginning of the trial, such communication is not possible at this time. During deliberation you will be able to communicate with me, but only by sending me written questions through the court officer, which I shall answer to you in court, in the presence of the attorneys for both sides. That is the only time, and the only way you may communicate with the court until after the deliberation is over and the verdict has been reached. Any communication at this time is wholly inappropriate and cannot be allowed.

"You understand, this is not an arbitrary decision on my part. It is one of the safeguards of the judicial system to ensure a fair trial. There is to be no communication of any kind which might in any way taint the jury and render them incapable of delivering an impartial verdict. I am sorry for anyone who did not know that.

"But you know it *now*. And should it occur, in light of my admonition, I should have to consider it contempt of court."

Judge Davis glared at us for a moment, then turned to Peter/Paul, the attorney for Veliko Tool and Die. "Mr. Wessingham. Call your next witness."

It was too much. She hadn't listened. She was going ahead with the stupid trial. Peter/Paul was going to call a witness and introduce new evidence. And I couldn't sit there and listen to it. Not in light of the murder case. But what the hell could I do?

As Peter/Paul stood up to call his witness, I suddenly gagged, clapped my hand to my mouth, stood up, hunched over, grabbed my stomach with my other hand and scuttled from the jury box and out the door.

The jury deliberation room was locked, of course. But Ralph was right behind me. I didn't want to talk to him in the hall. So I stayed scrunched up, pointed to the door, and muttered, "Bathroom! Quick!"

Ralph unlocked the door and pushed it open. I scuttled inside, waited for him to follow. As soon as he did, I stood up, turned around and said, "I'm not sick. I just couldn't listen to the testimony."

Ralph's eyes widened and his jaw dropped open. Then his face darkened murderously. "You are in contempt of court," he said.

"That's right, I am," I said. I held out my hands. "Why don't you handcuff me? That's the only way you're gonna get me back in that courtroom.

"But before you do, you better think about it. Judge Davis won't talk to me because she doesn't want to prejudice the jury. You take me back there in handcuffs, well, what do you think that's gonna do to them? You wanna bet there'll be a mistrial then?

"If that's what you want, fine. The judge may be pissed at me, but think how thrilled she's gonna be at you. You walk me through that door in handcuffs and the show is up. A week of testimony down the drain. A week of jury selection down the drain. And all on your head. If that's what you want, fine. It works for me either way. If I'm in contempt of court, then I'm gonna get my day in court. When I do, I'm gonna have my say. But I'm gonna have it one way or another, and at the moment I just don't give a damn.

"So it's your move. What's it gonna be?"

He didn't blow up as I'd expected. Underneath the stereotypical sour employee who hated his job, there lurked a human being, with all the requisite drives and feelings, curiosity chief among them.

"Why are you doing this?" he said.

"That's between me and the judge," I said. "If you want this trial to continue, I suggest you take her another note."

"That would be contempt of court."

"I'm *already* in contempt of court. The only issue now is whether this trial proceeds."

He thought that over. "What's the note?"

I tore a piece of paper off OTB Man's legal pad and wrote, "I can no longer sit on this jury. I ask to be excused from service."

Ralph took the note, read it. "You can't be excused from service," he said. "There's no alternate."

"I know that."

"Then what's the point?"

"As I said, that's up to Judge Davis. Just take her the note."

He hesitated, looked at me.

"Hey, you wanna handcuff me to a chair? I ain't running away from a contempt charge. I *want* to talk to her."

He frowned and went out, closing the door. He was back five minutes later, ushering in the jury. They came in looking at me as if I were from another planet. I couldn't blame them. I could imagine the whispered conversations they must have observed between Judge Davis and Ralph.

When they were seated, Ralph said, "Mr. Hastings?"

"Yes?"

"This way."

He opened the door for me and I walked out in the corridor. He pushed the door to the courtroom open. Aside from the jury, they were all still there. Judge Davis, the Silver Fox and Peter, Paul and Mary. I walked into the jury box, sat alone in my appointed seat. They were all looking at me. The looks were not friendly.

Judge Davis took a breath. She seemed to be controlling herself with a great effort. "Mr. Hastings," she said.

"Yes, Your Honor." That was a victory in itself, being able to speak out loud.

"I specifically instructed you regarding communications with the court. You disregarded those instructions. You are therefore in contempt of court. Do you understand that?"

"Yes, Your Honor."

"I am disregarding procedure in speaking to you now. I want you to know that the only reason I am doing that, is because there is no alternate in this case. If there were an alternate, you would not have this chance. You would be in custody, the trial would be proceeding, and the alternate would be sitting in your place. Is that clear?''

''Yes, Your Honor.''

''It happens that, unfortunately, no alternate is available. And we are well over a week into the trial. If you cannot serve, I will have to declare a mistrial. Which I am extremely reluctant to do. Which is why you are being afforded this chance. A chance you would ordinarily not be afforded the opportunity to take. You may consider yourself a very lucky man.''

I said nothing, waited.

Judge Davis held up my note. ''You sent me a note saying you cannot sit on the case, and asking to be excused from the jury. You must be aware of why I cannot grant such a request. For all the reasons I just gave you. To do so would mean declaring a mistrial, since there is no alternate to take your place. That is why, if there is any way possible, I would like to get by this unfortunate incident and proceed with the trial.''

''Yes, Your Honor.''

''I point out that in so doing, you would be able to clear yourself of contempt of court. But that, of course, should not be your primary motivation.''

''Yes, Your Honor.''

Judge Davis took a breath. ''Therefore, I ask you now. Are you able to proceed as a juror in this case?''

''No, Your Honor.''

''You are not?''

''No, Your Honor.''

''And why is that?''

I took a breath. ''Because I find I am prejudiced against one of the parties in this case.''

Judge Davis frowned. ''You are biased against one of the parties to this action?''

"Yes, Your Honor."

"May I remind you that you were informed about all aspects of this case during jury selection, and questioned as to any possible bias or interest in any of the parties involved. Do you recall that?"

"Yes, Your Honor."

"Since you were selected for the jury, you must have stated that you had none. Do you recall that?"

"Yes, Your Honor."

"Was that statement true?"

"Yes, it was, Your Honor."

"Then how do you explain your present position?"

"I became biased against one of the parties during the course of the trial."

"That's absurd," Judge Davis said. "There's nothing that's gone on that—" She stopped. Frowned. "I'm sorry," she said. "It's not my place to comment on the evidence. I'm afraid you have me so upset that I was about to." She took a breath. "Mr. Hastings. You say you are biased against one of the parties to this action?"

"Yes, Your Honor."

"Are you biased against Mr. Dumar, of Dumar Electronics?"

"No, Your Honor."

Judge Davis frowned. "But he is the only party to have given testimony so far. Well then, are you biased against Veliko Tool and Die, Delvecchio Realty, or the City of New York?"

"No, Your Honor."

Judge Davis stared at me. "You are not biased against the plaintiff, or any of the three defendants?"

"No, Your Honor."

"Mr. Hastings, against whom are you biased?"

I took a breath. "I am biased against the attorney for the plaintiff, Mr. Pendergas."

Judge Davis stared at me incredulously. "You are biased against one of the *attorneys* in this action?"

"That's right, Your Honor."

Judge Davis couldn't believe it. I could see emotions struggling over her face. It was almost comical.

She composed herself, took a breath. I could tell she was ready to explode.

"Mr. Hastings," she said. I swear she said it through clenched teeth. "Please try to understand. A trial is a very serious matter. It is not to be taken lightly. Bias is also a very serious thing, and not to be taken lightly. A biased juror cannot sit in court.

"But there are various degrees of bias. I point out that different lawyers have different styles. Some are pleasing, some are not. You cannot like everyone you meet, and you cannot necessarily like their style. That does not mean you are biased against them. It is a matter of personal preference. If an attorney has done something to irritate you, if you do not like his manner of presentation, that is something you must put out of your mind. You must consider only the facts of the case as they are being brought out in court. If you do not make an effort to do so, then you are not fulfilling your duty as juror.

"So, I am asking you—no, I might say I am begging you—if you have somehow developed a bias in this case against Mr. Pendergas, that you ignore it, do not let it influence you, and that you consider the evidence that you hear in this courtroom solely on its own merits."

"I'm sorry, Your Honor. I can't do that."

Judge Davis looked like a woman drowning. How could she reason with an irrational man?

She controlled herself, made one last effort. "I see," she said. "Then tell me, Mr. Hastings. Why are you prejudiced against Mr. Pendergas?"

"Because he killed my fellow juror, Sherry Fontaine."

41.

THERE WAS a stunned silence in the courtroom.
Judge Davis blinked, once, twice, then closed
her mouth, which had somehow involuntarily
opened. She wet her lips, blinked again. She stared at
me incredulously.

Then turned to look at Pendergas.

The Silver Fox was taking it much better than she
was. My words had to be as big a shock to him as
they were to her, only more so. But you'd never know
it. He looked calm, unruffled. He turned toward Peter,
Paul and Mary, and I could see his shoulders go up,
obviously as he shrugged at them to indicate his utter
bafflement. He turned back to Judge Davis with a be-
mused expression on his face. I swear his eyes were
almost twinkling.

Judge Davis looked at him, then at me. She took a
breath, seemed to get control of herself. "Mr. . . ."
she began, then broke off helplessly.

"Hastings," I said.

She rubbed her forehead, took another breath. "Yes.
Mr. Hastings. Are you aware of what you just said?"

"Yes, Your Honor."

"And the implications?"

"Yes, Your Honor."

"I'm not sure that you are. I'd like to explain them to you. You have just accused a reputable attorney at law of the crime of murder. You have done so publicly, in open court, in the presence of witnesses. On top of your other troubles, this lays you wide open for a suit for slander. And since the person you have slandered is a lawyer, there is little doubt that suit will be brought.

"Now, you are only a layman, and perhaps you do not understand the law. But do you realize that what you just said is slanderous?"

"I do not, Your Honor."

"You do not? But I just explained it to you."

"Begging Your Honor's pardon, but you pointed out that my remark could be considered slanderous. You didn't explain the laws of slander."

Judge Davis stared at me. "Are you asking for a legal definition?"

"No, Your Honor. That won't be necessary. I've already consulted Richard Rosenberg, of Rosenberg and Stone. In his humble opinion, what I've just said is not slanderous, for two reasons. One, to be considered slanderous, a statement must be made irresponsibly and *voluntarily*. Your Honor charged me with contempt of court, and called me to account for myself. You asked me *specifically* why I was biased against Mr. Pendergas. The statement that I made was in response to a direct question by you. I had no choice but to make it, since it was a directive by the court. In fact, had I *not* made that statement, I would be in contempt of court."

I paused and looked at Judge Davis, in case she wished to comment. She didn't. She merely blinked. I don't think she could have looked more surprised if

I'd suddenly sprouted wings and started flying around the courtroom.

I went on. "The second reason I'm not guilty of slander is, for a statement to be slanderous, it must also be made with flagrant disregard for the truth. Truth is always a defense for slander. The statement I made is true, and can be proven true, so there can be no slander involved."

Judge Davis stared down at me. "You've consulted a lawyer, Mr. Hastings?"

"Absolutely. I have no wish to go to jail, or to be sued for slander. I suddenly found myself in an impossible position, being on this jury and knowing Mr. Pendergas was guilty of murder."

Judge Davis looked as if her world were collapsing around her. This, in a simple civil suit. A simple case of property damage. Suddenly, here she was, dealing with a mistrial, contempt charges, a slander suit, and an accusation of murder.

"Mr. Hastings," she said. "You are making statements that have no foundation. How could you know any of this? I don't understand."

"That's because this is a civil case, Your Honor, and in a civil case the judge isn't present for jury selection. If you had been, you would know that I'm a private detective. And during the course of the trial, I developed a friendship with Sherry Fontaine. When she was killed, I naturally began investigating to see what had happened."

The "naturally" was pretty ballsy on my part, seeing as how it had taken my wife and MacAullif to push me into doing it.

But Judge Davis didn't know that. "You did?" she said.

"That's right," I said. "And I uncovered the information which leads me to my present position. I found a witness who identifies a picture of Sherry Fontaine as the young woman she observed last Wednesday during the noon recess, talking to a gentleman she did not know but whom she describes most vividly. You will note that Mr. Pendergas' appearance is rather striking. I have no doubt that this witness will have no problem picking him out of a lineup.

"I have another witness, who observed a gentleman of Mr. Pendergas' description leaving Sherry Fontaine's apartment house at approximately one A.M. on the night of the murder. From the description, I have no doubt that this witness will also be able to make the identification."

Judge Davis frowned. "That is hardly sufficient for making an accusation."

"I know that, Your Honor. But I also have the motive for the crime. I have the statement from Miss Velma Dawson of Cincinnati, Ohio, that ten years ago Mr. Pendergas was the attorney who represented her when she was the victim of a hit-and-run. She wasn't injured, but Mr. Pendergas got her a thirty-thousand-dollar settlement through the use of phony X-rays of a leg she'd previously injured in a skiing accident.

"It happens that Velma Dawson was an actress, who once took classes with Sherry Fontaine. When Sherry Fontaine was put on this jury, the name Pendergas was vaguely familiar to her.

"The records of the telephone company show that on Tuesday night, the first day of this trial, Sherry Fontaine put through a phone call to Velma Dawson in Cincinnati, Ohio. Miss Dawson's statement verifies the call. She also states that what Sherry wanted to know was if Mr. Pendergas was indeed the attorney who had represented Velma in that action. She also admits that the action was fraudulent, and that Mr. Pendergas had full knowledge of it.

"Which gives us your motive for murder. We know by the testimony of the witness, that Sherry Fontaine approached Mr. Pendergas during noon recess the following day. We can show by inference that she tried to blackmail him. She confronted him with what she'd learned from Velma, and demanded money for her silence.

"It can also be shown that that money was promised, but was not paid. It happens that Sherry Fontaine used cocaine. She didn't use much, but that was largely due to the fact that she didn't have any money. But it can be shown that Wednesday night—two A.M. Thursday morning, actually—after her rehearsal, Sherry Fontaine put through a call to the young man who was supplying her with drugs, ordering, not half a gram as she usually bought, but a quarter of an ounce. It can be further shown that Thursday evening, when Sherry Fontaine returned from court, she had an altercation outside her building with the young man who was bringing her these drugs, over the fact that she had no money with which to pay for them. Obviously, during the noon recess she approached Pendergas for the blackmail money he'd promised her, only he didn't pay. He stalled her, put her off until the next day.

"Only he had no intention of paying at all. He brought up paying her later that evening, and learned that she'd be away at rehearsal, getting back some time after midnight. So he went, he watched, he waited. He saw her arrive home and get out of a taxicab with a young man, an actor named Claude Breen who had romantic designs on her. Had she allowed him to go upstairs with her, she might be alive today. But she brushed him off, and he walked over to Broadway to catch a bus home. She went upstairs, hot and tired from the long rehearsal, and hopped in the shower.

"The doorbell rang. Well, that was a shock. She wasn't expecting anyone. Certainly not Pendergas, since he'd stalled her till the next day. If she'd thought it was him, she might not have opened the door. But no, as far as she was concerned, it was either young actor Claude being persistent and she'd have to tell him off. Or—and this was probably why she opened the door—it was her connection, coming by to apologize for the scene and to give her the dope.

"But it wasn't either of them. It was Pendergas. And he pushed his way in and strangled her."

I looked around the courtroom.

Pendergas, though still outwardly unruffled and dignified, seemed also tense and alert. The sly fox, scenting the wind.

Peter, Paul and Mary looked totally shocked, as if their guitars had suddenly vanished out of their hands right in the middle of a chorus of "Puff, the Magic Dragon."

Ralph was gawking at me with his mouth open, as if he couldn't quite believe his ears.

Judge Davis had regained her composure. "Have you communicated any of this to the police?" she asked.

"Absolutely, Your Honor." I pointed to the back of the courtroom. "I call Your Honor's attention to the two gentlemen sitting in the back of the court. They are NYPD homicide sergeants. On the basis of evidence I've given them, they have obtained a warrant for the arrest of Mr. Pendergas for the murder of Sherry Fontaine. They have that warrant with them, and they are waiting to make the arrest as soon as these proceedings are over."

I looked at the back row of the courtroom, where Sergeant Thurman and Sergeant MacAullif had been sitting, trying to look inconspicuous since the beginning of the courtroom session. They looked incredibly grim. Thurman also looked somewhat confused, but that was how he always looked. Sergeant MacAullif looked positively murderous. His eyes weren't just grim, they were smoldering.

I knew why. MacAullif was furious because everything I'd just said was total bullshit. They didn't have a warrant. And they couldn't have if they'd wanted to. There wasn't evidence enough for it. There were no witnesses. That was bullshit too. I'd made it up, just like the bit about the warrant.

I'd told MacAullif about my call to Velma Dawson, of course. And I'd told him my theory of the crime. He'd been sold enough to call Sergeant Thurman and get him down here, like I said. But Sergeant Thurman hadn't bought it. He agreed to come, just to see what was going on. But according to MacAullif, when he'd called me back last night, Sergeant Thurman's main interest in coming was to see if I'd spill something that might tend to implicate *me*.

So the grim looks on their faces were due to the fact that I'd just spun out a fine web of bullshit with absolutely nothing to back it up. They were grim, not because they expected to nail a murderer. No, the one they were angry at was me.

But the Silver Fox didn't know that. He looked at the back of the courtroom and he saw Sergeant Thurman and Sergeant MacAullif sitting there, looking as if they were ready for a hanging, and he thought the one they intended to hang was him. And then he looked at the front of the courtroom. And when he did, Ralph, god bless him, took one step to the side and planted himself square in front of the exit door.

The Silver Fox was still composed. He looked around, haughty, proud, disdainful. He was sly and cunning, the Silver Fox. He never turned a hair. But the fox could smell the hounds. And he thought they had him dead to rights on a murder rap. And so the fox turned tail.

It happened very fast. One minute he was sitting there, cool, dignified, every hair in place. The next moment he sprang from his seat and bolted up the aisle.

Which is when Sergeant Thurman shone. He was a stupid, obnoxious cop who could never have solved the case on his own, could never even have gotten close. And who probably didn't even understand it all now. But as MacAullif had said, he was on the side of the angels. And the man was tough, and the man was quick. Before Ralph or MacAullif or anyone else in the courtroom could move, Sergeant Thurman was on his feet.

Yeah, he was on the side of the angels, Sergeant Thurman was. And he vaulted over the back of the bench, and launched his body into the air, and he brought down the Silver Fox with the sweetest little flying tackle you ever did see.

42.

*L*OVE STRIKES OUT opened to rave reviews, moved to off-Broadway, and won an Obie.

Just kidding. But that was the thought that flashed on me while the waitress poured coffee for me and MacAullif at a small greasy spoon near the courthouse. MacAullif dumped in cream and sugar, took a sip and grimaced.

"Shit," he said. "You spoiled me with your damn uptown coffee. Now everything else tastes like shit." He took another sip, scowled at the coffee, set the cup down. "All right," he said. "Give."

"What do you mean?"

"I'm waiting for your explanation."

"Of what?"

"The case. What, are you dense? The case."

"You heard what I said in court."

"Yeah, yeah, yeah," MacAullif said. "I know what you said in court, and I know what you told me last night on the phone. I know what happened. I want to know why it happened, and how you figured it out."

"Why it happened?"

"Start with how you figured it out."

"Isn't that obvious?"

"No, it isn't. It's like you put two and two together and made twelve."

"No, it isn't."

"Then give. Hey, this should be fun for you. This is a milestone. This marks, to the best of my recollection, the first time in a case you've ever been right."

"That's not true."

"Let's not quibble. It's the first time you solved the case ahead of the investigating officer and dumped it in his lap. Now, that's admittedly not as big a deal as it seems, when you consider the investigating officer was Sergeant Thurman. But even so, it's a triumph for you. You figured it out, you did it right, you can take some pride in that."

"Thank you."

"You also left me in the dark, pulled a lot of shit in court you didn't tell me you were gonna do, and pissed me off utterly. If you hadn't been right, I'd have had your head. As it stands, you're right, so you win. And I wanna know how."

"How what?"

"How did you figure it out?"

"I told you how. Dexter Manyon remembered that Sherry had once mentioned a girl named Velma."

"Yeah, yeah, yeah," MacAullif said. "That's when you added two and two and got twelve. It was a small, insignificant detail. Why did that do it for you?"

"I don't know. I guess it was just that I'd been going under a misconception."

"What do you mean?"

"About what Sherry said, the first day I met her. You know how people always misunderstand each other?"

"I'll say."

"Because you always know what you *mean,* but the

other person only hears what you *say*. That's what happened. Sherry was talking about this girl, Velma, and she said, 'my girlfriend, back in Cincinnati.' *She* knew what she meant—it was her girlfriend, who'd moved back to Cincinnati—perfectly clear to her. But it was an awkward construction, see? Back in Cincinnati implies to the listener, who doesn't know, that Sherry lived there too. That's what I heard, and that's what locked in my mind—Sherry Fontaine came from Cincinnati.''

''So?''

''So, that's what did it. That's what jolted me. Dexter Manyon told me she lived in Atlanta. That short-circuited my thought process. Wrong. Couldn't be. Sherry Fontaine lived in Cincinnati. 'My friend, Velma, back in Cincinnati.' I'd heard that, and I'd heard about the insurance scam, and it was locked in my mind as something that had happened in Cincinnati when the two of them lived there before Sherry came to New York. It was all tied up in my mind.'' I ticked them off on my fingers. ''Sherry, Velma, insurance scam, Cincinnati.

''Dexter Manyon destroyed that. Not Cincinnati. Never in Cincinnati. Velma was someone Sherry knew from New York. That suddenly transferred the whole package here. Velma, insurance scam, Sherry, New York. A crooked New York lawyer who pulled an insurance scam ten years ago.

''And suddenly it all clicked. Sherry gets put on this jury. Something about it triggers her memory and suddenly she starts talking insurance scam. It had to be one of the lawyers. It didn't necessarily have to be Pendergas, though he was the most likely. It also could have been Peter, Paul and Mary.''

''Who?''

"The other three attorneys. We called them Peter, Paul and Mary."

MacAullif thought about that. "Oh. Yeah."

"But it *was* Pendergas. And that night she calls Velma and makes sure. The next day she tries blackmail."

MacAullif waved it away. "I know all that, I know all that. It's your deduction from Atlanta to Pendergas. That's what's bothering me."

"Well, Sherry had told me the whole thing. But I hadn't connected it in my mind with the murder at all, because I thought of it as Cincinnati. But then it wasn't Cincinnati. And what really woke me up, was the realization that I'd jumped to a conclusion and been terribly stupid."

"Yeah, but that must happen to you a lot."

"Fuck you. Anyway, that's what did it. And there was something else too."

"What?"

"The old man. Nathan Hargraine. My buddy from jury duty. That was a stupid idea, yes, but it put me in the right direction. 'Cause I'd been all wrapped up in the theatrical side of Sherry's life, the actors, her boyfriend, her connection and all that. But my buddy was the one who got me thinking that Sherry was also a juror on a court case, that maybe what happened to her was a result of that. It was dead wrong, of course, but it had me in the ballpark. So when this other thing came along, my mind was open to it."

MacAullif looked at me as if I'd just told him the earth was flat. He took another sip of coffee. He grimaced, set down the cup, pushed it away. "I can't drink this stuff. I gotta get back to the office. Okay, what's the rest of it?"

"The rest of it?"

"Yeah. Why? Tell me why?"

"You know why. She was blackmailing him."

"I know," MacAullif said. "But that's not an explanation. I mean, okay, maybe ten years ago this guy wasn't that hot. He probably wasn't. Attorneys had just been allowed to advertise, negligence was just getting big, this guy's probably had some lean years and rough sledding and was having trouble getting off the ground. Hence, the cuttin' corners on the settlements and the whole shmear. Now he's respectable, prosperous, what have you, he doesn't want that to come out. I know all that.

"But why kill her? It was a small deal. The blackmail couldn't have been that much. Murder is one hell of a drastic step. Why doesn't he just pay her off and leave it at that?"

"Well, for one thing, I don't think it was really blackmail."

MacAullif frowned. "What do you mean?"

"I think what she probably asked him for was the same thing she asked me. To pull an insurance scam for her. Just like he'd done for her friend, Velma."

"So?"

"Obviously, the guy wasn't about to do anything like that. He's secure and legit now, he doesn't need that kind of shit. He tells her no, but she won't quit. She's got the goods on him and she wants him to pull a scam. If there was blackmail, I'll bet you *he* was the one suggested it. He won't help her with her scheme, but he'll pay her off to forget about it."

MacAullif considered that. "Okay, so why didn't he? Why not pay her off and be done with it?"

I shook my head. "He didn't dare to."

"Why not?"

I knew the answer. It wasn't a complete answer, but

it was one that satisfied me. Well, satisfied isn't the right word—in fact, it's dead wrong—there was nothing satisfying about it. It was in fact a rather flip answer, and a rather inadequate epitaph for someone I had known and liked.

And not just liked. For someone who had bothered me, troubled me, for a girl who had tied me up in knots and rekindled all those old adolescent feelings of love/hate relationships, a girl as unobtainable as lost youth itself, a girl I couldn't *help* liking, despite how angry and frustrated and manipulated she made me feel.

So, no, the answer wasn't satisfying at all.

But for me it was an answer that made sense. In a kind of horrible way I understood.

And I figured MacAullif would understand too, when I told him. Alice hadn't, when I'd tried to explain it to her last night. I mean, she'd understood it intellectually, 'cause intellectually there wasn't that much to understand. But Alice was a woman, so she didn't quite get it. No matter how well I explained it, she didn't quite understand.

But MacAullif was a man. And, hard as it might be to realize, he'd been young once too, and gone to high school, and had girlfriends and adolescent problems and anxieties and the whole bit. He'd been young once, just as I'd been young once, just as the Silver Fox had been young once, so he'd know what I'd recognized, what the Silver Fox had recognized, and what, had he met Sherry, I'm sure he would have recognized too. So somehow I just knew he'd understand.

I smiled slightly. Sadly. Wistfully.

And answered his question.

"She was Trouble."

About the Author

PARNELL HALL, a part-time sleuth and former actor living in New York City, is particularly well-qualified to present the fascinating milieu of *Juror*—"Hall's swift, spare prose captures the grit of Manhattan. . . . He has also created a thoroughly credible character in the irrepressible Hastings," wrote the St. Louis *Post Dispatch*. Mr. Hall is currently writing the movie script for *Juror*.

MYSTERY PARLOR

☐ **THE DEAD PULL HITTER by Alison Gordon.** Katherine Henry is a sportswriter—until murder pitches a curve. Now death is lurking in her ballpark, and she's looking for a killer on the dark side of glory days and shattered dreams. (402405—$3.99)

☐ **HALF A MIND by Wendy Hornsby.** Homicide detective Roger Tejeda had an instinctive sense for catching criminals. But now he's working with a handicap: his last case left him with a skull fracture, black-outs and memory lapses—which make it that much harder to figure out who sent him a gift box holding a severed head. . . . (402456—$3.99)

☐ **THE CHARTREUSE CLUE by William F. Love.** Although a priest with a murdered girlfriend wasn't exactly an original sin, the irascible, wheelchair-bound Bishop would have to use leads that included a key, a letter, and a chartreuse clue to unravel the deadly affair. (402731—$5.50)

☐ **MRS. MALORY INVESTIGATES by Hazel Holt.** "Delightful . . . a British whodunit that works a traditional mode to good effect." —*Cleveland Plain Dealer* (402693—$3.99)

Buy them at your local bookstore or use this convenient coupon for ordering.

NEW AMERICAN LIBRARY
P.O. Box 999, Bergenfield, New Jersey 07621

Please send me the books I have checked above.
I am enclosing $_____ (please add $2.00 to cover postage and handling).
Send check or money order (no cash or C.O.D.'s) or charge by Mastercard or
VISA (with a $15.00 minimum). Prices and numbers are subject to change without
notice.

Card #_____ Exp. Date _____
Signature_____
Name_____
Address_____
City _____ State _____ Zip Code _____

For faster service when ordering by credit card call **1-800-253-6476**

Allow a minimum of 4-6 weeks for delivery. This offer is subject to change without notice.

There's an epidemic with 27 million victims. And no visible symptoms.

It's an epidemic of people who can't read.

Believe it or not, 27 million Americans are functionally illiterate, about one adult in five.

The solution to this problem is you... when you join the fight against illiteracy. So call the Coalition for Literacy at toll-free **1-800-228-8813** and volunteer.

Volunteer Against Illiteracy. The only degree you need is a degree of caring.